MW00582630

Forever Home

A Hometown Harbor Novel
Book 6

Tammy L. Grace

Praise for Tammy L. Grace

"*A Season of Hope* is a perfect holiday read! Warm wonderful and gentle tale reflecting small town romance at it best."

—*Jeanie, review of A Season for Hope: A Christmas Novella*

"This book is a clean, simple romance with a background story very similar to the works of Debbie Macomber. If you like Macomber's books you will like this one. The main character, Hope and her son Jake are on a road trip when their car breaks down, thus starts the story. A holiday tale filled with dogs, holiday fun, and the joy of giving will warm your heart.

—*Avid Mystery Reader, review of A Season for Hope: A Christmas Novella*

"This book was just as enchanting as the others. Hardships with the love of a special group of friends. I recommend the series as a must read. I loved every exciting moment. A new author for me. She's fabulous."

—*Maggie!, review of Pieces of Home: A Hometown Harbor Novel (Book 4)*

"Tammy is an amazing author, she reminds me of Debbie Macomber… Delightful, heartwarming…just down to earth."

—*Plee, review of A Promise of Home: A Hometown Harbor Novel (Book 3)*

"This was an entertaining and relaxing novel. Tammy Grace has a simple yet compelling way of drawing the reader into the lives of her characters. It was a pleasure to read a story that didn't rely on theatrical tricks, unrealistic events or

steamy sex scenes to fill up the pages. Her characters and plot were strong enough to hold the reader's interest."
—*MrsQ125, review of Finding Home: A Hometown Harbor Novel (Book 1)*

"This is a beautifully written story of loss, grief, forgiveness and healing. I believe anyone could relate to the situations and feelings represented here. This is a read that will stay with you long after you've completed the book."
—*Cassidy Hop, review of Finally Home: A Hometown Harbor Novel (Book 5)*

Killer Music and Deadly Connection are award-winning novels, earning the 2016 & 2017 Mystery Gold Medal by the Global E-Book Awards

"Killer Music is a clever and well-crafted whodunit. The vivid and colorful characters shine as the author gradually reveals their hidden secrets—an absorbing page-turning read."
—*Jason Deas, bestselling author of Pushed and Birdsongs*

"I could not put this book down! It was so well written & a suspenseful read! This is definitely a 5-star story! I'm hoping there will be a sequel!"
—*Colleen, review of Killer Music*

"This is the best book yet by this author. The plot was well crafted with an unanticipated ending. I like to try to leap ahead and see if I can accurately guess the outcome. I was able to predict some of the plot but not the actual details which made reading the last several chapters quite engrossing."
—*0001PW, review of Deadly Connection*

Forever Home
A Novel By
Tammy L. Grace

www.tammylgrace.com
Facebook: facebook.com/tammylgrace.books
Twitter: @TammyLGrace
Instagram: @authortammylgrace

Published in the United States by Lone Mountain Press, Nevada

ISBN 978-1-945591-15-0 (eBook)
ISBN 978-1-945591-14-3 (Print)
FIRST EDITION

Printed in the United States of America

Also by Tammy L. Grace

Below you will find links to the electronic version of all of Tammy's other books available online

COOPER HARRINGTON DETECTIVE NOVELS
Killer Music
Deadly Connection
Dead Wrong

HOMETOWN HARBOR SERIES
Hometown Harbor: The Beginning (FREE Prequel Novella)
Finding Home
Home Blooms
A Promise of Home
Pieces of Home
Finally Home
Forever Home

CHRISTMAS NOVELLAS
A Season for Hope: Christmas in Silver Falls Book 1
The Magic of the Season: Christmas in Silver Falls Book 2
Christmas in Snow Valley: A Hometown Christmas Novella
Christmas Sisters: Soul Sisters at Cedar Mountain Lodge Book 1
Christmas Wishes: Soul Sisters at Cedar Mountain Lodge Book 3

GLASS BEACH COTTAGE SERIES
Beach Haven

WRITING AS CASEY WILSON
A Dog's Hope

A Dog's Chance

Tammy would love to connect with readers on social media and her website at www.tammylgrace.com. Remember to subscribe to her mailing list for another freebie, only available to her subscribers. Follow this link to subscribe at https://wp.me/P9umIy-e and she'll send you the exclusive interview she did with all the canine characters in her Hometown Harbor Series.

Follow Tammy on Facebook at this link, by liking her page. You may also follow Tammy on BookBub by clicking on the follow button.

Dear Readers,

After so many notes and emails from loyal readers, I decided to write another book in my Hometown Harbor Series. If you've read the other five books in the series, this one picks up where *Finally Home* (Book 5) ended. Like readers who have taken the time to reach out to me, I love the characters in these books. They truly feel like old friends and the setting always makes me feel like I'm in the San Juan Islands.

If you're a new reader and this is the first Hometown Harbor Novel you have picked up to read, there will be spoilers throughout the story, that will ruin some of the surprises in each of the previous five books. Some readers don't mind reading out of order, but I always recommend starting at the beginning with *Finding Home*, for the most enjoyable and satisfying experience. There is also a free prequel to the series, *Hometown Harbor: The Beginning*, where you can meet Sam, the main character in the first book, through excerpts from her personal journal over the years and before the story that takes place in *Finding Home* begins.

Each book features a different heroine and her story. I've chosen to craft most of them as more seasoned, with rich life experiences. All the books in the series are listed in order below, so if you missed any, you can easily click through and download them.

I hope you enjoy Izzy's story in *Forever Home* and can't thank you enough for reading and sharing your love for these characters, human and furry, and their stories.

Happy Reading,
Tammy

This one is for my loyal readers...thank you for reading, sharing, reviewing, and supporting me

Tammy L. Grace

Forever Home

A Hometown Harbor Novel
Book 6

Table of Contents

Chapter 1

IZZY BROUGHT THE warm chai tea latte to her lips, tempted by the enticing aroma of the huge slice of cinnamon-laced fresh apple pie sitting in the middle of the table along with three forks. With the Harvest Festival over and the bulk of the work done at the winery, she had the day to herself and was enjoying the quiet afternoon, pondering an idea that had been nagging at her since she came to visit the island earlier in the summer.

With the sun glinting off the water, she glanced out the window to the outdoor seating on the deck, and regretted not taking the opportunity to enjoy the perfect weather. She had too many things on her mind when she placed her order and visited with Sam, stationed behind the counter of Harbor Coffee and Books.

Her lawyer colleagues from all those legal and leadership workshops over the years, where the personality and strength surveys always pegged Izzy as reliable and stable, would be shocked at her idea now. What she'd been contemplating and the spontaneity of it, went against her natural instincts. The truth was, she was feeling guilty and a bit selfish for even considering it.

The chimes on the front door announced the arrival of her brother, Blake and his new bride, Ellie. They joined her at the table, where their steaming drinks awaited.

Both of them sported huge smiles. "We finished tallying the sales from the weekend and the festival, and it exceeded our wildest expectations." Blake squeezed Ellie's hand. "It will get us through the lean months at the winery after the holidays."

"That's wonderful news." Izzy pointed at the pie. "Sam gave us this gigantic slice to share."

Ellie held up her hand. "Only one bite for me. I did some cheating this weekend and need to get back on track."

Blake took a bite and raised his brows at his sister. "So, what did you want to talk about? You've got us intrigued."

Izzy took another sip and put her cup down. "I've been giving some thought to making a change and wanted to run it by the two of you. The lease on my little cottage is up this month, so my time here was supposed to come to an end. The thing is, I'm not sure I want to go back to the Tri-Cities. I've been toying with the idea of moving here, but I don't want to do that if it would cramp your style. I know it's not always easy to be living close to family."

Ellie's eyes danced with excitement, and she jumped from her chair to wrap Izzy in a hug. "We'd love to have you nearby."

Blake grinned at the two of them and nodded toward his wife. "What she said. It's been wonderful to have you here, Izz. Not only have you helped us so much, but it's comforting to have you here." He reached across the table and rubbed her arm. "You don't need our approval or permission to move anyway, but you've got it."

Izzy smiled and shrugged her shoulders. "I didn't want you to feel weird having your big sister around. I feel so at home here. I'll miss being close to Mom and Dad, but with me actually looking to retire, it seems like a great time for a whole new start. Having you and Ellie here would be a true gift."

Blake rested his fork on the pie plate. "Are you going to sell your place?"

Izzy nodded. "I'm talking to my realtor now and if I go ahead with it, need to find a place here. Something easy to take care of and not too demanding. I'm tired of having a large place to worry about and this will help me downsize." She plucked her phone from her purse and turned it toward them. "I've been looking online and really like this one on the golf course. I wouldn't have to worry about yard work, it's all part of the homeowner association fee, so no maintenance, and while it's not on the water, it has a lovely view of the greens, nice walking paths, and tons of amenities. At first, I had my heart set on a property along the beach, but I save a bundle avoiding the water view."

Blake nodded and showed the photos to Ellie. She pointed at the screen with an excited look in her eyes. "Oh, I like the shingled siding. We should go see it."

Izzy nodded. "I thought I'd call Nate's dad and arrange a visit. From what I can see from these online photos, I like it."

"We can go with you when you get an appointment, if you want," offered Blake.

"That would be terrific. I'd love another opinion. I'm not usually this spontaneous."

Blake finished off the last bite of pie. "So, are you really thinking you'll actually retire from practicing law?"

Izzy wrinkled her nose. "Well, I can do contract work or some small jobs working out of a home office. I don't want to have a practice or work for a firm. I want some freedom. I like helping you at the winery and working with Kate at her shop, but I'd like to step away from the bulk of my legal work and not feel tied down to my clients. One more reason to leave the Tri-Cities—it's easier to say no to clients from a distance."

Blake nodded. "I get that. Have you told Mom and Dad? They're gonna miss you."

Izzy's smile faded and her stomach lurched. "Not yet. I wanted to talk to you first. I know they'll miss me, but Esther and Lauren are nearby, so they'll be okay." She kept telling herself this same thing, but it didn't do much to suppress her guilt.

Blake nodded. "I can help you move things. We can commandeer one of the winery delivery trucks and make a trip out of it."

She tucked a stray piece of hair, more salt than pepper lately, behind her ear. "That's the part I'm dreading. I need to only bring what I really want to keep." She pointed at her phone. "Some of the furnishings in this house stay with it as part of the sale, so that's another thing I like. The idea of moving is a bit overwhelming, but I've given it some thought over these last few months."

Blake reassured her with a kind smile. "I would never doubt any of your decisions. You always analyze everything. We can help you, so don't worry about that. It's good timing. Call Jack and set it up. He'll probably jump at the chance to show it to you today or tomorrow."

Izzy nodded and tapped the screen on her phone. Within minutes, Jack had agreed to meet them at the house, saying it was empty and he could swing by the office and pick up the keys.

Izzy led the way. When she drove down the driveway and saw the first glimpse of the Cape Cod style house, it felt like home. Blake and Ellie pulled in behind her, and Jack arrived a few minutes later.

Jack greeted them with a hearty smile, and pointed out the maintenance free weathered shingle siding that looked like wood, but was a composite. Upon opening the front door, gleaming cherry hardwood floors welcomed them into the open floor plan. A subtly curved staircase, directly across from them, led to two guestrooms, a bathroom, and a study, explained Jack.

He led the way into the great room, then the huge kitchen, which boasted a large granite counter that could be used as an eating area, and adjoined to a larger dining space. Oversized windows and glass patio doors ran along the entire back of the house, showcasing a gorgeous view of the rolling greens.

Ellie lingered in the kitchen, while Blake and Izzy followed Jack into the large master suite with a walk-in shower and separate garden tub. There was a deck off the master where Izzy pictured herself enjoying her morning coffee, plus a patio off the living area that would be perfect for alfresco meals.

She checked out the large laundry room with plenty of storage and the attached garage before heading upstairs. The study would make a perfect office and even had doors leading out to a small balcony overlooking the golf course.

Izzy thought it was exactly what she wanted, even before Jack pointed out that the window treatments would stay with the house, as well as the built-in cherry bookcases in the study, and the floating shelves in the living area. The large dining set and matching buffet that fit perfectly in the space also stayed with the house, as did all the outdoor patio furniture and grill.

They rejoined Ellie in the kitchen, who was sitting at the counter angled across the space. "I love this kitchen, Izzy."

"It will be a bit of a waste on me," she said, laughing. "My cooking days are behind me, thank goodness."

Jack cleared his throat. "The owners lowered the price on this one last week, so I know they're motivated. If you're interested, you might want to put in an offer soon, as the lower price could attract more buyers."

Izzy nodded. "This is exactly what I was looking for. Can I sleep on it and come by your office tomorrow?"

"Of course. The office is closing in a few minutes, so not to worry about any offers tonight. I have a feeling it will go quickly now that the price is so attractive."

Izzy asked a few more questions and made sure there were no other homes available in the same price range before walking outside for one more look around the yard.

The house, although twenty years old, was in immaculate condition, with mature landscaping that Izzy wouldn't have to tend and could just enjoy. After Blake had checked the HVAC systems and appliances, he continued his careful examination in the yard. The only thing he discovered that could use a bit of maintenance was the wooden deck off the bedroom—but it was nothing a coat or two of stain wouldn't fix. Everything else looked brand new.

Jack wished them all a good evening and told Izzy to call with any questions. When he was gone, Izzy stood admiring the house, noticing the wide covered porch that circled the entire building, and the lovely wooden bench and flowerpots by the door that added to the welcoming vibe. She could see herself here, starting a new chapter.

Blake put his arm around her. "You like it, don't you?"

She nodded. "I do. It seems like the right place for me."

"How about we treat you to dinner at Lou's, and talk more about the logistics of all of this?"

"That sounds wonderful." Izzy lingered for a few minutes after Blake and Ellie drove away, soaking in the view and the peaceful neighborhood. Houses were on both sides of this one, but the way they were situated, with none of them in a straight line and all the lots oddly shaped, plus the well-planned landscaping, she didn't see or hear anyone else. She could get used to this peaceful haven.

Her thoughts drifted to the friends she had made over the summer months she had spent on the island. Choosing to live here meant not only would she have Blake and Ellie, but the women and men she had come to think of as family, who had welcomed her with open arms. Sam, who owned the coffee shop and her wonderful husband, Jeff, whose family owned Cooper Hardware; Linda, the florist and nursery owner, and her new husband, Max, who was a renowned cardiothoracic surgeon; Regi, who with her husband, Nate, had adopted sweet little Emma not long ago; and Kate, who owned her lovely antique shop and tempted her longtime friend, Spence, to join her on the island; they all surrounded her with kindness. Their friendship and warmth had enticed her to make this quaint place her home.

With Mia immersed in her schooling, and from what Izzy could discern based on her daughter's infrequent and brief texts, doing well, and with her foolish ex-husband seemingly set on marrying Barbie, his latest, far-too-young love interest, Izzy was ready for a fresh start in a new place. A community where she wouldn't be encumbered with old memories or old friends who were sure to learn about John's upcoming wedding. Despite him living in California now, he still had ties to the Tri-Cities and visited his dealerships often.

She shook off thoughts of her ex-husband and smiled as she drove away with the tingle of excitement of a new adventure awaiting her.

Chapter 2

IT WAS A packed house at Lou's for Monday night football, but Lou led them to a table and took their order personally. Blake and Izzy discussed the trip to Richland while they waited for their orders.

Blake reached for a piece of fresh sourdough bread from the basket on the table. "It would be best to make the trip as soon as possible, since we'll want to avoid any bad weather."

Izzy nodded. "I know, I should have thought of this a few weeks ago. I could take the money from my savings and borrow anything I need from Mom and Dad, and then I won't have to worry about selling my house first. It'll probably sell for close to double what I'll be paying for this one, so there isn't any real risk. I need to figure out what to do with all the stuff in it though. It's too much for me and honestly, when we divorced, I took it from John because he offered and I knew he really loved it."

Blake grinned. "John deserved to lose it, and he knew it. And, it's been a great investment. You'll be able to do whatever you like when you sell it."

Tears formed in Izzy's eyes, which surprised her. She was set on moving, but thinking about leaving her house behind stirred up old memories. John had been so excited to build the huge stone and stucco home soon after he had started making enough money at his first dealership. Mia had been a sweet and precious five-year-old then. Those had been happier days. Ten years later, the marriage was over, broken by John's unfaithfulness.

John had wanted away from Izzy so badly, he had been eager to offer her the sprawling home. He agreed to pay for maintenance on the home, and even supplied Izzy with a new car each year. She knew it was out of guilt and his way of trying to appease his conscience, but she took it all anyway. Part of her didn't want anything from the lout, other than for him to leave, but her lawyer brain overrode her heart and she happily signed the papers agreeing to the compensation he offered.

Mia, who had always been a daddy's girl, blamed Izzy for the divorce and elected to move out and live with John and whichever bimbo of the month he was with at the time. That left Izzy with six-thousand square feet and a four-car garage on the side of a hill, alone. She threw herself into her work, and gravitated toward her family, thankful she had never changed her name and would always be Isabelle Griffin.

Despite the excitement and anticipation surrounding her new start, it would be difficult to leave it all behind, and even harder to be so far away from her mom and dad. She could still handle anything to do with the business and all of their personal legal work, but she wouldn't be only a few miles away. She couldn't pop by for a visit and a cup of tea or a glass of wine. She took a deep breath and buttered a slice of bread, hoping it would settle her stomach.

Blake brushed her hand with his finger. "Are you okay, Izz?"

She refocused on him, and sighed. "Yeah, thinking too much."

"You deserve to be happy. All these years, you've been the one to take care of everyone, solve our problems, both personal and business, and help Mom and Dad all the time. I know you feel responsible for everyone, but you're not."

She couldn't stop the tears from sliding down her cheeks. "Thank you for saying that. Mom and Dad are going to be tough. They're not getting any younger, so I'll have to make sure I schedule trips to go visit them often."

"I need to do the same. I've been so focused getting this winery in top shape and then with the wedding and everything, I haven't been the best son lately." He glanced at Ellie. "We'll make a trip soon, maybe spend some time with them over the holidays."

Ellie nodded. "We'll be there for the anniversary celebration of the family winery in February, too."

Lou interrupted with the arrival of their entrees. He glanced at Izzy and said, "Is he picking on you? Brother or not, I can take care of him if he's bothering you." He winked at her and put his hand on Blake's shoulder.

Izzy laughed and gestured him away with her hand. "He's my favorite brother and no, he's not picking on me. I'm living a little too much in the past right now."

"I hear ya. Best to stay focused on right now, believe me. I lived through my past once, I don't need to revisit it." He turned his head at someone calling his name, and said, "You guys enjoy. I'll bring you something sweet to cheer you up in a bit."

As they ate, Blake talked about how much they could fit in one of the large trucks from the winery and his personal truck. "We could probably talk Nate into making the trip with us in his delivery truck if we need it."

"I think I can confine myself to what will fit. I'll have half the living space and less storage area in the garage. Maybe I can do like the owners of the new house and include some of the furnishings in the sale."

"The church always collects for their massive yard sale, so you could donate anything you can't sell," said Blake. "Mom would know who to contact."

Izzy nodded. "I think I'll go home this weekend and talk to Mom and Dad. What do you think about coming too, while the weather is nice?"

Blake looked at Ellie, who nodded. "It's doable for me. Ellie can drive my truck back, and we can load your SUV, along with the delivery truck."

"I'll call Mom and Dad, so they know what's happening before we get there."

"Don't forget Esther and Lauren." Blake scooped up a forkful of crab-laced macaroni and cheese. "Lauren was looking forward to Sabina having her Aunt Izzy close by, but she'll also be fine if you're not there."

"Don't forget Shannon," said Izzy, mentioning their third sister. "Although, it won't have any impact on her. She seems to float around from place to place and doesn't come home often."

Blake rolled his eyes. "Until she needs something. I'm done with her and if I were you, I'd let Mom and Dad tell her. We never know where she is anyway."

Shannon was the square peg in a family of round holes. All the siblings were hardworking and responsible, dedicated to family, traditions, and their community, but Shannon, the youngest daughter of Gene and Helen, was anything but traditional. It could be argued that the baby of the family always got away with more, but Blake was technically the baby, so nobody quite understood what had happened with Shannon.

Blake was sure she had been switched at the hospital. He had gone the rounds with their parents about the way Shannon behaved and her lifestyle of nonconformity, but it had no impact. Izzy attempted to reason with them and tried her best to instill some sense of responsibility in Shannon, but failed on both fronts. They indulged Shannon and she let them. Her hatred of authority and capitalism had started when she was young, going to college in Oregon, paid for, of course, by her parents. Everyone assumed she would outgrow it, but she was now forty-one and still had no permanent address or job, preferring to be a professional protestor, traveling from cause to cause, but never able to articulate what she was actually protesting.

Blake deemed Shannon an embarrassment and never missed an opportunity to tell her so. Izzy took a more rational approach with her, but all her advice fell on deaf ears. Esther never said much either way, always trying to keep the peace. Lauren, who had always been closest to Blake, took his side in everything, but had been too preoccupied with her pregnancy and baby, Sabina, to get involved in Shannon's recent rantings.

Her stomach roiled at the thought of breaking the news to her whole family that she would be leaving her hometown. Then, there was Mia. Her daughter had never been especially close to her, so Izzy couldn't imagine Mia would care where her mother lived. But that didn't mean Mia wouldn't be upset. Until very recently, she still worshiped her father and rarely contacted Izzy, usually choosing not to return her calls or reply to texts with only one-word responses, when she replied at all. Then, after Izzy, with Max's support, helped Mia enroll in the medical imaging program at the University of Washington, she had been warmer towards her mother, but still elusive when it came to regular communication.

Lou delivered a brownie sundae and three long spoons to the table when he collected their empty plates. "On the house. I hope your week gets better, Izzy."

"How sweet are you? I'm sure it will. I've decided to buy a place here and move, so that's why all the serious faces earlier. I'm worrying about how my decision will impact my family."

"That's great news for us. We can never have too many smart beautiful women on the island." He winked at her and added, "I'm happy to hear your news." A loud crash caused Lou to roll his eyes. "I've got new help in the kitchen. Enjoy your evening, folks." He hurried away from the table.

Ellie pushed the sundae closer to Blake and Izzy. "I've overdone the sugar lately, and my insulin levels are a bit high for any more cheating right now."

Not convinced the sugary sweetness would sit well, but not wanting to ignore Lou's kind gesture, Izzy took a few bites, but left the bulk to Blake, who had no trouble eating every last drop. They heard a yell from the kitchen and turned at the sound of Lou's voice yelling a string of expletives. Blake darted through the tables, followed closely by Izzy.

They found Lou with a bloody gash across the inside of his palm, holding a towel to his hand. "Oh, boy. You're going to need some stitches," said Blake.

Lou grimaced and muttered. "I also need to fire my latest hire." He glared at a young man in a dirty apron. The boy's mouth gaped open as he watched Lou's blood drip onto the floor.

Izzy gripped Lou's shoulder. "I'll drive you to the emergency room, come on." She ushered him through the kitchen and out the back door.

Blake hollered, "We'll stay here and keep an eye on the place."

Izzy walked with Lou to her car, and they hurried through the streets to the emergency room entrance at the hospital. Despite Lou pressing on the towel the entire time, it was drenched with blood. His normal sarcasm and teasing, replaced by silence and a sheen of sweat across his pale face, worried Izzy.

She put her arm around him and led him through the doors. Luckily, the waiting area wasn't full and the woman at the counter ushered Lou through to the treatment area.

Izzy paced the hallway while she waited. She glanced at the wall clock and shrugged. "No time like the present," she whispered as she hit the button on her phone to connect with her parents.

She found a quiet corner outside the closed laboratory and settled into a chair. Both her mom and dad were on the phone as she explained her decision about moving to Friday Harbor. Much to her surprise, they didn't sound upset and only encouraged her. They told her they would miss her, but they understood her wanting to slow down, and after attending Blake's wedding, they appreciated the charm and alure of the small island.

Before she could ask about borrowing any cash, her dad offered it. They were excited about the prospect of a visit that weekend and Gene volunteered some helpers from the winery. "You can store anything at the warehouse until you're ready for it," he added.

"Plan on eating here at the house when you're in town. I'll call your sisters, and we'll have a celebration," said Helen.

Izzy promised to send photos of the house on the golf course, and disconnected, feeling like a heavy weight had been lifted from her shoulders. She loved her parents and would never do anything to hurt them. Hearing the genuine excitement in their voices eased the concern that had formed a knot in her stomach.

She wandered back to the emergency room reception, and heard Lou laughing. A few minutes later, Andi came through the door. "Izzy, come on back, if you'd like. Lou is almost done."

"Oh, I forgot you work here on Mondays." Izzy stepped through the door, smiling at Andi, who also helped out at

Kate's shop, and followed her to a cubicle, where Lou was resting on a bed.

Andi tapped her watch and said, "Almost done for the day. I'm off in a few minutes."

Izzy noticed Lou's hand wrapped in gauze. "How's the hand feeling?"

He shrugged. "Not too bad." He turned his eyes toward Andi. "She's an angel. I barely felt a thing, plus she held my good hand the whole time." He wriggled his brows at Andi, and she blushed.

The nurse smiled and waved her hand in the air. "I never realized what a flirt Lou was. I only knew he had the best crab cakes on the island."

Izzy's phone chimed with a text alert. She glanced at it and smiled. "It's Blake, checking on you. He and Ellie are still at the restaurant."

"We're waiting for the doctor to sign off and then Lou can get out of here." Andi craned her neck to look around the corner. "In fact, I can give Lou a ride. I'll be leaving myself in a few minutes."

"Are you sure?" asked Izzy.

Lou turned to her and his eyes widened. "She can give me a ride, and I'll treat her to a late dinner. All the crab cakes she wants."

Izzy stifled a laugh and put her hand on Lou's shoulder. "If you need anything let us know, okay?"

"I'll be fine. Thanks for bringing me in. Sorry I ruined your evening."

She shook her head. "You didn't ruin anything. Take care of yourself and for once, follow directions, will you?" She gestured to his hand and arched her brows at Andi.

Andi narrowed her eyes at Lou. "I'll make sure he does as he's told." She stepped closer to Izzy. "You're working tomorrow at Kate's, right?"

"Yes, I'll be there. I was telling Lou at dinner, I've decided to buy a house and move here, so I'm hoping to be signing some papers with Jack, but I'll be at work. I'm going to need Kate's help figuring out furnishings."

"That's so exciting. I'm thrilled you've decided to make Friday Harbor your new home. We'll have such fun decorating." Andi peppered her with questions about the style of the home as she walked her to the main door.

Izzy waved goodbye as she slid behind the wheel and steered for her tiny beach cottage that would soon be replaced with a real house. A place she alone had chosen where she would start her new adventure, in the small community she had begun to think of as home, filled with friends she had come to cherish. She breathed a sigh of relief. With the weight of telling her family behind her, she could let the guilt go and make room for excitement.

Chapter 3

L AST NIGHT, Izzy hadn't been able to resist texting Jack as soon as she got home from the hospital to let him know she wanted the house. He suggested she stop by the realty office on her way to Kate's shop, which was where she found herself signing papers and putting down a deposit. Jack recommended she offer the current asking price and she agreed.

He added the paperwork to the crisp new folder on his desk and shook her hand. "Okay, we're off and running. The owners live over in Redmond now, so we should be able to make quick work of this, especially with a cash offer. I'll get moving on it and will stop by the shop with any updates."

Izzy thanked him and drove the few blocks to Alexander's. With the busy season behind them, Tuesdays were quiet in the shop. After calling her realtor in Richland to list the house and fax her the signed paperwork, Izzy spent most of her time dusting and rearranging things to give the shop a fresh look. As she placed pillows and trinkets in new locations, she thought of how she would decorate her new home.

Her house in Richland was ornate, almost gaudy, with rich, dark colors, lots of tile and decorative columns, and it felt heavy. She wanted her new home to have a lighter, airy, more carefree vibe. When she'd first walked in, and had seen all the natural light and the white walls, she'd known it was what she wanted. Perhaps it was a metaphor for what she hoped her life would be like—relaxed and cheerful.

The decision to spend all that money on her first house had been John's, and she'd let him handle the details, including the furnishings and décor. John's tastes had tended toward gilded luxury. With those years behind her, she now realized his self-worth was wrapped up in showing people how well off he was with extravagant surroundings and purchases. At the time, she hadn't cared much, as she was focused more on her work and knew how excited he was to be able to afford such a home. But the house, although beautiful, wasn't her style. It was too lavish, too rich.

Instead of being paid by Kate, she earned store credits and had built up enough to warrant stashing a few of her favorite things on a shelf in the back room. She had fallen in love with the subtle blush color of pink, featured in several accent pieces, and planned to make it the focus color in her bedroom.

Of the things tucked away, she wanted Kate to help her decide. Kate had such an eye and was sure to have some fabulous ideas. Izzy could hardly wait to tell her about the house. Kate and Spence had taken a short trip over to Orcas Island to get away for a couple of days. After her old friend Maggie's death, she had been in a bit of a slump and Spence surprised her with the much needed escape.

In between tidying the shop, Izzy sold a few small items and visited with some window shoppers. Late in the afternoon, Jack came through the door, sporting a huge grin. "Great news, Izzy. They've accepted your offer, so we'll be going through the escrow process. I don't foresee any issues, and I'll prod the title company to hurry it along."

A sense of peace settled around her as she closed out the register for the day and prepared the deposit. Despite having John removed from her life for the last fifteen years, she'd continued to live the life they had built, in the house he coveted, in the neighborhood he'd chosen, albeit alone. Now, she would do things her way.

She picked up dinner to go from the Jade Garden and settled into her cottage to make a list of all the things she needed to bring from her old house. She had talked to Lauren and Esther last night; both of them were excited for her and told her not to worry about their parents. They both assured her they would be around to help them with anything they needed.

It had lightened her heart and eased the regret that plagued her each time she thought of abandoning them. They were in their mid-seventies, and while healthy now, she knew there might come a day when they wouldn't be, and it made her doubt her decision. She should have done something like this years ago, but like with everything, hindsight provided perfect clarity.

At times, Izzy lamented the fact that she had wasted her youth with John and then when their marriage dissolved, felt stuck. In the years after the divorce, she chose not to think about it much and despite her outward strength, deep inside, she suffered silently. Not only did her husband leave her, but in a show of support for him, her own daughter chose to discard her. Izzy had never felt so alone, deserted and neglected by the two people she assumed would be with her forever.

After John and Mia left, she fell back into the embrace of her loving parents and family, immersed in their loud and jovial dinners, taking care of the winery business, helping her siblings and their friends with legal matters, and building up her clientele in her own law office. She put all her energy into her practice. It was far easier to work until she was exhausted and then fall into bed, than it was to sit alone and think of all she had lost.

She glanced in the mirror when she walked into her tiny bathroom and was startled at the expansion of silvery strands into her dark hair. After much thought and a long conversation with Jen a few months ago, she decided to quit coloring it and let it go natural.

It might seem like a trivial decision to some, but until she started giving it serious consideration, Izzy didn't realize how much of her identity was wrapped up in her dark hair. She'd been coloring it to keep the gray at bay for the last twelve years, and the time between visits had been decreasing. Jen explained, as she painted on lowlights in the crown during Izzy's recent visit, they would obscure the line of demarcation as the process of growing out her gray hair continued.

Jen had warned her it was a long haul, especially since Izzy wasn't a fan of short haircuts and preferred her below the shoulder length. As she studied her image, she wondered if she shouldn't reconsider cutting it shorter. Jen reassured her she could always revert back to coloring her hair if she didn't like the color of her gray or changed her mind. It was a risk-free decision, but one more adjustment for Izzy to accept.

She was at the age when drastic changes were taking place in her body. The vivid memory of a conversation with her doctor, two years ago, flashed in her mind. That was the day she learned, much to her dismay, perimenopause could last for years. The information was inexact and inadequate as to causation and treatments. In exasperation, Izzy had demanded to know, if we could make computers the size of thumbnails and send people into space, why couldn't modern medicine get a grip on this transition that impacted millions of women. The look on his face, one of exasperation, made her chuckle now.

THE HOT FLASHES had wreaked havoc with her, until she found a specialist who turned her onto the magic of progesterone cream. As she thought about her doctor, doubts crept into her mind. She would have to find new doctors and a dentist, or face making a long trip each time she needed one. She added that to another list and while still excited about the future, felt a bit more overwhelmed.

WHEN IZZY WOKE early the next morning, she packed a few things and called Blake to let him know she had decided to head back to Richland a few days early to start packing. She checked her texts, hoping Mia would have replied, but nothing yet. She had tried calling her daughter to tell her the news and left a voicemail, and texted her as well, since it seemed to be the only way Mia communicated these days.

She stopped by Sam's coffee shop on the way and bought a large chai tea latte and a fresh bear claw for the trip. On the ferry, she left her SUV on the car deck and went upstairs to enjoy her breakfast and the view of deep green islands dotting the waters. In addition to the larger inhabited islands, the area consisted of almost two hundred islands, some quite small, but all gorgeous.

The eight o'clock ferry didn't make any stops, and got her to Anacortes a bit after nine. She had a five-hour drive ahead of her and set off for the interstate. After only about forty minutes on the busy road, she cut off at Everett and headed east. Over the years, she had learned to avoid the clog of traffic that always surrounded Seattle, and rather than make herself crazy sitting or inching along for what could be hours, she elected to take the slightly farther, but more scenic route, that in the end would be quicker than traveling through the city. The last thing she needed was more stress.

As she drove, her decision to find a local doctor strengthened; she didn't want to make this trek for routine appointments. Maybe she could enlist Max's help to find a good doctor on the island, or at least closer to her. She stopped in Leavenworth, a cute Bavarian styled town known for its extravagant Christmas celebration. After a quick bite to eat and fuel she got behind the wheel for the last stretch of her trip.

When she pulled up to her house, she saw her mom and dad's car in the driveway and the Griffin Winery truck backed up to one of the garage doors. She should have known her parents would have already organized things. When she walked in, she saw a mountain of boxes her mom and dad had taped together in preparation for packing and heard their voices coming from the kitchen.

"Hey, you two," she said, putting down her purse and hugging each of them. "Thank you for getting a head start. I didn't expect you to do all this, but I'm grateful."

Her dad put his arm around her shoulders. "We didn't have anything else to do, and when you called and said you wanted to get started, we thought we should help. We picked up some moving boxes."

Her mom smiled and added, "Your dad has a couple meetings, but I'm free this week and can help you wrap and pack. It'll be fun, and will give us more time to spend with Blake and Ellie this weekend." She glanced at her husband. "Your dad has organized some staff from the winery to come over and load the truck Saturday and Sunday, if need be."

Izzy pulled a package of colored sticky notes from her bag and gave her mom instructions on what to pack in the kitchen, before setting out to tag things to take with her. Her office furnishings and all the contents would be moving to the island. She had decorated her office with soft neutrals and loved the fabric couch and oversized chaise chair.

She tagged a few pieces of furniture throughout the house, but would be leaving most of the heavy dark furnishings behind or selling them. As she surveyed each room, she was convinced it would all fit in the delivery truck. After tagging everything she wanted, she set about boxing up her office.

Several hours passed before she wandered into the kitchen, where she found her mom and dad still emptying cupboards and a neat stack of labeled boxes in the corner. Izzy let them finish the box they were working on, and then insisted they call it a day with her treating them to dinner at their favorite Italian restaurant.

After a delicious and fun-filled dinner, she spent a few more hours boxing up mementos, taking her time going through old photograph albums, reliving happier times, and shedding more than a few tears watching Mia grow up among the pages. After her daughter had left home, there were fewer and fewer photos of her, or any of them. It was when the life Izzy had known ceased to exist. She wasn't sure she could pinpoint the exact moment she had lost Mia, only that the end result had been her daughter's sneering look as she left with her father that day so long ago. Izzy had thought Mia would change her mind and want to come back, but the fissure between them had only expanded over time.

Izzy had quit counting the number of times Mia would agree to visit for a family dinner, a birthday, or Mother's Day celebration, and then at the last minute, cancel or worse, not show at all. Some of Izzy's friends had told her it would blow over and Mia was a typical teenager acting out, but the sweet girl who had held her hand and loved to snuggle and read stories with her, was gone forever.

Izzy had fond memories of taking Mia to the park and the river, running through the vines at the vineyard, sipping ice cream sodas at the shop downtown, and field trips with her elementary school classes. The loss of all of that and the open disdain Mia had for her defied logic. Izzy never imagined the closeness they had shared for all of those early years would disappear and be replaced with such contempt. Try as she might, she'd never been successful in repairing the rift.

The trip down memory lane prompted her to check her phone again.

Nothing from Mia.

She tapped in another text message, asking her to get in touch. Izzy wasn't sure how Mia would react to her selling the house or moving, but if past experience held true, she was prepared for an outburst of some sort. In Mia's eyes, everything Izzy did was wrong, so there was no reason to expect anything different with this situation. After leaving to live with John, Mia never expressed an attachment to the house, but she rarely missed an opportunity to start a quarrel.

Sadly, Mia was another reason Izzy wanted to move to Friday Harbor. She would be more removed from her daughter's constant drama and the distance would make it more difficult for Mia to pop in with her latest problem— although, Izzy had been surprised when she showed up on the island this summer, unannounced. Mia hadn't been as abrasive on that visit, but she had been desperate, so it made sense. Sometimes, Izzy wondered if her daughter truly hated her as much as she seemed to.

Chapter 4

AFTER A FEW days of hard work, hours of snuggling with baby Beanie, and lots of help from her family, Izzy fought back tears and hugged her parents goodbye early Sunday morning. She, along with Blake and Ellie, promised to make it back for a visit during the holidays.

Things were in motion with the realtor. Her family was handling an estate type of sale for the furnishings she didn't want, some items would stay with the house, and her mom would coordinate donating any remaining items. Izzy had urged them to take anything they wanted from the house prior to the sale.

She led the way in her SUV, followed by Blake driving the delivery truck, with Ellie bringing up the rear in Blake's pickup. Izzy scolded herself as she made her way to the interstate, tears streaking her cheeks. She was always the strong one, the logical one. She hated getting emotional, and didn't think she had any attachment to her house, but leaving it behind was harder than she anticipated. Leaving her parents was heart wrenching. Despite the smiles on their faces and their excitement, they couldn't hide the tears in their eyes. Her dad had never hugged her so tightly, and all she'd wanted to do was call the whole thing off.

Blake had urged her forward, making plans for their parents to come to the island and stay a few weeks in the summer. They both perked up at the suggestion and started chatting about the best time to come. As they walked away,

Blake whispered, "You have to focus on new memories and making fun plans. Don't get stuck in the past."

He was right, and wiser than she sometimes realized. As she dried her tears, she quieted her mind, resisting the thoughts of self-doubt and guilt, and pushed her brain into organizing fun activities for her dad and mom. Her dad enjoyed golfing, so her new house would be perfect, and she hoped they would be able to make a few trips a year and stay for several weeks each time. The long drive worried her. They weren't used to the heavy traffic around the city, so she made a mental note to check flights that might work for them.

The trip back to the island was a bit slower, with the big truck. They stopped only for fuel and a late breakfast, and boarded the ferry that would get them back to Friday Harbor before four o'clock. They chose a table by the window, and Izzy let the gentle motion lull her and closed her eyes.

She appreciated Blake and Ellie making the trip with her. It made it much easier to have their company and the distraction of their conversation, along with their enthusiasm for her decision to move. They spent the hour-long crossing talking about ideas for the winery, the upcoming weddings they had for the fall and winter, and getting Izzy moved into her new house. Blake was going to park the delivery truck at the winery until they got the go ahead from Jack to move in.

Kate and Spence had invited the three of them to dinner tonight, knowing they wouldn't feel like putting a meal together after a long day. Kate and Izzy had texted back and forth over the weekend, and Kate already had some ideas on furnishings and couldn't wait to help Izzy make her new house a home.

As the island came into view, and Izzy spotted the colorful buildings along Front Street and the ferry landing, her heart swelled with peace. This tiny slice of the world delivered the serenity she craved, along with the love of support from the circle of friends she coveted. She was almost home.

IZZY DROVE DIRECTLY to Kate's house, while Blake and Ellie headed to the winery. Kate welcomed Izzy inside with a long hug. Spence was in the kitchen, cooking something that smelled delicious, with Roxy keeping watch.

Kate led Izzy into the living room, where she sunk into a comfortable chair, relaxing for the first time since she embarked on her journey several days ago.

She swallowed several sips of refreshing iced tea mixed with a bit of lemonade and let out a long sigh. "This tastes wonderful."

"Spence is grilling some fresh salmon for us. I've got some appetizers ready," Kate said, moving into the kitchen. She returned with a tray of mini quiches and bacon wrapped dates. Izzy took a couple of each and pronounced them delicious.

Kate retrieved some magazines from the coffee table and flipped to a few pages she had marked. "I wanted you to take a look at some of these concepts for your new place."

The doorbell interrupted them, and Kate rose to lead Blake and Ellie into the house. The foursome chatted about Izzy's new house while they continued to snack. As Spence called them to the dining room, Izzy's phone buzzed. She was surprised to see an actual call from Mia.

She stepped out the front door to take the call, telling them all to go ahead and start eating without her.

"Hey, Mia, I'm surprised you're calling instead of texting." Her greeting was met with silence. "Mia, are you there?"

Sobs came through her speaker. "Mom," Mia mumbled.

"What's wrong?" More sobbing and muffled words Izzy couldn't understand came from her daughter. "Are you okay? Where are you?"

Fear rippled through her, as she listened to Mia blubber. It took patience, but Izzy finally understood Mia was at her campus apartment and was safe, but distraught. Izzy listened, letting Mia's heaving sobs subside, trying not to press her while horrible thoughts of what might be wrong filled her mind.

Mia tended to be dramatic, so Izzy tried to ignore the clenching pain in her stomach and hoped whatever was going on was something related to school or a new boyfriend, and not anything serious.

It took several minutes until she heard Mia take a long breath. "I'm pregnant."

Izzy's heart sank and she reached for the side of the house. "Oh, Mia." She wanted to ask her how she could be so careless, but knew it wouldn't help the situation. "What can I do to help?"

"Nothing, nothing at all. I called Dad and he went totally ballistic. Told me I was irresponsible, like you, and shouldn't count on him to rescue me like he had to do for you. He told me to call you."

Of course, he did. Izzy gritted her teeth as she seethed with rage at her ex-husband. He was great for handing out money and showering Mia with gifts and attention, making her dependent, until it wasn't convenient for him. Now, their daughter was thirty years old, irresponsible, had never held down a job, never paid her own way, and had only buckled down in the last few months with her interest in the medical imaging program. A baby would throw a wrench into the midst of those plans.

Like with so many things surrounding John, Izzy was left to clean up the mess. Mia couldn't even take care of herself, and Izzy had no idea how her daughter would care for a baby. "Did you go to the doctor and confirm the pregnancy?"

"Yes, I went to the health center today. I want to go home. I don't want to be here. I don't know what to do. Dad told me I couldn't come back to the house."

"I know it's scary and not something you wanted to happen, but going to your dad's house isn't going to change things. It's important you keep up with your studies."

"Can I come back to your house in Richland?" Mia's voice took on the childlike tone she had perfected with her father. It had never worked with Izzy.

"I'm afraid I'm selling the house. That's why I tried to call you so many times this past week. I'm moving to the island."

"What?" Izzy held the phone away from her ear at the shrill sound of Mia's voice. "How can you sell our house without even asking me? I can't believe you and Dad are both so selfish and awful."

Before Izzy could respond, Mia disconnected.

Izzy's head throbbed as she tucked her phone in her pocket and went in through the door. Any hope for a good night's sleep after the exhaustion of the last few days evaporated as she thought of her daughter.

She slipped into her chair at the table, and the laughter came to a halt. "Izzy, what's wrong?" asked Kate.

She looked across the table at her brother, who was frowning at her, concern in his eyes. "Izz, what is it?"

"Mia. She, uh, well, there's no easy way to say this. She's pregnant."

A collection of serious and concerned faces stared back at her. "She called John first, and he hit the ceiling and offered no help or support, and told her she was irresponsible, like her mother." Her throat burned, and she took a long swallow from her iced tea.

"He has always been such a jerk, Izzy. Don't let him get to you." Blake reached for her arm.

"Mia wanted to come home to the house in Richland. I told her it was for sale and she blew up. I'm not sure what to do, but taking the ferry back tonight and trying to reason with her doesn't appeal to me." Every muscle in her body ached and she was too tired to think of solutions.

Blake glanced at Ellie. "I could call her or maybe Ellie could try talking to her. You could take a few days, go over later this week and check on her, help her figure out a plan."

Izzy nodded. "I'd be of no use to her tonight, and she's in a mood I'm sure wouldn't be receptive to any advice I have to give. I'm so furious with John right now. He's lucky I'm far away from him."

"It's a shame this is happening. She seemed excited about the program she's in," said Kate. "It's a two-year degree, right?"

Izzy nodded. "Yes, and she needs to stay focused and get it completed as soon as she can, now that she'll have a baby to raise. If John would have supported me in making her buckle down years ago, she'd be in a better position. Now, she's going to have to take time off and drag out her education before she can get a decent job. It's exasperating."

"I'm sure she's feeling overwhelmed and lost," said Ellie. "I'd like to call her and see if I can help."

"That's nice of you, and I'm sure you'll get further than I will." Izzy sighed and added, "I care for her so much, and worry about her. But I've played this game for far too many years and honestly, I'm exhausted."

They finished their meal with Izzy picking at and rearranging the food on her plate, but not eating much. Blake and Ellie hugged Izzy goodbye and thanked Kate and Spence for dinner before leaving. Ellie promised to call Izzy as soon as she was able to talk to Mia.

Kate brewed tea while Spence talked Izzy into a small slice of pumpkin cake, while she petted Roxy, their beautiful golden retriever, a lighter blonde, almost white color. She was a retired explosive detection dog Spence had acquired from the police department in Seattle. Izzy watched Kate pour the golden colored liquid into one of her vintage teacups. "I'm sorry to put such a damper on your lovely meal. You probably think I'm a horrible mother."

Kate shook her head. "Not at all. Her news would be jarring, and I know she hasn't been the easiest child. Being a mother is so hard. You want what's best for them and you want to save them from all their mistakes, but it's impossible." Kate knew that more than anyone. Losing her beloved daughter, Karen, to suicide had left a hole in her heart forever, and the recent events with Maggie's visit and subsequent death brought all of those old memories bubbling to the surface for her.

Tears filled Izzy's eyes. "Mia thinks her life is tough now. She has no idea what adding a baby will do to it. I was entirely too young when I had her, and looking back, I'm not sure how I was able to accomplish everything I did." She took a sip of tea before continuing. "I'm good at finding solutions to problems, but our relationship has never been great, aside from when she was young. Once she decided I was the enemy in the divorce, it's been dicey. We tolerate each other, but only for short periods. Part of me wants to take care of her and the other part wants to give her the tough love treatment."

"That's understandable." Kate's compassionate eyes held hers. "I think you need some rest. Let Ellie and Blake talk to her, and you can figure out a plan tomorrow, after you've had some sleep. You could always text her and let her know you're there for her when she's ready to talk."

"You're right, of course. I need to separate my anger at John, and be gentle with her. I remember what it felt like to be pregnant when it was the last thing I wanted."

Kate squeezed Izzy's hand. "I know you want to teach her to be strong and responsible, but right now she needs a soft place, and you're the only one who can provide it."

Hearing her words, Izzy didn't trust her voice and reached for her tea, letting it soothe her suddenly dry throat.

Spence nudged Kate with his elbow and raised his brows at her. Kate turned her attention to Izzy. "It seems like the wrong time to mention this, but Spence obviously thinks I should. I had intended to invite you to a getaway. I'm going to head over to a trade show next week. I have a friend I met at the same show a few years ago, Cyndy, who lives in Driftwood Bay. She suggested I spend a few days there and tack on a day or two, so I made a reservation at her friend's bed and breakfast. It's called Glass Beach Cottage and looks delightful. Cyndy highly recommends it and I thought it would be nice for you to come with me."

"That sounds heavenly," said Izzy. "I'd love to go, if I can make it work. It depends on Mia."

"Of course. We'll play it by ear."

Izzy hugged them both goodbye and sat in her car for a few minutes texting her daughter before she headed back to her cottage. Kate's advice had been sound, and she only hoped Mia would take some small comfort knowing Izzy was there for her. As she pulled into her parking area and noticed the sliver of the moon hanging in the sky, it reminded her of one of Mia's favorite books from her childhood, *Goodnight Moon.*

"Goodnight, Mia," Izzy whispered as she crawled into bed, hoping the morning would bring a brighter day.

Chapter 5

AFTER BEING AWAKE until the wee hours, searching for answers in the soft glow of the moonlight that filtered through her window, Izzy slept later than usual, right through an early morning text from Ellie. As she later scrolled the message, she learned Ellie had texted with Mia off and on throughout the night, and had convinced her to come to the island at the end of the week. Mia would arrive on the Thursday evening ferry, and Ellie and Blake were prepared to let her stay with them.

Tears of relief clouded Izzy's eyes as she tapped in a reply, thanking Ellie and apologizing for not seeing it earlier. She took a long shower and let the hot water cascade over her shoulders, hoping to melt the tangle of muscles across her back. When she got out, the coffee she had started brewing was ready, and she poured herself a full mug, breathing in the rich scent as she carried it outside.

No sooner had she swallowed her first sip when her phone rang. Jack's name popped up on her screen. As she listened, a smile filled her face. "Thanks, Jack. I can meet you there this morning. See you in about an hour." Shame at the good news from Jack washed over her. How could she be happy when her daughter was suffering?

As she drove to her new house to collect the keys and sign a form to allow her to move her things in a few days ahead of the official closing date, Mia continued to weigh on her mind. While trying to sleep last night, Izzy had decided she would offer Mia a room in her new home, so she would have a place to stay once she had to take a break from school. She would help her daughter figure out a plan on how to arrange for child care, so she could finish her degree when she could go back.

Kate's advice last night had hit home, and she knew she wouldn't have made it through her own pregnancy without her mom and dad's support. John had been there too, though he wasn't much help—but she hadn't been alone. Though gripped by the deep fear that Mia would use this as an excuse not to finish school, Izzy knew that her daughter needed help more than a lecture.

After giving her a quick overview of the mechanical systems in the house, Jack gave her the keys, and let her know she had an appointment at the title company on Friday morning to sign the documents to make it all official. After seeing him out, she slipped into the chair at the dining table to savor the delight of sitting in her new house, gazing at the manicured greens.

Izzy texted Blake to see if he had time to drive the truck with her belongings over to the new house. The house was quiet and calming, full of gorgeous morning light. Although her excitement of her new adventure was dampened by the thought of Mia's situation and the possibility of having her stay, she reveled in the peaceful feeling the house brought her. Being a mom, she knew, required sacrificing for your children, and her mother had been a wonderful example. If Izzy had a good relationship with Mia, it would be different, but she worried about spending that much time together and dreaded the bickering that was sure to ensue.

She had so many questions and had to remind herself not to treat Mia like a client, probing for all the details. She knew she had to curb her tendencies to solve problems, and be present for her daughter. She wasn't sure how long Mia would continue to go to school, or when the baby was due, but hoped she could get through two quarters and then be able to resume school in the fall.

At least, in this house, they'd each have their own space. Mia's room would be upstairs. Both guest rooms were large enough to accommodate a crib. She would add it to the list of furnishings she needed to purchase. While she was thinking about it, she texted Kate to see if she had time to stop by and help her decide on a few pieces. From all of her years in the city, Kate had contacts everywhere and could find anything a customer desired. As soon as she finished composing her message, she saw a reply from Blake saying he would be there with the truck in the late afternoon and would bring a crew if she would provide pizza.

She laughed and put in a call to Big Tony's, and ordered several pizzas for pick up in the early evening. Next, she tackled getting the utilities transferred to her name and organizing Internet service. While she was finishing her call, her phone chimed. She disconnected and saw a text from Mia. *Thanks for your message. I'll see you Thursday.*

The breath Izzy had been holding, floated between her lips while she read the message again. She was tempted to ask a question, but instead sent a heart emoji and celebrated what was the longest text she ever remembered getting from her daughter.

After calling her parents to let them know Mia's news and to thank them again for loaning her the funds to make her house a reality, she spent the rest of the morning and early afternoon getting ready for the delivery, figuring out how to organize the kitchen, and adding to her never-ending list. Her parents had taken the news about Mia's pregnancy in stride, but she sensed the disappointment in their voices, and was sure they were remembering the day she had told them she was pregnant and would be marrying John. Mia hadn't even mentioned the father. Times had certainly changed.

She took a break to grab lunch and pop by the store to get a few essentials and when she arrived back at the house found Kate and Spence had parked in her driveway.

She gave them a tour of the house and watched as Kate scribbled in her notebook, sketching out ideas and making a list. Spence spent time admiring the view from the patio and checking out the grill. While he was outside, he made himself useful and used some of Izzy's newly purchased products to clean the table, chairs, and firepit table.

Kate and Izzy sat at the dining table and discussed options and color schemes until Blake arrived, along with Nate, Charlie, Jeff, and Max. They got busy unloading the truck and told Izzy their better halves would be joining them for pizza later. Izzy explained how to situate her office furniture and left them to it.

Kate helped Izzy select all the bedroom furniture, then got on the phone with one of her suppliers to check stock and get the orders in motion. Kate had guided Izzy to wooden pieces the color of driftwood, more casual and relaxed than her old furniture had been, and perfect for creating the coastal atmosphere Izzy desired.

Spence offered to run to town and get the pizzas, while Izzy and Kate unpacked boxes in the kitchen, leaving the younger men to do the heavy lifting. In between stocking her cupboards and drawers, the two chatted about the upcoming trip to Driftwood Bay.

Kate tackled organizing the silverware drawer. "I hope things work out with Mia, so you can come with me. It's perfect timing for you to find some great decorative pieces and accents at the show, and Cyndy has a lovely shop you can browse."

"I've been afraid to ask Mia any questions, but when Ellie gets here tonight, I might know more. I'm assuming Mia will stay for the weekend, since she doesn't have classes this

Friday, and will probably head back Sunday. I really want her to get as far as she can with her coursework before she has to take time off for the baby." Izzy flattened another empty box. "It's probably not the best time for a mini-vacation," she said, and gestured to the space around her, "with all this work, but I could use a break from reality."

"I feel the same way. These last few months with Maggie and Mitch's accident wore me out. I'm one of those people who is good during the crisis, but crumples afterward. That's why Spence distracted me with a trip over to Orcas."

"He's definitely a keeper. You two give me hope. I've avoided any type of romantic relationship after John, but I miss the companionship, having someone to lean on at times."

Kate smiled at her friend. "Spence is top shelf, always has been. We've been friends for so long, and things morphed into more after Karen's death and my divorce. He was there for me through it all. He's seen me at my absolute worst and helped me back from the edge of despair. I wouldn't have made it without him."

"You're lucky to have him. I was so hurt by John and Mia, dedicated myself to work and my family, thinking I would meet someone who would sweep me off my feet, but it never happened. My family, of course, tried to set me up with eligible men, but nothing clicked and honestly, I wasn't ready. Mia hated me already and I knew if I ever got serious about a man, she would come unglued." She finished another cupboard and opened a new box. "Then, it became easier to be alone, not take a risk. Now, here I am at fifty-one, never imagining my life quite like this."

"Age doesn't matter," said Kate, with a sly wink. "If you meet the right person, nothing matters and your whole world will feel right, like whatever you've been missing has been found." She smiled, with a faraway look in her eyes. "It's nothing short of magical."

Spence came through the door carrying a tower of pizza boxes, followed by Sam and Linda. A few minutes later Ellie arrived with Regi, toting little Emma, who was thriving despite the loss of her grandmother and guardian, Maggie, who had enlisted Kate's help to arrange for her adoption before she passed away. Izzy abandoned her work and conversation, and joined in welcoming each of them with hugs and thanks. The early October weather was perfect and allowed them to set up dinner on the patio. Jeff started the fire pit and showed Izzy the switch and how it was piped into the natural gas that fed the house.

Charlie had plans with Hayley and wished them all a good evening. Izzy thanked him and hugged him goodbye, making him promise to come back for a proper housewarming party. The friends gathered around, toasting Izzy's new house with plastic cups of iced tea and soft drinks.

The men had made quick work of emptying the truck, setting her furniture in place, and delivering all the boxes to the appropriate rooms. Jeff and Charlie even hung her artwork and installed the flat screen televisions in her bedroom and the living room. Once they finished the men escaped to the patio to discuss golf, while the women toured the house, leaving Kate to mind Emma in the dining room.

Izzy was still deciding on living room furniture, but was leaning toward Kate's recommendation of the light beige couches and chairs, and using pillows and other items to add color. Kate had shown her several choices and Izzy pictured each of them in the space. As she took in the space, she made her final choice, opting for the models Kate had told her were the most comfortable. That's what she wanted more than anything – a comfortable home. As she led the group back downstairs and eyed the empty space, she knew she had to make the trip with Kate work so she could pick out some other things for the house.

While they were making their way back to the dining area, Regi slipped an arm around Izzy's shoulders. "Ellie told us about Mia's situation and I wanted you to know, we've got all of Emma's things and are happy to gift them to you for Mia when the time comes, so don't rush to buy anything. Maggie had two of everything."

Izzy tightened her grip around Regi's waist. "That's so kind of you. I'll know more when I talk to Mia this weekend, but it sounds terrific. I was going to get a crib, but hadn't thought much further."

"Emma's going to be getting a bed soon, so we can give you the crib, if you like it."

"That's fabulous. I'll discuss it all with Mia. I'm going to offer her a room here so she can recuperate and I can help her with the baby." She shrugged and pursed her lips. "Not sure if she'll be agreeable, but we'll soon find out."

Regi smiled at her. "Mothers and daughters, huh? It's always more complicated than it looks."

Blake toted all the flattened boxes to the garage, while Izzy and the others made quick work of emptying those remaining and putting things away in cupboards and drawers. Jeff and Max made sure the firepit was turned off and all the patio furniture straightened before they collected their wives. Izzy thought it would be fun to have a Halloween party as an open house and vowed to work on planning one. One by one, the couples made their exit and Izzy was left alone.

She would have loved to stay the night, but didn't feel like sleeping on her office couch and technically wasn't allowed to occupy the house yet. It was beginning to feel more and more like hers, and had Mia's situation not been at the forefront of her thoughts, she would have felt more like celebrating.

BY THURSDAY AFTERNOON, Izzy had things organized for Mia's stay, stocked the fridge and pantry at the new house with groceries, and borrowed a temporary bed and couch from a client of Jack's, who was moving off the island and listing his home.

In addition to hosting Mia that weekend, Ellie and Blake were making dinner to celebrate her arrival. Izzy sipped the smooth café mocha Sam had fixed her, while she waited for the ferry to arrive. She was early, but planned to use the time to relax and coach herself on how to interact with her daughter. Sam slipped into the chair across from Izzy and slid a plate with fresh brownies to her. "I thought you could use some chocolate fortification."

Izzy smiled and took one. "Chocolate cures everything, right?"

"I know you're dealing with lots of emotions right now." Sam placed her hand on Izzy's arm. "You're lucky to have each other. I would give anything to have my mom around to talk with about a problem. Remember that." Tears pooled in both of their eyes.

"You're right. No matter how much she irritates me, I'm thankful I have a daughter, and I'm lucky enough to still have my mom. I can't imagine how you got through everything you did without having yours."

"We do what we have to do, I suppose."

Izzy took a long swallow from her cup. "I'm the last person to lecture her about getting pregnant. I'm surprised at her age, she was so reckless, but it happens. I want her to look to the future and not have this alter her course. Now, a good job is not only a good idea, it's a necessity."

"Try be gentle with her. Imagine how scared she is."

Izzy nodded. "I know, I've been giving myself a pep talk all week. With all the words of wisdom I've been getting from Kate, Spence, Max, and you, I guess Blake's assessment of me being bossy is correct." She chuckled. "I'm going to do my best to keep my advice to myself until she asks for it." Izzy's eyebrows rose as she rolled her eyes. "Wish me luck."

Sam chuckled, and squeezed Izzy's arm. "You'll do fine. Chances are it won't all be solved in the next few days."

"Thanks, Sam. I think part of me is mourning what I had hoped would be a new chapter in my life, here, without old memories, and without the stress Mia typically brings to my doorstep. It sounds selfish, but if I'm honest, she's done it again."

Sam nodded, and took a sip from her own cup of tea. "That's understandable. Remember, we'll all be here for you and Mia, no matter what happens. We'll see you at Lou's for dinner Saturday night. I've got to get back to the kitchen." Sam rose from her chair and hugged Izzy.

Izzy sighed as she finished her mocha and gazed out the window at the harbor. She had made reservations for the whole group at Lou's, hoping Mia would feel everyone's love and acceptance and would know they were there to support her through this journey. She was also prepared to call it off, should Mia not be open to the idea of a large gathering.

Izzy had gone up against tough judges and opposing counsel over her career, but nothing delivered the self-doubt and fear coursing through her body like the thought of spending a few days with her own daughter.

Chapter 6

IZZY HAD PARKED close to the landing, and when she saw the ferry heading toward it, she waved goodbye to Sam and walked down the street. She stopped to pick up a dessert from the bakery and slipped it into the backseat. Although it could be inconvenient, Izzy loved that the ferry was the only way to access her new home, unless you took a boat or seaplane. There was something romantic in the nostalgia of the arrival of a ferry, the waiting and watching, the anticipation and the slowness of the entire process, whether as a passenger or the person waiting on the dock.

Izzy spotted Mia, noticing her usual smile was missing. She'd always had the posture of a ballerina, but today, her shoulders sagged as she lugged her suitcase down the ramp. Izzy stepped forward and waved. "Hi, Mia, let me grab your suitcase."

Her daughter flinched at Izzy's hand. "I'm not an invalid. I can do it myself."

"I'm parked over here," Izzy said, and led the way. With no question about Mia's current mood, Izzy ditched the idea of offering to take her to see her new house on the way to Blake's. Mia wouldn't be interested.

On the short drive, Izzy made small talk, holding true to the promise she had made to herself about not asking questions. It took all her verbal skills to elicit more than a one-word response from Mia. She pulled into the driveway, feeling the knots tighten in her shoulders and the beginning of a headache, and Mia had only been on the island for thirty minutes.

Her daughter exited the car, slammed the door, and made a beeline for the front door. As Izzy retrieved Mia's suitcase, she shook her head. Her daughter's newfound independence had been short-lived. Izzy carried the bakery box and tugged the case up the steps. She deposited the luggage in the guest room and slipped the cheesecake into the fridge.

The aroma of meat on the grill drifted from the patio, and Izzy followed the scent where she found Ellie with her arm around Mia. Both of them were sitting on the cheery green cushions of the curved outdoor couch with the flames flickering from the firepit table in front of them. The deck was decorated with white twinkle lights, as were the trees and bushes. Colored solar garden lights with whimsical butterflies and birds dotted the planters and only added to the charm of their lush back yard.

"Something smells wonderful," said Izzy, making her way to the grill at the other end of the deck. Blake lifted the lid as he wiggled his brows at her, revealing sizzling steaks and chicken.

"How's Mia seem?" he asked.

Izzy's eyes widened and she shook her head. "Insolent and irritated. Glad she's staying with you." She tilted her head towards the house. "I need wine."

Blake gave Izzy some directions on getting the side dishes from the kitchen and within a few minutes she had everything on the table, already decorated with candles and miniature lights in pretty glass containers. Had she been more confident in the company, Izzy would have said it was a perfect evening for a get-together.

Mia didn't say much as they ate the delicious meal. After drinking a glass of wine while she helped with dinner, Izzy had left her glass and the rest of the bottle in the kitchen, not wanting to tempt fate and risk an argument with Mia about drinking while pregnant, and opted to fill their glasses with iced tea instead.

Blake raised the topic of Izzy's new house, and Ellie chimed in saying how lovely it was. "You get to stay in it starting tomorrow, right?" Blake turned to his sister as he reached for another dinner roll.

"Yes, I'm looking forward to it, though it will be better when I have some furniture."

Mia's eyes narrowed. "What happened to all the furniture from your other house?"

"I'm selling most of it. The style doesn't fit this new house. It's all too bulky and ornate."

With a roll of her eyes and a huff, Mia dismissed her comments. Izzy was dying to ask Mia when the baby was due, but didn't dare. Ellie must have read her mind and posed the question.

Izzy held her breath, waiting for Mia to erupt. Instead, she said, "April first."

It took a huge effort not to blurt out something sarcastic about April Fool's Day, and Izzy reached for a drink of iced tea to keep her mouth occupied. Ellie smiled across the table and said, "Spring is such a beautiful time of year, that will be wonderful."

Izzy cleared her throat. "I wanted to make sure you knew there was plenty of room for you at the new house and you're welcome to stay there when the time comes. I can help you with the baby until you're back on your feet."

"Like that's real convenient with you living out here in the middle of nowhere. I'm sure Dad will come around. I'm going to call him and see if I can move down there." Mia's snarky tone reminded Izzy of her high school years.

She could feel Blake's eyes willing her not to say anything, so instead of telling Mia what she thought of the idea, she took another sip from her glass. She set the tea on the table and said, "Okay, well, the offer stands."

Despite all the tea she had gulped, Izzy's throat was dry. She had been foolish to think Mia would appreciate her help or be willing to accept it. As usual, she gravitated toward John, which Izzy was sure would result in further heartbreak, but it was a lesson Mia would have to learn the hard way.

Izzy didn't say much more, but listened as Ellie steered the conversation to safer topics. As the other three chatted, she learned Mia was taking the morning ferry back on Sunday. That bit of news lifted her gloomy spirits, knowing the path would be clear for her to accompany Kate to Driftwood Bay.

Mia didn't mention much about school, beyond the fact that she liked the program. If she was considering a move to California, she had no intention of finishing her degree. Mia, in her naivety, assumed John would pay her bills indefinitely. Part of Izzy, the part she didn't admire, hoped that if Mia disliked her so much, that she did move. Then she would be John's problem.

The pit in her stomach made eating the lovely meal difficult. She hated feeling that way about her own daughter, but it was clear Mia wasn't willing to put forth any effort into building a better relationship with her. She wondered how long it would take her to conclude that John was not the answer to her future. That glimmer of hope Izzy had kindled this past week, thinking she and Mia could bond over this ordeal was nothing more than a dying ember.

Izzy took charge of clearing the table and rushed the dessert process, anxious to leave and free herself from the tension and forced conversation. Blake packed up containers of leftovers, including a healthy slab of the cake he knew she loved, and a bottle of wine, and put everything in a sturdy bag.

He handed it to her with a long hug. "Sorry, Izz, I know this hasn't been easy tonight. She's acting like a brat, but maybe it's the hormones. She doesn't look pregnant, but she's three months along."

Izzy nodded, but didn't trust her voice. He held her close for a few minutes before she whispered. "I'll see you tomorrow. I'm going to say goodnight and get some rest."

"Try not to worry. I'll call you tomorrow and let you know how it's going."

Izzy walked to the patio and caught Ellie's eye. "I'm going to call it a night. I'll see everyone tomorrow. Thanks for a lovely dinner."

Ellie hurried from her chair and enveloped Izzy in a hug. As she did so, she whispered in her ear, "I'll talk to her a bit more. Don't worry."

"Goodnight, Mia. See you tomorrow." Izzy waved at her daughter, hoping for a reply, but received only an indifferent nod.

Izzy trudged to her car. She steered it toward the road and her last night in the tiny cottage she had enjoyed. Tonight, she had imagined sitting on the patio, enjoying the lovely yard and fire pit, sipping a bit of wine, helping Mia come to terms with the changes she would be facing, with the support of Ellie and Blake. Instead, she was alone, again.

Chapter 7

EVEN AFTER A late night glass of wine and some cheesecake, Izzy was up early, had her car loaded with the last of her personal possessions, left her keys to the cottage in the drop box at the main house, and set out for her appointment at the title company.

Although she hadn't bought a home in decades, her legal background made her familiar with the process and various contract documents. The cash sale eliminated much of the usual stack of paper requiring signatures, and she was in and out within thirty minutes.

While she was downtown, she stopped by the coffee shop and picked up two drinks to go, taking one to Kate at Alexander's. When Izzy walked in, Kate was ringing up a customer, so she left her drink on the counter behind her. As soon as the door shut behind the woman, Kate's voice beckoned Izzy from the back room.

"I signed the papers for the house, and wanted to stop by and tell you I'll be able to go on the trip with you Monday."

"That's wonderful news, and thank you for the coffee." Kate raised her paper cup to toast Izzy. "It will be so much more fun to have you with me. I'm wondering if we should take your SUV, since it's more spacious, and then if you find some things you want, you can bring them home."

"I'm happy to take my car, and do some shopping for the new house," Izzy replied with a smile.

"I've got a reservation on the early morning ferry, and that should put us in Driftwood Bay around noon, provided we can catch the right ferry out of Coupeville."

"I'll pick you up around seven."

"You haven't mentioned Mia. How did it go last night?"

Izzy shook her head. "Not great. She's treating me like she always has, and she's angry I'm selling the house and moving here. I was quite restrained and didn't bite when she baited me, but had a hard time when she said she plans to convince John to help her move down to California with him."

Kate's eyes widened. "Oh, dear. That won't end well, will it? Not with a new bride in the picture."

"I offered to let her stay with me when she's ready to have the baby and let her know I'd help her until she could get back on her feet, but she rejected the idea straightaway. I'm at a loss and right now, a week away, doing something besides worrying about her is exactly what I need."

Kate patted Izzy's hand. "I'm sorry you're having to deal with this. Give her time. She may come around."

"It seems like each time in my life I start to think things are improving between us and we can have a real relationship, something happens to derail it. I'll never understand why she harbors so much animosity toward me still. I accepted she chose John over me in the divorce, but that was so long ago." Izzy's voice cracked and she took a long swallow from her cup.

Kate reassured her with a smile. "I finally learned I can't be responsible for anyone's happiness but my own. Mia knows you're there for her. She came here, so there must be a tiny part of her that wanted to see you. She might need more time, and if you're right about her father, she's going to need you more than ever when she faces his rejection."

Izzy shut her eyes and shook her head. "I don't even want to think about it. I thought about calling him, but I don't want to get in the middle of it. It's time Mia learned what he's really like."

"Keep your chin up. You'll get through this." The door chimed as a customer came through it. "Are we still on for the group dinner at Lou's tomorrow?"

Izzy nodded. "I'm not sure how it'll go, but we're still on. I'll see you there." She waved goodbye, and despite having a refrigerator full of groceries, picked up lunch to go and headed for her new house.

After lunch, she tackled syncing the garage door opener with her car, set up her wireless connection and tested it on her phone, televisions, tablet, and laptop. She unloaded her car and put everything away as best she could. Without a dresser, her things were stacked in the walk-in closet.

Her office was the only fully furnished room, so she sat at her desk and perused the local news. An article caught her eye about the local prosecutor's office getting budgetary approval to contract with outside attorneys. Not knowing how Mia's situation would unfold, she had been toying with the idea of keeping some clients or finding some work to generate extra income to support Mia and the baby. With the busy season behind her, Kate wouldn't need much help at Alexander's, not that working there added anything to Izzy's bank account, but she'd have even more free time. This opportunity might be the answer.

She checked the time, changed into one of her suits that she wore to court, touched up her hair and makeup, and retrieved a copy of her resume. She hopped in her car to make the short trip to the courthouse, a couple of blocks from the coffee shop. The two-story brick building was in a complex that housed the courts as well as the auditor, clerk, treasurer, and prosecuting attorney for San Juan County. Izzy found the office on the first floor and stepped to the reception counter.

She introduced herself to the older woman in the flowered dress behind it, mentioned the article, and asked if Mr. Randall was available to answer some questions. Hazel, as she introduced herself, returned Izzy's greeting with a smile, her plump cheeks bulging beneath her head of wavy gray hair, and suggested Izzy have a seat while she checked with the prosecuting attorney to see if he had time for a visitor. Less than five minutes later, Hazel returned and ushered Izzy into his office.

Mr. Randall's office was cluttered with files and paperwork and his hair looked like he'd been running his hands through it, with wisps sticking out here and there. Izzy saw intelligence in his eyes, and his friendly smile welcomed her to a chair he had finished clearing of files. "Hazel tells me you're interested in some contract work?"

"Well, I wanted to know more about it. I've moved here from the Tri-Cities, where I first worked in a firm and then had my own practice for the last almost twenty years. I'm not interested in continuing at that pace, but when I read the article, the idea of doing some contracting appealed to me."

He nodded his head and explained they had been understaffed for several years and finally convinced the powers that be to augment the budget to allow some help. He had hoped for a permanent position or two, but would have to make do with what they'd approved. She could work from home and have access to all the resources of the office and the law library. He told her the hourly rate they could pay, which was much lower than her usual fee.

As they chatted, she handed him a copy of her resume and business card. He perused it and nodded, noting he knew some of her references. "Let me do my due diligence and check into your history, but if it's what I suspect from the caliber of the colleagues you've listed, I'm prepared to offer you the job. I'm sure I can give you a firm offer on Monday."

Izzy smiled, shook his hand, and said, "That sounds great. The weekend will give me time to think about it and make sure it's a good fit."

He walked her to the door and said, "We can always tackle it on a trial basis, and if you're not happy, you can walk away. No hard feelings, no problem. I was worried I wouldn't be able to find anyone on the island and have to do all of this long-distance, so I'm thrilled you're even interested."

He insisted she call him Cliff and promised to be in touch soon, before wishing her a good weekend. Izzy thanked Hazel, and drove to the coffee shop to reward herself with a chai tea latte on her way home. Sam wasn't working, but Hayley was behind the counter. While Izzy waited, Jen came through the door.

"Hey, how are you?" Jen hugged Izzy, and said, "I need to come and see your new place. I was working late the other night when everyone was there to help."

"Come by anytime. I'd love to have you. I'm gone next week with Kate, but hope to have my furniture the following week, so wait until I have it done. I'm toying with the idea of a Halloween housewarming party."

"Sounds wonderful. Sean and I will be at dinner at Lou's tomorrow night, so we'll see you then. Jeff said Mia's here and things aren't easy for you. I'm sorry. I know how tough it is being a single mom."

"It's a bit of a roller coaster at the moment. I'm trying to give her some space and see what happens." Izzy rolled her eyes and added, "It goes against every instinct I have, since I like to dig into problems and solve them, but I'm doing my best."

"As a mom, sometimes doing nothing takes the most effort." Jen hugged Izzy again, and collected her drink. "We had a cancellation for two pedicures tomorrow morning, if that's something you think Mia would enjoy. You could bring her?"

Izzy grimaced. "That would give us an hour of no escaping each other. Could be good or quite horrible. I'll test the waters and let you know. Thanks, Jen."

When Izzy got home, she hung up her suit and changed into her soft pajamas before she started cutting up vegetables for a pot of soup. She was excited to try out her new kitchen, and although she didn't cook much for herself, the activity would occupy her mind. Blake had asked her about joining them for dinner, but after last night, she wasn't in the mood to experience the cold shoulder from Mia and wanted to think more about contracting for the prosecuting attorney.

Although the hourly rate was a far cry from what she was used to, she wouldn't have any overhead and it wouldn't take more than twenty hours a week, based on the allocated budget. Despite Mia assuming John would support her, Izzy wasn't convinced, and the idea of stashing some money to help Mia and the baby made sense. Of course, that was going to be another difficult conversation because Izzy wasn't going to support her forever.

As she washed the celery and carrots, she thought more about Jen's idea for pedicures. It had been a long time since she and Mia had enjoyed time together. Maybe it would open a door to a conversation they needed to have.

She dried her hands and tapped out a text to Mia, inviting her. Experience had taught her not to expect an immediate reply, so she flicked on the television and scrolled to the streaming service with the series she'd been meaning to watch. She loved how the kitchen had a great view out into the open living and dining area, making it easy to watch the screen while she worked.

She left the pot on the cooktop, and settled into her borrowed couch to finish the episode of *Shetland*, an intriguing mystery set on a small island north of Scotland. Her phone chimed and her heart beat a bit faster, anticipating Mia's response, but it was a message from Blake asking her to dinner again. She smiled as she sent her reply, letting him know she was in for the evening. He promised to call her later.

After the episode ended, she forced herself to gather together the clothes and things she would need for her trip with Kate. The prospect of spending time away helped mask the fact that she couldn't even get her daughter to reply to her texts. She assembled a collection of casual clothes, adding one dressier outfit in case they went somewhere more upscale for dinner, and loaded her travel toiletries into a suitcase.

She was glad Kate had talked her into going, and also happy Blake had suggested a group dinner with all their friends while Mia was here. He thought Mia would be on her best behavior in front of others, as opposed to family. Mia had seemed to enjoy her time during the days she had spent on the island this summer, and Blake thought being with everyone would remind her of the support she would have if she took Izzy up on her offer to stay after the birth.

Izzy couldn't agree fast enough. Having everyone there would be much better than facing Mia alone. She hoped it wouldn't end in an embarrassing evening. When she finished with her packing project, she checked on the soup and let it simmer while she watched another episode.

As she was slicing the fresh bread she had picked up at the bakery, her phone chimed and she saw a reply from Mia.

It was another one-word reply, *NO*.

Izzy shook her head and tossed the phone on the counter. She would have felt hurt had it not been for years of constant rejection, all of which trained her to expect it.

She ate dinner seated at the large granite-topped island in the kitchen. During the next episode of the series, Blake called. Mia had spent the day at the winery, with Ellie and him. He brought her up to date on their conversations, and confirmed Mia was counting on her dad to let her come and live there, and wasn't thinking much beyond that. Lauren had called and offered Mia her maternity clothes and was going to send them to her.

"We hinted she might want to have a backup plan in case that didn't work, with John getting married in June. It's hard to imagine his new bride would be excited to have her and a baby with them, but Mia shrugged it off." He paused and added, "She does seem genuinely interested in the medical imaging coursework, so there is at least that."

"I really hope she will finish the program. She could have a great career. With regard to John, I know she won't listen to anything I have to say, so I'll have to wait for the fireworks when he bursts her bubble. Talking to her is counterproductive, and she clearly doesn't want to engage with me."

They chatted more about her new house and her upcoming trip with Kate. "We'll see you tomorrow night if not before. Ellie thought we might be able to convince Mia to stop by and see your new place sometime tomorrow."

Izzy rolled her eyes. "Don't force it. It's not that important." She wished her brother goodnight and thanked him again for taking care of Mia.

The mental effort of dealing with Mia was exhausting. She poured herself a glass of wine and snuggled under her favorite blanket, intent on watching as many episodes as it took until she fell asleep. Instead of the happiness she had imagined spending her first night in her new house, she felt only despair. No matter what she did, it was always wrong when it came to Mia.

IZZY WOKE WITH a stiff neck from sleeping all night on the couch. She elected to walk the golf course and followed the pathway outside her backyard, making the loop. She welcomed the burst of color from the changing leaves along with the solitude, both of which helped soothe her wounded heart.

She breathed in the cool, damp air, and let the magic of nature wash over her. A brilliant red strip of color flashed along the edge of a thick grassy patch. As she got closer, she saw the color came from delicate leaves that had blown from nearby bushes, and become trapped in the sturdy blades of grass. She didn't know much about plants, but was sure Linda could tell her what the beautiful red bush was, and find her one.

During the walk, she decided to take the position with the prosecuting attorney's office. It would give her something to do, plus she could bank several months' worth of salary to help with Mia's support costs. A bit of excitement bubbled through her at the thought of welcoming a new grandchild, but she pushed it down. Instead of being a thrill, it would only become another painful dilemma she would have to solve.

The beauty of the manicured grounds and the connection with nature boosted her mood and comforted her from the worry she felt about Mia and the baby, and by the time she returned home, she felt ready for the day. After a few days with nothing to do, she realized she was too young to actually retire. The work at the prosecutor's office was something she was more than capable of handling, plus with Cliff mentioning a trial period and his enthusiasm for finding someone with her skills, she knew it was the right decision.

She composed an email to Cliff stating she would accept the contracting position, and proposed a start date in two weeks, giving him plenty of time to vet her, and giving her time to get her house organized with the new furniture that was due to arrive when she returned from Driftwood Bay. The doorbell rang before she could send the email.

She opened the door to the group of women she had come to think of as family: Sam and Jen toting drink carriers, Linda carrying a huge bouquet of gorgeous flowers, Regi holding little Emma, Kate and Ellie balancing pastry boxes, and lastly, Mia shuffling behind the others.

"We came to shower you with a bit of a sweet welcome to your new home," Sam said, setting the drinks on the island. Linda positioned the vase of rich autumn colored flowers in the center of the counter.

Izzy's throat tightened with emotion as she gazed upon her smiling friends, then her gaze caught Mia, eyes glued to her phone and doing her best to ignore her mother, and her heart sank. "Wow, this is so kind of all of you," she said, forcing sadness out of her voice. Kate opened a cupboard and pulled out plates while Ellie popped open the pink boxes filled with decadent treats from her old bakery.

Between the dining table and dragging in a couple of the high chairs from the island, Izzy had enough seating for the group. As they chatted and laughed at Emma licking whipped cream from her hot chocolate, Izzy noticed Mia was wearing sandals with freshly painted toenails.

Ellie put her arm around Izzy and scooted her foot next to Mia's. "Aren't our toes gorgeous? Mia suggested we get pedicures this morning down at Jen's shop. They had an unexpected opening so it worked out."

Ellie continued on her way to the kitchen to brew some tea. Feeling as if she had been punched in the stomach, Izzy met her daughter's cold eyes, detecting the hint of a smirk on her face. A kick to the stomach would have been easier to take. Mia's obvious delight in hurting her only added to the misery. But Izzy had practiced for the last fifteen years; she wouldn't let Mia see the pain she caused.

"That's a beautiful color you chose. The perfect plum for fall," said Izzy, glancing at Mia's toes. Her profession had helped condition her not to react, and she garnered every ounce of training to hide the utter sadness she felt as another piece of her heart broke off, adding to the pile Mia had amassed since her teenage years.

Kate described the furnishings that would be arriving and went around the room to point out where each piece would go, talking about the blending of a coastal feel with a more modern twist. Mia wandered outside onto the patio, while the others chatted about décor and all the things they loved about Izzy's new house.

Izzy focused on her daughter, who was tapping on the screen of her phone, leaving Izzy to wonder for the umpteenth time why her adult daughter harbored such animosity toward her, and doubting if they would ever find a way back to each other.

Chapter 8

SUNDAY DAWNED WITH a more hopeful outlook, as Izzy set out for another morning walk, early enough to have plenty of time to get to the Front Street Café for breakfast with Mia, Ellie, and Blake, before Mia took the ferry back to the city. Izzy ran Cliff's reply to her email through her mind as she walked. He'd made it clear how happy he was to have Izzy on the team and looked forward to working with her in two weeks. Although pleased to have a new purpose and something to keep her occupied, she hoped it didn't create too much stress with Mia's situation up in the air.

She hated she was relieved at the prospect of Mia heading back to college today. She thought about Kate, and the fact she had lost her daughter forever, and how much she adored her grown son, and loathed to see him go after he visited the island. Why couldn't she and Mia have a relationship like that?

Then she remembered Regi's mother and Ellie's mother, both of whom were awful to their daughters and didn't have any kind of a relationship with them. They were missing out on two wonderful young women, and what distressed Izzy even more was she knew Mia was capable of kindness and had a good heart when it came to others. That made the sting of her rejection hurt even more.

Punishing Izzy and favoring John as she came to terms with their divorce was one thing; Izzy always thought it would wear off as Mia grew up. But she was thirty. How much longer could it possibly take?

Part of the problem had been John, of course, taking the easy road of being the fun parent who won Mia over with indulgences, and leaving Izzy to be the disciplinarian and the realist. It made Izzy resent her ex-husband even more, since his failings left her with an even more difficult job. Regardless, she was steadfast and not one to take shortcuts, so she stood her ground with an often raging teenager, convinced she was doing the right thing, and Mia would mature into a responsible adult.

Over the years, Izzy had talked to John, always trying to reason with him, to get him to understand the importance of his actions with Mia. Everything she suggested fell on deaf ears or was discounted almost immediately. On the few occasions he agreed to her ideas, they were short-lived and he always surrendered to Mia's desires. Mia knew this and had mastered manipulating him.

After suffering through dinner last night, which would have been a lovely meal without Mia's attitude and churlish behavior, Izzy hoped John would be predictable, as she would like nothing better than to see Mia on her way to Los Angeles. There, her dad could indulge her every whim, and leave Izzy to her own quiet life. She knew it was wrong to wish for such an outcome, and in her heart suspected John's focus would be on his fiancée and not his daughter, but it would make her life much less complicated. John had always been selfish, and she didn't expect that to change.

At the dinner, Lou's hand was still bandaged, and Andi was hanging out at the restaurant, helping him at the register and sticking close to him. Izzy had noticed Lou slip his hand around her waist a few times and the secretive and knowing looks that passed between the two of them throughout the evening.

It made her heart happy to see them together. Lou, although harmless, was a nonstop flirt, and it seemed the cut on his hand had led to a fortuitous opportunity with a lovely woman. Andi's smile and laughter at Lou's jokes and teasing were wonderful to see and hear. Over their previous chats, Andi had shared how much she had been struggling after her husband was killed in Afghanistan, and Izzy was thrilled to see her blossom at Lou's attention.

Andi, who had wanted children, but suffered a miscarriage years ago, doted on Emma, checking on her and visiting the table often, making sure she had anything she wanted, including her favorite macaroni and cheese, and chocolate sauce on her ice cream after dinner. She even hinted she was more than happy to babysit her anytime Regi and Nate needed it.

Several times, when Mia wasn't focused on glaring at her mother, Izzy observed her laughing and enjoying herself. None of Izzy's friends pressed her about the baby or college, so it made for easy and fun conversations. Only when Mia addressed Izzy, did she put on her mask of cruel indifference, discounting her, rolling her eyes, or huffing at anything Izzy said. It reminded her of their conversations when Mia had been fifteen.

It was embarrassing, but Izzy ignored her and focused on chatting with everyone else, and tried to avoid engaging Mia directly to save the uncomfortable situation it created for the others. It had been an exhausting evening, which was why she welcomed her daughter's departure and couldn't wait to head out with Kate on Monday. The trip would give her brain something to ponder besides the fractured and failed relationship she had with Mia.

Later that morning, when Izzy emerged from her shower, the house seemed darker. She glanced outside and noticed the gray clouds had rolled in and obliterated the earlier sunshine. Opening the door to the patio, a cool breeze blew in and made her shiver. She dressed in her favorite black sweater and a fashionable silvery poncho with metallic threads woven through it that reminded her of her hair.

She was the last to arrive at the restaurant, and found them at a table, where she slipped into the chair across from Mia. Blake and Ellie carried the conversation as they ate, talking about upcoming events at the winery and prepping for the fancy wedding slated for the following weekend.

Almost done with her plate of food, Mia let out a long sigh. "I don't know how you stand to live on this tiny island. The ferry is so inconvenient and you can't leave whenever you want. It's such an outdated way of travel and so annoying."

She was itching for a battle, which was her modus operandum when she was leaving. Izzy smiled, and said, "I rather like it. It's relaxing and living here is wonderful."

Blake and Ellie agreed, citing the excitement of seeing tourists arrive, and remarking they had learned to work around the schedules.

Izzy took a sip of coffee. "Have you heard from your dad yet about moving down to LA with him?"

Mia wouldn't meet her eyes. "He and Barbie are in Palm Springs for a vacation, and he said he'd talk to me when they get back next week. I'm sure he'll agree."

"Well, if not, you're welcome to come here." Knowing she wouldn't have to deal with the fallout for long, Izzy pressed forward. "Are you going to finish the second quarter at school in March, so you can get that behind you before the baby arrives?"

Mia looked as if Izzy had horns growing out of her head. "No, I'm going to move to Dad's as soon as possible, so I can get settled and established with a doctor down there. If I decide to finish the program, I can do it at UCLA."

Izzy resisted the urge to raise her voice. "It's important for you to finish, don't you think? It would give you such a great opportunity for a career that could carry you well into the future, and it seems you like it."

"I think I know what I'm doing. I don't need your advice or approval."

Her derogatory tone prompted Ellie to raise her eyebrows and Blake frowned at her. "You know," he said, "your mom was asking and pointing out the importance of thinking ahead. She's offered you a place to stay and help, and all you've done is act like a brat to her. You need to lighten your tone a bit."

Mia threw her napkin across her plate and stood. "This is exactly why I want to live with Dad. He doesn't try to control me. I don't need Mom's help or yours." She stormed down the aisle and out the door of the restaurant.

"Sorry," Blake murmured and glanced at his sister.

Izzy shook her head. "Don't be sorry. You spoke the truth."

"I'll go get her suitcase out of the car," he offered. "She won't get far without it."

Izzy collected the check and paid the bill, steeling herself for one more conversation with Mia. She couldn't figure out why her daughter bothered coming to the island, since it was clear she had no intention of talking to Izzy about her situation and only resented her involvement.

She wandered to the ferry landing, where Ellie and Mia were sitting on a bench, the suitcase at their feet, and Blake standing at the railing watching the ferry arrive. Izzy slid into the space next to Mia and put her arm around her. "I'm not sure why we always struggle so much, but I want you to know I love you and care about you and the baby. If you need me, I'm here. Always."

Mia squirmed away, and Izzy noticed the glint of tears in her eyes. Mia turned her attention to Ellie and hugged her goodbye, thanking her for letting her stay. She collected her suitcase and met her mother's eyes. "I'll let you know when I get settled at Dad's."

Izzy nodded and watched her walk to Blake, where he put an arm around her and drew her closer. Izzy and Ellie joined him at the railing as Mia made her way onto the ferry. "How can one girl be so nice to me and treat you the way she does?" asked Ellie.

"I'm used to it, but I don't understand it. I'm sure Blake has told you our relationship has been strained for years. She tries to get under my skin, and I try not to let her know she has. Like yesterday with the pedicure. I had asked her to go with me, hoping to chat and connect, but she said no."

Ellie gasped, and put her hand to her mouth. "I had no idea. I'm so sorry."

Izzy chuckled, and shook her head. "Don't apologize. It's Mia's way of needling me and trying to upset me. Like I said, I'm not sure why she feels the need to cause me pain, but she delights in it, and has since she was fifteen."

Blake and Ellie each slipped an arm around Izzy. "She doesn't know how lucky she is to have you for a mom. My aunt was a wonderful substitute, but I would have given anything to have my mom love me and care about me." Tears welled in Ellie's eyes. "I'm so sorry, Izzy."

Izzy's emotions were all over the map. She loved her daughter more than anything, but sometimes Mia's actions toward her, like today, caused her physical agony. Her head throbbed and her chest hurt. She leaned her head against Blake's shoulder, and let the warmth of his and Ellie's love comfort her.

She never wanted Mia to feel alone and without support, but there were times, like the last few days where she made it almost impossible to like her. Izzy longed for a relationship like so many mothers had with their grown children – one without all the unnecessary angst where they could enjoy each other's company and be more like friends. She wanted so much to be excited to welcome a grandchild, but at the same time feared that Mia would use the baby as a weapon against her. She worried the child would become just another extremely effective way to reject her.

Rather than get excited about the idea of a baby to spoil and play with, she vowed to push those thoughts away, hoping if she didn't get attached to the idea, it wouldn't hurt as much when she didn't get to be part of the baby's life. There was a tiny chance motherhood would change Mia and lead her back to Izzy, but it was the weakest flicker of hope.

She kept her eye on Mia as her daughter continued onto the ferry. Right before Izzy was ready to walk back to her car, Mia turned and waved at them. Maybe there was still hope, but if this visit was any indication, it was going to take all the patience Izzy could muster. That was one virtue she didn't possess.

Chapter 9

THE CLOUDS WERE gone and the sun shone Monday morning, when Izzy picked up Kate and drove the few blocks to the ferry. While they were waiting in the vehicle line, Spence appeared at the passenger window toting a bag and two steaming drinks from Sam's coffeeshop. Roxie was with him, holding her leash in her mouth. Kate rolled down the window and he handed her the goodies and drinks, giving her a sweet kiss. "Thought you ladies could use a snack for the trip over."

"Aww, that's so thoughtful. I'll let you know when we get there and check in with you on our way." Kate kissed him again, and Izzy waved to him, echoing her thanks and telling Roxie goodbye.

Kate steadied the drinks as the line began to move and Izzy steered her car onto the ferry, following the instructions and parking on the exterior car deck. They toted their breakfast upstairs, and found a window table.

Over moist pumpkin muffins and lattes, they chatted about Izzy's new position and enjoyed the scenic view. Izzy had texted Mia last night to make sure she arrived home safely, and received a thumbs up emoji, but nothing more. She shuffled her thoughts about her daughter to the back of her mind, intent on enjoying her time with Kate.

There was something so calming about floating across the water, and it never failed to ease Izzy's worries. She likened it to listening to the piano music she turned to in times of stress or intense work deadlines. The slowness of the movement helped soothe her frazzled thoughts and she began to relax. Before they knew it, it was time to head downstairs and get ready to disembark.

The process went smoothly, and Izzy was on the road to Coupeville in no time. Kate texted Spence with updates on their progress. His career in law enforcement fed his need to know where Kate was and that she was safe. She finished her text and glanced at Izzy. "Sometimes checking in can be inconvenient, and there are times I forget and he calls me, but I know it eases his worry when I'm away from home. Too many years of seeing the worst side of humanity, I guess."

Izzy nodded. "I think it's sweet he loves you enough to worry and wants to know you're okay. Not only that, he brought us breakfast this morning. He's a definite keeper."

Kate chuckled and smiled. "He is my rock and my true soulmate. I'm so happy he decided to follow me to Friday Harbor. I think I'm the luckiest gal there."

Izzy didn't know what it felt like to have such a close relationship to a man. Even thinking back to when she was first married to John, she wasn't sure they were ever really soulmates. Her family had been her rock over the years, but she doubted she'd ever find an actual partner who would be like Spence.

It had been years since Izzy had spent any time driving on Fidalgo or Whidbey Island but the beauty never failed to take her breath away. A bit of fog lingered over the water and clouds dimmed the sunshine. As they came upon the sign for Deception Pass State Park, Kate checked the time and suggested they take a quick detour, and park at the lot after they crossed the bridge, so they could capture some photos. The bridge was walkable with a sidewalk on each side, and they set out to admire the stunning view. The wisps of fog hanging close to the water and drifting along the edge of the island made for some gorgeous photos. They didn't have the time to hike the trail below, but captured the gorgeous scene from the bridge and even managed a selfie of them smiling together with the stunning background. Kate texted it to Spence.

Their scenic stop didn't take long, and they made the line for the ferry with plenty of time to spare. The crossing took over thirty minutes and Kate navigated, while Izzy drove the short distance to Driftwood Bay. Years ago, when Izzy and her family had visited the Olympic National Park, they had driven through the area, but she had never spent any time in Driftwood Bay.

The picturesque downtown and the waterfront reminded her of Friday Harbor, but this community was larger, more sprawling than the tiny island town she had chosen to call home. Still, it had the same relaxed vibe and feel, the hint of salt in the air, and the inspiring beauty of the surrounding waters.

They stopped for lunch at a spot Kate remembered from her last visit, The Busy Bee Café. Breakfast was served all day, and they opted for savory scrambles, homemade hash browns, and fresh focaccia toast with berry jam.

After lingering over tea, they wandered down the sidewalk of the quaint downtown to Bayside Gifts, took a moment to admire the display window filled with autumn hues in cookware, vases, kitchen towels, and silk flowers, then went inside. Cyndy was behind the counter and hurried from around it when she spied Kate.

She embraced Kate in a long hug, and then surprised Izzy by doing the same to her. "Wonderful to meet you, Izzy, I'm Cyndy and I'm delighted you made the trip with Kate. We'll have so much fun together."

Izzy glanced around her shop, and said, "I'm thrilled to be here and in the market for some things for my new house."

"Did you have lunch yet?" Cyndy asked, as Izzy began to wander through the shop.

Kate nodded. "Yes, finished and we're stuffed."

"I'm cooking for us tonight and also invited Lily, the owner of Glass Beach Cottage, where you're staying. Actually, she and Mac, my brother, are both coming."

"That sounds lovely," said Kate, as two customers came through the door. "I'll go help Izzy browse."

Cyndy's laughter filled the store as she visited with the women shopping for birthday gifts. Izzy's eyes sparkled with interest as she showed Kate a few things she liked. She found some textured pillows in delicate sea glass colors that would be perfect for the accents she and Kate had discussed adding to her neutral furniture.

Izzy began making a stack of items, and Cyndy offered to put them aside for her. "I'll hold these, but you might find more at the show this week, so I'll wait until you decide."

They whittled away a couple of hours visiting and shopping, with Cyndy giving them directions to her house before they left to settle in at the guest cottage. Glass Beach Cottage was only a few blocks away, and Izzy parked her SUV at the side of the main house.

As they were retrieving their luggage, a woman with caramel blonde hair came from around the corner. "You must be Kate and Izzy? I'm Lily." She glanced at the puppy on her leash and the other golden retriever standing next to her. "Fritz here is the oldest, and Bodie is the puppy I'm training to be a hearing assistant dog."

"They are such sweeties," said Kate. "I'm a friend of Cyndy's, and she's the one who told me about your place. It's lovely here."

Izzy was busy petting Fritz and Bodie, who were happy to be the center of attention. Lily led the way into the backyard, pointing out the keypad security on the gate. "It's our slow time right now, so you're the only booking and I've put you in the second cottage, the one with the bright purple door. You'll be able to admire Cyndy's touches everywhere. She's got such a talent with decorating and helped me with all the cottages."

Kate smiled. "I'm not surprised. She is a natural, and such a warm person. I'm looking forward to spending time with her."

Lily smiled as she unlocked the door. "I'm sure you'll have great fun together. I don't have a clue about home décor or any other décor for that matter. I'm fortunate to have met Cyndy when I moved here."

She showed the two of them around the space, then as she left, pointed to a door in the back of the main house where they would find the common room that contained a television, refrigerator, washer, dryer, and other amenities. "Also, I host a casual gathering around the firepit on weekends, so I hope you'll be there on Friday."

It didn't take them long to unpack and settle into the gorgeous cottage, where they admired all the beach inspired touches while the coffee brewed.

Outside, at the small patio table, they took their first sips. "Aah," said Izzy. "Nothing like the sound of the water lapping at the sand, a gorgeous view of the beach, and a good cup of coffee." She laughed, and added, "Well, maybe a glass of wine."

"Cyndy is a wine lover, so she'll have plenty of choices for us tonight, I'm sure." Kate took in the view of the water through the bushes and trees. "This beats a stuffy motel, for sure. It's such a serene spot."

They chatted about the schedule for the trade show that would start tomorrow, as they looked over the information Lily provided in the cottage, along with the coupons she included for breakfast each day.

Kate tapped in a text to Spence to let him know they were settled in at the cottage, and then turned to Izzy. "Cyndy offered to drive us to the trade show tomorrow. She has a large SUV, so we'll have lots of space to bring anything back we find."

"That sounds great. As excited as I was to get a new house, everything with Mia sort of squelched the enjoyment." She sighed as she gazed at the vista. "But, being here I feel better already."

Kate patted Izzy's hand. "I know it's impossible to take your mind off of her. I had my share of turbulent times with Karen, and when I lost her, I wasn't sure I'd survive it. I'm not sure why some daughters seem to make a point of causing their mothers such pain, but it seems they do. I hope being here brings you a bit of peace."

Izzy nodded. "It will. I don't like uncertainty, so her situation and even more, her lack of communicating with me drives me nuts." Her brows arched. "Which she knows, and is part of the reason she's keeping me in the dark, I'm sure."

As they chatted and decompressed after the trip from the island, dusk settled over Driftwood Bay and reminded them they had dinner plans. They took their cups inside and set out across the beautiful yard, spying Lily up on the deck. "I was going to come down and let you know I'm heading over to Cyndy's. I'm taking the dogs, otherwise, I'd offer you a ride."

Izzy waved and said, "Not a problem. Cyndy gave us directions, so we'll see you there." She and Kate pulled away from the house before Lily, and drove downtown, stopping at a local store to pick a couple bottles of wine for dinner. Lily's car was in the driveway when they parked in front of Cyndy's beautiful Victorian home.

Lily greeted them at the door, a delicious aroma wafting around her. "Cyndy's in the kitchen. Come on in, we're visiting while she cooks."

Izzy and Kate followed her through the black and white tiled entry, passing by the beautiful wooden staircase, and into the large kitchen. Cyndy stirred something on the cooktop. When she saw them, she waved them in. "Hello, you two. Welcome and meet my brother, Jack MacMillan, who goes by Mac."

Mac greeted Izzy with a warm handshake, and turned to Kate. "I remember you visiting a few years ago."

"Yes, I came to see Cyndy several years ago and we were introduced."

Izzy noticed his blue eyes, and as she studied him, realized he looked much like Spence, though a slightly younger version. He offered to pour wine for the ladies or fetch them other drinks. Lily and Kate opted for iced tea, and Izzy took a glass of red.

They visited as they watched Cyndy put the final touches on the meal. When Lily excused herself to check on the dogs, Izzy followed to get a look at the porch and backyard. She recognized Fritz and Bodie, but as she joined Lily on a bench, she was also welcomed by a large golden retriever Lily introduced as Sherlock, Mac's dog, and a smaller golden with the beginning of a sugar face named Sunny.

"Mac is a veterinarian and took Sunny in at the end of last week. She's a longtime patient of his, and her owner is ill and can no longer take care of her. She's been so sad, so he's hoping Sherlock will cheer her." Sunny wandered over to the porch and put her head on Izzy's thigh, looking up at her with gentle brown eyes.

Izzy petted her soft head and was rewarded with a tail wag. As Izzy stroked the ears of the sweet dog, she couldn't help but smile. Lily glanced at the dog, still resting against Izzy's leg. "Looks like you've found a friend."

"Aww, she's such a sweet soul. The last week hasn't been my easiest one, so sitting here, like this, is wonderful."

"Dogs have a way of knowing exactly what we need, don't they?" Lily looked across the yard at the other three dogs romping with each other. "I would have never made it through my husband's death without Fritz. I know I wouldn't have had the courage to move all the way across the country without him. He's been my rock and such a comfort when I wasn't sure what the future held."

Izzy gasped, and said, "I'm so sorry about your husband, Lily. That puts my problems in perspective."

"No matter your struggle, when you have a dog, you're never alone." Lily turned at the sound of Mac's voice at the door.

"Dinner's ready, you two." He held the door for them, noticing Sunny's attraction to Izzy. "I'm looking for a forever home for her. Are you interested?"

Izzy's eyes widened. "I've never had a dog, except as a kid. I hadn't even considered it."

"You're missing out on the best friend you'll ever have. Sunny's a special girl and suffering from missing her owner. She's a certified therapy dog and loves people. It's a sad situation."

They sat around Cyndy's beautiful table, decorated in purples and greens, as they chatted and ate her lovely meal. The butternut squash soup and beef dip sandwiches, piled high with thinly sliced roasted rib eyes and melted cheese on delicious crusty bread, along with homemade au jus, made for the perfect fall meal.

Cyndy offered dessert, but the group was stuffed and opted to wait. Lily and Mac suggested Izzy accompany them while they took the dogs for a walk, and Kate stayed behind to help Cyndy with the dishes.

Mac gave Izzy Sunny's leash. With a smile and a chuckle, she took it in her hand. "You're a bit like a car salesman. My ex-husband sells cars and whenever customers showed the slightest interest in a car, he'd deliver it to their house and tell them to drive it around for a few days."

"Smart marketing, I'd say," said Mac, as he took hold of Sherlock and Bodie, leaving Lily with her faithful Fritz.

They meandered the sidewalks, taking in the few blocks around Cyndy's home. Sunny stayed close to Izzy's side, the dog's steps matching her pace. She never pulled or tugged on the leash, and whenever Izzy stopped, Sunny sat down. "How old is Sunny?" she asked Mac.

"She's almost five now. She's been well cared for, up to date on all her vaccinations, and went through some training when she was younger, plus did some therapy work at local hospitals, schools, and libraries, so she's well behaved. She's the perfect dog, but needs to find a new owner to love her."

As they made their way back to Cyndy's, the idea of keeping Sunny began to take hold in Izzy's mind. She had plenty of room and now, more than ever, she could use a friend. Having a dog would tie her down, but with all her friends and Blake having dogs, she was sure to find a place for Sunny to stay should she have to make any trips off the island.

They continued walking, side by side, and when they returned the dogs to the backyard, Sunny gave Izzy's hand a quick lick when she removed the leash.

"How long are you ladies staying in Driftwood Bay?" asked Mac.

"We go home Saturday." Izzy continued to pet the top of Sunny's head.

"How about I bring her over after work one evening, and you can get to know her a bit more and see what you think. I'll even go so far as to say, if you take her and it doesn't work, I'll bring her back here."

Izzy looked into the dog's eyes, deep with adoration as they sparkled in the porch lights. "I'd like to get to know her better, and really am considering taking her home. She's so sweet and hard to resist." She met Mac's eyes and chuckled. "Not to mention, you missed your calling in sales."

After enjoying slices of fresh apple pie, Kate and Izzy thanked Cyndy for her hospitality, and Izzy gave Sunny lots of snuggles before they headed back to the cottage. As they climbed into Izzy's SUV, Kate smiled at her and said, "I think you've found your forever furry friend."

Chapter 10

OVER THE NEXT few days, Izzy and Kate started their mornings with scrumptious breakfasts at the local café, with Cyndy joining them before she drove them to the fairgrounds event center, about an hour away from Driftwood Bay.

They combed through row after row of displays and booths, admiring furnishings, gifts, and home décor items. Cyndy and Kate made several orders for their shops, and Izzy collected some beautiful pieces to add to her new home. While Izzy was busy and occupied, Mia didn't dominate her thoughts, but in the evenings when she and Kate settled in at the cottage, it was a different story.

On Thursday evening, after a delicious meal along the waterfront, they bumped into Lily on their way to their cottage. She was downstairs finishing some laundry, followed by Fritz and Bodie. She invited them to join her upstairs, since they were the only guests.

"Choose a bottle of wine from the stash and come on up," she said, pointing to the counter. "There's some white in the fridge and red in the cupboard." She toted a laundry basket up the stairs, followed by her two loyal companions.

Izzy selected one bottle of each, and they met Lily in her beautiful kitchen that opened onto her deck with the lovely view. Lily retrieved glasses from the cabinet, and put the kettle on for tea. Izzy and Kate opted for wine, while Lily brewed a cup of green tea. She ushered them into the great room, where the two dogs settled in beside her recliner.

Izzy smiled as both Fritz and Bodie looked up at Lily and she reassured them with a soft stroke. "Watching your sweet dogs really has me thinking about Sunny."

Lily smiled over the rim of her cup. "Bodie was a surprise. Mac asked me to foster him and help train him. He's involved with the regional organization that works to train and match dogs with hearing impaired candidates. Mac pulled some strings to pair Bodie with a local young man I know." She ran her hands over Bodie's ears. "I'm not sure I'll be able to give him up next year. He's such a sweet one."

She took another sip from her cup. "Fritz is such good company, especially with my son so far away. He's also such a strong connection to my husband, Gary. I'd be lost without him, and now Bodie is an extra bit of fun and great company for Fritz."

"So, I wouldn't be the first woman Mac has charmed into taking on a dog?" Izzy grinned as she sipped her wine. "Like you, I'm alone, and the idea of having someone who is always there is appealing." She sighed, and added, "My life is a bit chaotic at the moment, which is the only thing holding me back."

"When I agreed to take Bodie, that's how I felt. Actually, my life is still a bit chaotic. At the same time, I was also asked to take in a nineteen-year-old woman who had lost her family and was essentially homeless. Her name is Mel and she lives downstairs in one of the guest rooms. It has been a bit of a roller coaster ride."

Kate and Izzy's eyes widened. "Wow, that makes a dog sound easy," said Izzy. "I've got a daughter and nineteen is not the easiest age." She chuckled and added, "Actually neither is thirty."

"My son is in college back in Virginia, so it hasn't been long since I've had a teenager around, but Mel...is a challenge."

The three women sipped and lamented the joys and heartaches of motherhood. Izzy shared her recent worries about Mia and her angst about what the future held. When Lily learned Kate had lost her beloved daughter to suicide, twenty years ago, tears spilled onto her cheeks.

After Kate finished sharing more about Karen and admitted she still struggled with the grief, Lily nodded and swiped her finger under her eyes. "I understand. My husband was killed in the line of duty a year before I moved here. I just couldn't stay there. The memories were too much for me, and with me also being a police officer, I couldn't escape them. This was a chance for a new start."

She explained her uncle had passed away and left her the property she had always loved and visited as a teenager. "With Kevin going to college, it seemed like the best idea and a sign." She reached down to run her hand over Fritz. "That's how Fritz and I ended up here, running Glass Beach Cottage."

Kate stood and reached to hug Lily. "Second chances are the best. Trust me, I know."

"Some days are harder than others. I'm sorry," said Lily, with fresh tears trailing from her eyes. "I don't normally act like this with guests."

Kate patted her shoulder. "You needn't worry about that."

Izzy noticed Fritz move closer to Lily, placing his head in her lap, offering his comfort. As it had been for so long now, she didn't have anyone at home, only her work. Blake and Ellie and her wonderful new friends in Friday Harbor were what made Izzy want to make her home there, but seeing how Fritz soothed Lily, she knew she had to give Sunny the same chance at a forever home.

FRIDAY, INSTEAD OF accompanying Kate and Cyndy to the trade show, Izzy drove to Mac's veterinary clinic. Mac met her out near the pond, with Sherlock and Sunny in tow. Both dogs greeted her with wagging tails and Sunny sat at her feet leaning into her leg.

Mac smiled. "I'd say you've definitely taken a shine to one another." He joined Izzy on the bench. "I was so glad when Lily called last night and said you wanted to give Sunny a home."

"Watching how much love Fritz and Bodie offer to Lily inspired me. Right now, despite the turmoil in my life, I could use a friend, someone who will be there no matter what. I haven't had that kind of roommate for a long time."

"Sunny here will be perfect," he said, stroking the dog's back. With this being Izzy's first dog, outside of those she had grown up with at the old house next to the winery, Mac went over how to care for Sunny, showed Izzy her health records, and writing down the type and amount of food she liked.

"These sweet dogs are easy to overfeed as they get older, so take it easy on the treats. Use tiny ones or break up larger ones. This girl loves apples, carrots, and berries, so use those instead of store-bought treats."

"My sister-in-law is an ex-baker, but she still makes popular dog treats for friends. I know she has a pumpkin dog cookie that is quite popular."

Mac grinned. "Sunny will love it. She's a huge fan of pumpkin, and as a special treat gets a spoonful of the puree added to her food." At Sherlock's invitation, Sunny joined him for a sprint across the grass to the edge of the pond.

"You can spend as much time as you like here with her and take her back to Lily's if you want. I've got all her toys and bedding back at the house. I'm coming to Lily's tonight and can bring it all, so you have it when you're ready to leave tomorrow. I'll put these records along with her spare food and bowls from the clinic in your car, so you can take them with you."

"That sounds great. Lily said I could keep her in the cottage tonight."

He handed Izzy a leash and a squeaky ball. "These are hers. She loves to play fetch, and if you need any help when you're ready to go, pop in and ask. Sunny is used to going in vehicles, so she'll be fine. I've got to get back to my patients, but I'll see you tonight." He stood, and Sherlock followed him back to the clinic.

Izzy tossed the ball for Sunny, who bounded after it, returning it each time with her lips curled into a smile. After several romps through the grass, Sunny returned with the ball and plopped down at Izzy's feet. Game over, for now.

Izzy rested with her and let her mind relax as she took in the tranquil scene of the lush fields, the mixture of colorful and still green leaves on the trees, and the ducks floating atop the pond. Her stress melted away as she breathed in the fresh air. She captured a photo of Sunny, and texted it to Blake. Last night, he and Ellie had encouraged her to adopt Sunny, offering to help care for her and already planning a playdate with Oreo, Ellie's border collie.

She clipped Sunny's leash to her collar and began walking toward the clinic. Sunny led her to a fresh bowl of water along the pathway, where she lapped up a long drink. They walked around the perimeter of the building, where Izzy guided Sunny to her car. She opened the back door, and without any direction, Sunny jumped onto the seat.

"What a good girl," said Izzy, smiling at the dog, who eased herself down across the seat.

Izzy steered onto the main road and glanced in the mirror periodically to check on Sunny, as she made her way to the downtown waterfront. The dog never moved and looked quite relaxed with her eyes almost shut.

She found a spot to park and Sunny sat up, her eyes focused on Izzy. "Let's find an outdoor table at The Busy Bee, and have a late breakfast."

The dog waited for Izzy to get hold of the leash and didn't leave the car until Izzy said, "Okay, Sunny, let's go." As they walked, Izzy was already enjoying the company of her new friend, and with Sunny's impressive manners, she was sure she could get the hang of dog ownership.

While Izzy ate her favorite egg scramble with homemade focaccia toast, her new furry friend nestled at her feet, resting in the sunshine warmed patch on the patio. Gabby, the young waitress that Izzy and Kate had come to know from eating at the café every morning, brought Sunny a bowl of fresh water and a homemade dog cookie as a reward.

Gabby smiled as she stroked Sunny's ears. "She's such a sweet one. I love it when customers bring their dogs. I keep wanting a dog, but I live in an apartment that doesn't allow pets."

"Sunny's owner is unwell and can't care for her, so I'm taking her. She's the first dog I've had in decades, but I can tell she's a professional, so we'll be fine." Izzy smiled at the dog, basking in the extra attention she was receiving.

Although there was a bit of a chill in the air, the sun was shining and Izzy spent most of the afternoon in Lily's backyard letting Sunny play with Bodie and Fritz. They made what Izzy suspected were hundreds of loops around the perimeter of the yard, playing and chasing each other. A little later, she selected several colorful balls and squeaky toys and threw them out into the yard. The three dogs romped through the grass and took turns retrieving them.

Sunny was the first to call it a day, and in the mid-afternoon stretched out on the cool concrete near the door. Fritz soon followed suit, and Bodie, without his friends to play with, snuggled next to them.

Izzy let the snoozing dogs be, and made her way upstairs to Lily's deck, where she looked through the glass door and saw her at work in the kitchen. Izzy tapped on the door, and Lily waved her inside.

"Wow," Izzy said, taking in the huge charcuterie board on the granite counter. "Looks like you've been busy. Is there anything I can do to help?"

"I need to add some berries and I'll be done with this, but I'll put you in charge of our wine selections tonight. I'm not much of a connoisseur, but I know with your family's business, you can handle it. There's the stash downstairs and a few more bottles up here in the pantry."

Izzy stepped into the pantry, and surveyed the labels on each bottle. "It's the three of us, plus Mac and Cyndy tonight, right?"

"I invited Nora to join us. She's a previous guest who moved here, with her daughter, Bree, and now is a local police officer. Bree and Mel are going to a reception and lecture sponsored by the library tonight."

Izzy toted the wine downstairs, and at Lily's suggestion, made sure there were a few bottles of beer in the fridge for Mac. By the time she helped Lily organize some plates and napkins, and got the fire going in the firepit table, Cyndy and Kate came through the gate.

The three dogs greeted them. "How was the last day of your shopping palooza?" Izzy asked, carting the wine glasses to the firepit.

"Long, but fruitful. I think we're shopped out." Kate looked to Cyndy who bobbed her head in agreement.

"I'm ready to get off my feet and sip a huge glass of wine." Cyndy made her way to the chairs gathered around the firepit, as Izzy selected a bottle and poured several glasses. She delivered one to Cyndy.

Lily came out the door, toting the spread of cheeses, meats, olives, crackers, and fruit she had prepared, and placed it on the table. "Oh, that looks lovely," Kate said, taking a slice of Havarti. "I was thinking I'm too tired to even go anywhere for dinner, so this is perfection."

Lily smiled and took her seat. "The fire is perfect for these chilly evenings. I've got plenty of wraps and blankets if anyone gets cold."

The sound of the gate opening drew their attention to Nora, followed by Sherlock and Mac. Mac carried an oversized dog bed and had a plastic tote under his arm.

As all three dogs ran to greet Sherlock, Izzy hurried from her chair to help Mac with Sunny's supplies. She grabbed the tote and opened the door to the cottage so he could place the dog bed in the living area. "Thanks for hauling all her stuff over here."

"Not a problem. I've got a bag of her food and her bowls from the house that I can put in your car."

"Are you sure Sherlock couldn't use the food?"

"She's a fussy eater, so this is all she'll eat, and Sherlock is on a different type."

They walked back to join the group and he smiled at the four dogs running around the yard, leaping over each other. "That's the best part of owning a dog. That sense of fun and all the smiles they bring to you. The joy they have for life is contagious."

Lily handed Mac a cold beer and introduced Nora to Kate and Izzy. As they snacked on the savory appetizers, the conversation turned to Nora's daughter and Mel.

Nora waved away the offer of more wine. "One glass is my limit. I promised I'd pick up the girls after the lecture tonight." She helped herself to another piece of cheese and a handful of olives. "I'm glad she's doing something and not sulking at me tonight. Teenagers." She shook her head and shrugged.

"I feel like Mel is finally on a straight path. I hope she is, anyway." Lily sipped from her glass and raised her brows at Mac. "She's going to the local community college and seems to like it. She's had so much trauma in her life, and although she's technically an adult, she's quite immature emotionally and socially. It makes it tough."

Mac patted Lily's arm. "I've had my own struggle with my daughter, Missy. After my wife passed away, Missy and I had a difficult relationship. She's grown and moved away now. We manage, but we're not close like we used to be. Losing her mom changed our lives forever. Mel, well with her losing both of her parents, her situation is even worse. Lily's a terrific mentor to her. She's given her a safe place and a purpose."

Lily slipped her hand in Mac's. "Loss and the grief that follows are so difficult, and the experience is different for everyone. It's devastating to lose a spouse, and then to try to be strong and comfort your child when all you want to do is crawl in a dark hole, is even harder. It took all I had to be there for my son after my husband was killed. I can't imagine Mel being alone and having nobody."

Nora nodded. "She's lucky to have you, Lily. As difficult as adolescent girls can be, someday she'll realize that." She plucked a strawberry from the table. "I keep telling myself the same thing about Bree. She can be so horrible to me and say the most hateful things. I hope when she grows up, we can be friends."

"I wouldn't count on it." Izzy's thoughts blurted out of her mouth before she could stop herself. She brought her hand to her lips and shook her head. "I'm sorry, I shouldn't have said that. I've been struggling with my daughter, Mia, since she was about fifteen and her father and I divorced. She's thirty now, and we still can't seem to tolerate each other."

Izzy took a long swallow from her glass. "Mia is finally back in school, focused on a career path that could be wonderful for her, but she just announced she's pregnant. I'm not sure what's going to happen, but doubt it will be good. Her dad has always indulged her and I've always been the realistic one, so Mia is certain her dad will come to her rescue again. I'm not so sure, but chances are I'll be the bad guy again."

Nora nodded her head in understanding. "Bree's dad wears the white hat in our family. She resents me for the divorce and for moving away. I understand what you're saying. Being a single parent is tough and it sounds like it may not get easier."

Mac raised his bottle of beer. "I agree. Over the years, Missy has made it abundantly clear how her life would have been better had I been the one to die instead of her mom. I know she didn't always mean it, but the chasm between us that developed so long ago is still there."

Izzy glanced at Kate, who had been quiet throughout the discussion. She caught her eye and raised her brows at her friend. Kate, knowing she was checking to see if she was okay, nodded at her.

"Izzy and Lily know I lost my daughter to suicide when she was in college, over twenty years ago now. I'm also divorced and understand the hardships that come with single parenting. I'm lucky I still have my son and a loving relationship with a man who has been my best friend since our school days." She smiled at Nora. "My son, Mitch, and I are quite close and I love having a friendship with him as an adult. He was my whole reason for living after Karen's death. The grief of losing her still reaches out and grabs me, sometimes when I least expect it. I don't think that emptiness inside of you ever goes away, but time dulls the pain of it."

Tears filled Lily's eyes as she bobbed her head. "Losing Gary was something I wasn't sure I would survive, and like you say, the anguish still takes over some days, but I can't imagine losing a child. That would be so much worse." She dabbed at her eyes. "Seeing you, I have hope. I would have never guessed you live with such sadness. It's not always easy to imagine a future, but your story renews my faith."

Izzy raised her glass. "Here's to all of us, struggling to get it right in this crazy world. My heart goes out to Kate, Lily, and Mac, for the losses you've all endured. I'm lucky enough to still have my daughter in my life. Thank you for reminding me of what's important."

Chapter 11

SATURDAY MORNING, KATE and Izzy loaded the SUV, adding their luggage to the boxes of items Izzy had purchased from Cyndy's shop and the trade show. She made sure to leave an empty space on the backseat and covered it with an old blanket she kept in the cargo area, giving Sunny a comfortable place to sleep on the way home.

They each hugged Lily goodbye, along with making sure Fritz and Bodie received lots of belly rubs and ear scratches. Lily walked with them to the car. "It's been wonderful to meet you. I'm delighted you came and spent some time here and hope you come back soon."

Izzy smiled as she leaned against the driver's door. "Your property is lovely and was the getaway I needed. If you get time to sneak away, come over to the island. You and the dogs are welcome to stay with me anytime."

"I may take you up on that. It's the slow season, so if I get a block of free time, I'll let you know. I'd love to visit the San Juan Islands."

Kate leaned across the console to see Lily through the open door. "You're always welcome, and between all of us, you'll have a place to stay no matter when you come."

"Safe travels and please keep in touch." Lily waved until they turned the corner and headed toward downtown.

After a quick stop at Muffins & More, where they had breakfast and took a box of muffins and pastries for snacks on the road, Izzy set out on the highway. She stopped often to let Sunny take a break, but even with the extra delays, they made it to the ferry landing in Anacortes in plenty of time to catch the mid-afternoon ferry that would get them back to Friday Harbor.

Sunny hadn't traveled by ferry, but she stayed close to Izzy and never even tugged on her leash. They made their way to the deck outside where animals were permitted, and found an empty bench while Kate stood in line and got each of them a cup of hot tea to go with their box of muffins.

Izzy removed Sunny's water bowl from her tote and filled it from a bottle. The dog slurped up the cool liquid and then stretched out in front of the bench. Kate and Izzy sipped tea and snacked on carrot cake muffins topped with sweet cream cheese frosting. As Izzy looked across the water that never failed to calm her, she breathed in the air and let peace wash over her.

The trip had been a welcome distraction and as she gazed upon the shimmering golden fur of the dog sleeping at her feet, she smiled. She never imagined finding a new best friend, but she knew Sunny would live up to her name and be the bright spot in each of her days. The dog's gentle eyes delivered calm, and she had a perpetual smile on her face, which Izzy found irresistible. She couldn't wait for everyone to meet her.

As she thought about Sunny, she slipped her cell phone from her purse to text Jeff about putting in a doggy door and an enclosure outside. She shook her head when she saw the screen. No service. She'd have to remember to get in touch with him when she got back to the island.

She leaned back and soaked in the tranquility of her surroundings. The lush green swells of the tiny islands that dotted the waterway, the blue sky, the dark, smooth water, all reminded her why she had decided to call this gorgeous corner of the world home.

And yet, despite her peace, her heart still ached for Mia. She understood all too well how scary a pregnancy could be, especially an unplanned one. It had helped to listen to Mac and Nora talk about their daughters and the hardships they faced, and were still facing. Izzy had realized she wasn't alone or the only parent struggling with her adult daughter.

She'd never failed at anything, but those feelings of inadequacy and defeat nagged at her almost constantly when it came to her performance as a mother. Part of her felt guilty she had elected to move away, somewhere that would make it harder for Mia to visit, somewhere where she would have to make an extra effort to see her mother. Izzy loved Mia and would always love her, but she longed for a friendship and closeness like so many other mothers and daughters shared. She had that with her mom, and until coming to the island saw her daily.

A new wave of guilt washed over her as she thought about her own mother and what she must be feeling with Izzy so far away. Her parents supported her and wanted her to be happy, and her sisters assured her they would watch over them, but it felt strange to be absent from them.

Thoughts of her old life, her old house, her old normal, inevitably turned her thoughts to John. She still harbored so much blame toward him, and although she knew it wasn't healthy, in times of stress or strife with Mia, those angry thoughts bubbled closer to the surface.

His selfishness had led to the demise of their marriage, her relationship with Mia, and so much more. She hated that he still invaded her thoughts, still captured her attention, albeit in a negative way. Why couldn't she let him go? Because of Mia.

It was one thing to betray her, but he had ruined their daughter. His inability to be a real parent had made Mia into a spoiled and irresponsible teen, and now a misguided and damaged young woman. She would never understand how he had convinced Mia, even now, that the sun rose and set upon him. Izzy loathed the fact Mia viewed her dad in such a good light, but now she feared even more what was to come if he failed to come to her rescue this time. It could send Mia over the edge.

It only took a glance at Kate to remind Izzy how lucky she was. Mia was still here. Izzy was ashamed for even voicing her complaints to Kate. A woman who no longer had the luxury of grumbling about her daughter shouldn't have to listen to her friend whine about her troubles, but Kate was so kind and loving, she never mentioned it. Izzy forced herself to focus on what she had, not what she'd lost.

They finished up the last of their snack, and decided to get together to decorate Izzy's house that week, then chatted about the upcoming furniture delivery slated for Monday. Soon the harbor came into view, and as they climbed back into Izzy's car, her peace faded away even more—until she caught Sunny's loving gaze. Maybe things would be different now; she wasn't alone.

AFTER DROPPING KATE home and introducing Sunny to Spence and Roxy, Izzy set out for her new house. As she drove, she talked to Sunny, who was sitting up and looking out the window, no doubt taking in the new views.

She had texted Blake before they got on the ferry to let him know when she would arrive home, so it was no surprise to see his truck parked in the driveway. He and Ellie, along with Oreo, a black and white bundle of energy, were sitting on the porch.

Blake smiled as he made his way to Izzy's SUV. "Welcome home," he said, as his sister opened her door. "We wanted to be here to meet Sunny, and we brought some stuff for dinner."

"That sounds perfect. Let's get Sunny out and let her run around and play." Izzy opened the rear door, and Sunny waited until Izzy told her it was okay before bounding onto the ground. Oreo bolted for her and after the two of them gave each other a thorough sniffing, they darted onto the lawn, chasing each other and playing.

"She's a sweetheart," said Ellie, watching the two of them.

"That reminds me, I need to text Jeff and see if he can create some type of enclosure or fence in the backyard that won't go against the HOA rules, plus add a doggy door."

Blake nodded. "I can help him if he needs it. You go ahead and I'll grab your things and unload for you."

Ellie linked her arm in Izzy's. "We can visit while we put together dinner." She stopped at Blake's truck, and they picked up the shopping bags from the cab.

Izzy found a corner in the living room for Sunny's bed, giving her a view out to the patio. Ellie took care of dinner, while Izzy directed Blake in placing all her packages and Sunny's supplies.

She eyed the stack of boxes in the corner. "I'll be glad to get some furniture on Monday and then get a bit more organized." She set up Sunny's bowls in the laundry room and called to her, so she'd know where to find her food and water. Oreo followed her new friend and they each proceeded to inspect and sniff every inch of the house.

When Izzy went back in the kitchen, the spicy aroma of garlic chili sauce wafted through the air. Ellie gestured to a stack of plastic containers on the counter. "I made dog cookies today, and stocked you up for Sunny."

"You are my favorite sister-in-law." Izzy chuckled and slipped into one of the chairs at the counter. "Despite only driving and sitting today, I'm pooped. Thank you for treating me to dinner."

"Of course. We figured you'd be tired from your day of travel and we couldn't wait to meet Sunny. This is a simple garlic chicken stir fry."

As they sat down at the dining table, Izzy's cell phone rang. She smiled at the screen. "Hey, Mom." As she listened, her smile faded, replaced by a furrow in the middle of her forehead. "Slow down. You're saying Shannon is in jail?"

Blake rolled his eyes and slammed his fork onto his plate. "You have got to be kidding me?"

Izzy grabbed a pad and pen and asked her mother several questions, jotting down notes. "Okay, Mom, let me make a few calls, and then I'll get back in touch with you." She shook her head as she disconnected the call.

"What now?" asked Blake.

"Shannon was involved in some sort of protest in a small town about thirty minutes south of Olympia. She's in jail, along with several others, for assault on a police officer and destruction of property. Mom couldn't remember everything, but Shannon called her and wants to get bailed out."

Blake slammed his hand on the table. "Of course, she does. I'm putting my foot down this time." Sunny and Oreo both raised their heads at the strain in his voice. "This is exactly why we set up the trust for the business and all the family assets. If it was up to Mom and Dad, they would use it all to get Shannon out of whatever mess she manages to make."

Ellie offered to take the dogs outside, as Izzy nodded and tapped the screen on her phone. "Let me contact the police there and see what I can find out."

After several transfers and waiting on hold, Izzy finally reached a person who could give her the information she needed. She glanced at her brother and then at her notes. "Her bail is $7,500. She's been charged with assault against a police officer, resisting arrest, theft, and property damage."

Blake shook his head. "Not a dime, Izz, not a dime. She needs to sit her ass in jail and think about her life and her choices. It's time she faced a consequence. She's forty years old, for goodness sake."

"I agree, but Mom and Dad are going to have trouble with our decision."

"I don't care. They put the two of us in charge of decisions and we sign the checks, so that's it."

In sharp contrast to her brother, Izzy's voice was calm and matter-of-fact. "Yes, logically, that's it. But we still have to deal with their emotions and what this will do within the family."

"Let's get Lauren and Esther on the phone and talk to them, so we're united in this. Mom and Dad signed over the decision making to us. They understood they were giving us the reins."

Izzy nodded. "You go ahead and call them. Remember, Mom and Dad have the means on their own to pull together her bail money, without the trust, so they may elect to do so. I agree we need to say no bail from the trust, but we also need to convince them to leave Shannon there and make her face the weight of the charges."

Blake pulled out his phone as Izzy left him to go to her office. She sat at her beloved desk, where she had tackled far more complicated legal problems over her career, and looked out the window. She was tired and hungry, although her appetite had disappeared when she heard the angst in her mom's voice.

With it being Saturday, Shannon wouldn't see a judge until Monday, so that meant two nights in jail. Izzy imagined she may have a new attitude come Monday, but only if their parents agreed not to intervene.

She knew Esther and Lauren would agree with Blake, so it would be the four siblings against Shannon. Her mom and dad never tolerated bad behavior from any of them, but with Shannon, all of their expectations went out the window. It reminded her of John and Mia, and how he let her get away with anything. She shuddered at the thought of leaving Mia in a jail cell for two nights. As much as she understood it was necessary, she could also empathize with their parents.

She summoned all her strength, knowing she would have to be the one to convince their parents to leave Shannon in jail. Blake was too angry, Lauren was busy with little Beanie, and Esther would cave to whatever the last person she talked to suggested, wanting everyone to be happy, and not liking to make decisions or waves.

Izzy didn't want their parents taking matters into their own hands and driving across the state either. That would only make things worse. Her dad had no business navigating the busy roads outside of Seattle, and the whole situation could end in a disaster. If they insisted, she or Blake would end up having to go to take them. That was the last thing she wanted to do, so she had to appeal to their parents and convince them it was the right decision.

She heard Blake's footsteps before he rounded the corner to her office. "Lauren and Esther agree not to use the trust funds for Shannon's bail and that she needs to stay in jail and go through the system."

"We might need them to keep an eye on Mom and Dad, if we can convince them to let this all play out."

He nodded as he slumped into the chair in front of her desk. "Yeah, we talked about it, and they both said they would go over to the house, so we can all talk together via a video chat. They're on their way now, and Lauren said she'd text when they're ready."

Izzy bowed her head and ran her fingers through her hair, massaging her scalp. "This is about the last thing I need right now." She took a deep breath. "You need to promise me you'll be calm and not yell at Mom and Dad. We don't need to get them any more excited or worried. I don't want them to feel like we're blaming them for Shannon's behavior."

He nodded. "I know. She makes me so damn mad. But I'll control it."

ELLIE APPEARED IN the doorway with two mugs of tea and a plate of cookies. Izzy smiled and took a cup. "Are those Sunny's cookies?" She grinned and winked at her sister-in-law.

Ellie laughed and said, "These are human treats. I made a few of them along with the dog cookies. Hopefully, I didn't mix them up." She put her hands across the top of Blake's shoulders. "I'll be downstairs with the pups."

"Thanks, sweetie. I'm sorry about all this." He brought her hand to his lips and kissed it.

His phone chimed, and Ellie kissed the top of his head. "Best of luck, you two," she said, making her way to the staircase.

Izzy opened the video chat screen on her computer, and Blake moved his chair around so they sat next to each other. Several minutes later, they saw their parents flanked by Esther and Lauren.

Izzy's heart broke for their parents, who looked frail and small, their pale faces devoid of color except for the red around their eyes. "Hey, Mom and Dad. I've got the information from the local police." Izzy spelled out the charges and watched as her horrified parents reacted.

Her mother's shoulders shook, and she kept clutching her hand to her throat. Izzy took a deep breath. "These are serious charges and I'm going to approach this like I would any of my clients and give you my best advice." She continued to explain with it being the weekend, Shannon would need to stay in jail until she saw a judge on Monday. "Sometimes our kids make poor decisions, bad choices, and the only way they learn not to make those same mistakes is to let the impact of their choice play out. I know you would never condone assault, much less against a police officer. This is reprehensible behavior we can all agree is not acceptable and never warranted. Shannon needs to understand this, and for some reason, she seems to be living in a different world. I think this may be an opportunity for us to hold strong, and not give in to her and bail her out right now. She needs to understand her responsibilities to society, to her family, and to herself."

Izzy glanced at her brother. "Blake and I have discussed this at length and included Esther and Lauren. We have responsibility for the family trust and as you know, Shannon does not have a seat at the table, by design. None of us felt she was responsible enough to play a role in the trust when we created it. Mom, you and Dad gave the authority to manage it to Blake and to me. As hard as we know this is for you, we cannot and will not approve funds from the family trust for Shannon's legal issues."

Tears streamed down her mother's face, and her father put his arm around her. He looked at Lauren and Esther, and then back at the camera. "How can you leave your sister in jail? Family is always there for you no matter what. What does that tell her?"

"It tells her she needs to suffer the consequence for her awful actions." Blake's voice boomed in Izzy's office. She patted his thigh and gave him a disapproving eye. He lowered his voice and moved closer to the screen. "Do either of you really believe it's okay for us to go around assaulting police officers, stealing from companies, smashing windows and cars, and demolishing furnishings in businesses? What if someone did that to the winery?"

Blake's words hung in the air as their parents ducked their heads. Helen's voice cracked and broke the silence. "She'll think we're coming for her. How can we leave her there?"

Gene cleared his throat. "What happens Monday in court, Izzy?"

"She'll have to appear before a judge for arraignment. She can post a bond and bail, but without any assets, a bondsman will most likely require a cosigner. The alternative is all cash bail. The person putting up collateral or providing the bail money is guaranteeing she will appear in court to face charges. She'll have to enter a plea Monday, and employ a lawyer to defend her or ask the court to appoint a public defender, if she doesn't have the funds. Since she has no job, other than her monthly stipend from the business, and no assets, she could probably get a public defender."

Helen shook her head. "No, Izzy, you have to be her lawyer. I know what you all think of Shannon, and I understand this is serious and she has made a horrible mistake, but she deserves a good lawyer, not some public defender who won't have time to help her." Her mother looked to Gene. "We can put up the bail bond money ourselves without using the trust, and guarantee she will appear."

Blake cleared his throat. "I understand you're willing to put up your funds to bail her, but with your generosity, don't you think it would be a good idea to attach some expectations? For instance, she could have to stay at home until her court date, so there's no risk of her running off with those dirtbags she hangs around with and forgetting to go to court. She could work at the winery and try to pay you back or get an actual job. This has got to stop. She is an absolute embarrassment. What would you do if she did this in Richland or Yakima?"

Gene's shoulders slumped even more, and Helen sobbed. Gene cleared his throat. "I hear what you're saying, son. We are mortified, and don't understand why Shannon does the things she does. We keep hoping she'll grow out of this phase and get her life figured out, settle down, find something she enjoys doing."

Blake started to speak, but Izzy interrupted. "We all hope so, Dad. The problem is, until she gets uncomfortable, she's not going to change. In her experience, each time she gets herself into a pickle, we rush to get her out of it. She hasn't had to work, so why would she? Do you understand what we're saying?"

Lauren mumbled something to their parents, which wasn't clear, but they both nodded their heads. "Lauren's right, we don't want this to escalate," said Gene. "Come Monday, do what you have to do, Izzy, and get her home to us here where she can stay until her court date. We'll pay you for your time."

"No, Dad. Shannon can pay me for my time. She could never afford my actual rate, but I'll make her a reduced deal and explain she will have to get a job to pay the bill. I suggest you do the same with the bond money. If she has any funds in her account, they need to go toward bail and my fee. I will ask her that first, as I think it's wise she understands the impact of all this."

Thoughts of trekking there and back and dealing with Shannon filled Izzy's mind. She had planned to work on her house and take delivery of her new furniture, and now with Sunny in the picture, it only complicated things. She also had her doubts the district attorney would go easy on someone assaulting a police officer.

As much as she didn't want to take this case, she couldn't refuse the pleading looks from her parents. Despite being close to the last thing she wanted to do, refusing to represent

Shannon would only cause them more pain. She would do it for them, not for Shannon.

Chapter 12

JEFF AND SAM showed up at Izzy's door on Sunday morning with fresh lattes and still warm pastries. They brought Zoe and Bailey to meet Sunny and play together, while Jeff came up with a plan for a doggy door and set about taking measurements to build an enclosure for the backyard. The homeowner's association didn't permit high fences in the yards, so the options were limited.

She greeted both of them with a hug, and led them to the dining room table. Jeff took a turnover and stepped outside, the three dogs at his heels. "My furniture situation will improve tomorrow." She turned toward Sam and gestured to the mostly empty space. "As luck would have it, I have to catch the ferry tomorrow, so Kate is going to handle the delivery and placement for me while I'm gone."

Sam frowned. "Is Mia okay?"

Izzy nodded. "As far as I know. I'm going because Shannon is in jail and needs an attorney." She took a sip from her latte. "It's a long story, and I'm not at all happy about it. I'm doing it for my parents."

The doorbell rang, interrupting their conversation. Izzy's brows rose. "I'm not expecting anyone. I'll be right back."

She opened the door to a smiling man holding a gift bag. "Ms. Isabelle Griffin?" he asked.

"That's me." Izzy took the bag, decorated with a beautiful copper colored ribbon. "This is a surprise."

"I'm Colin Sinclair, the general manager here at Sunset Bay Golf and Tennis Community. I wanted to welcome you to the neighborhood."

Izzy had always had a weakness for Sean Connery, and Colin's voice carried the same Scottish accent. That, coupled with his brilliant blue eyes, made her pulse quicken and her throat tighten.

"Please call me Izzy, and thanks so much. The gift bag is so kind of you." She opened the door a bit wider and gestured to the house. "Please come in. I'm not settled, still waiting on furnishings, but you're welcome to come in. My friends dropped by with fresh pastries and coffees."

He shook his head. "I don't want to intrude. I did want to make sure you knew about the Halloween party coming up at the end of the month." He nodded to the gift bag. "There's a flyer along with an event calendar in there, but I hope you'll come. It's at the large event pavilion connected to the golf course."

Izzy moved her head toward the kitchen. "Please, come in, and you can tell me all about it. I was gone this past week and haven't had time to do much exploring of the clubhouse or events center."

The man, dressed in jeans and a Henley sweater the same blue of his eyes, stepped through the door, and Izzy led him into the open kitchen. "Sam, this is Colin Sinclair. He's the general manager of Sunset Bay."

Sam smiled, and said, "I know Colin. He's a regular at the coffee shop. So nice to see you."

Izzy presented Colin with the box of pastries and offered him a chair at the dining table. "There's an untouched latte, so please help yourself."

He smiled and slid his tall frame into the chair, glancing outside as he plucked a cinnamon roll from the box. "I see Jeff has his toolbelt on. Already doing home improvements?"

Izzy took the chair next to Colin. "He's going to install a doggy door for me and come up with something in case Sunny, she's the dog I adopted, needs to stay outside."

Colin reached for a latte and took a sip. "What breed of dog did you adopt?"

"Sunny's a golden retriever and she's almost five and very well behaved, fully trained."

"Ah, that's my favorite breed. You know they originally came from Scotland?" His grin softened his strong jaw line, shrouded in a short, dark beard, flecked with generous streaks of silver, like his temples. "I've always had dogs and have a golden myself, Jethro. We'll have to get them together."

Surprised at the flutter in her chest, Izzy nodded. "That would be wonderful. She's the first dog I've had on my own, so I'd welcome your expertise."

Sam gestured outside as the three furry friends ran by the windows. "I probably wouldn't have been brave enough to move here without my best friend, Zoe." She turned her eyes toward Izzy. "It won't take you long to wonder how you ever managed without Sunny. She's such a sweet one."

Colin nodded as he swallowed the last bite of his cinnamon roll. "Dogs are the best. Not only are they perfect playmates and friends, but also the best therapists."

Sam bobbed her head. "That's an understatement."

"Jethro and I go for a walk every morning. You're welcome to join us." Colin cradled the cup in his hands. "I live less than half a mile down the road, right near the third green. We could pick you up tomorrow around six-thirty?"

Izzy frowned. "I can't make tomorrow, I've got to catch the early ferry and get to Olympia for some business, but perhaps later in the week after I get my furniture organized?"

"Of course, whenever it works for you. What line of work are you in?"

Izzy explained she was a semi-retired attorney and had taken on a contract position at the prosecuting attorney's office, but had a client who needed her in court tomorrow.

Sam stood and moved toward the patio door. "Izzy's brother, Blake Griffin, runs the Island Winery, and Izzy came to visit and fell in love with this gorgeous island and decided to stay." She gestured outside and added, "I'm going to run and check on Jeff and the dogs."

"I'm new to the island myself, but have heard great things about the winery," said Colin. "I've worked for the parent company that owns Sunset Bay for my entire career. I ran one of their clubs in Scotland for years, and then when my son was grown, I took a job that moved me to the United States and managed a club in Bend, Oregon before moving here last month."

"Golf is definitely in your blood." Izzy moved to the kitchen and filled the kettle with water.

"Are you a golfer?" he asked in his gravelly voice, making Izzy's legs weak, as he moved to sit at the large granite counter.

She shrugged and said, "I'm almost embarrassed to admit it, especially to you, but no, I don't golf. I fell in love with the house and was looking to downsize and find something I could afford, where I didn't have to worry about yardwork."

He chuckled. "Well, maybe I can teach you to love the game. We offer some great membership rates for homeowners and even give you a few months free, so you can try out all the amenities. There's a pool, although it's closed for the season, but saunas and hot tubs are open all year, as are the exercise facilities."

"I'll probably stick to walking the trails and visiting The Bistro, where I can indulge in my love for wine and eating." Izzy laughed as she grabbed a mug for tea. "Would you like some tea? I'm having Earl Grey."

"What kind of a Scotsman would I be if I refused tea?"

The patio door opened, and along with Sam and Jeff, the three dogs came bounding inside, making a beeline for Colin. He petted each of them, talking to them, scratching behind their ears and under their chins before they wandered off to the laundry room and slurped up water from Sunny's bowl.

"Morning, Colin," said Jeff, nodding toward him as he slipped his tape measure into the pocket of his tool belt.

"Izzy says you're working on some improvements for Sunny."

Jeff moved to the counter and unfolded a piece of paper. He pointed at the lines and said, "I think we can add a doggy door in the laundry room and I can build a narrow dog run along the side of the house, which won't violate any rules. That will give her a safe place, should you have to leave her home. I'd recommend one of those electronic doggy doors, where Sunny would wear an electronic collar that activates the door when she approaches it."

Izzy studied the sketch Jeff had done. "Makes sense. Go ahead and get everything you need ordered."

"Sounds good. I'll stop by in the morning on my way into town and pick up Sunny. We'll take good care of her tomorrow. Call when you're home, and we'll bring her by for you." He whistled for Bailey and Zoe, and they came running.

Sam hugged Izzy. "Good luck tomorrow. We'll see you when you get home."

Izzy saw them to the door and gave Bailey and Zoe two of Ellie's homemade cookies for the road.

Colin was putting his cup in the sink when Izzy returned. "Thank you for the tea. Well, I don't want to keep you. I was going to offer to look after Sunny for you tomorrow, but it sounds like Sam and Jeff are going to watch her. If you ever need a dog sitter, call me. My yard is set up to allow Jethro in and out and sometimes he comes to work with me."

"Aww, that's kind of you. Sunny was staying with a vet who had another golden, so I'm sure she would love to get together with Jethro. As soon as I get organized here, I'll get in touch and we can set up a walk or something."

She and Sunny walked with him to the door and onto the porch. He started walking down the driveway toward the road, and then turned around and jogged back to Izzy. Sunny pranced over to him, thinking it was a game.

He held both hands open in front of him. "I hope you don't think I'm being too forward, but you mentioned your love of wine and food. Perhaps one night this week, you'd consider being my guest at the Bistro and we can chat some more?"

It had been so long since Izzy had felt the rush of excitement or the flutter of interest, it took her a few moments to respond. "I'd like that, Colin. I'll give you a call later this week."

His smile reached all the way to his dazzling eyes, making tiny crinkles at the outer corners of them. "My cell number is on my card in the gift bag. Call anytime." He started walking backward as he talked, prompting Sunny to trot after him.

Izzy called her back and she returned, but not before getting a scratch behind the ears from Colin. Izzy led her inside and shut the door. "Well, he was an unexpected surprise. Colin seems like a nice man, doesn't he?" She looked into the gentle dark brown eyes focused on her.

Sunny beat her tail against the floor, and Izzy laughed.

MONDAY MORNING, JEFF arrived before dawn and collected Sunny. Izzy gathered her things and hopped in her SUV. She opted to take the early ferry, to make sure she had plenty of time to navigate the traffic through Seattle. She hated driving in the city, and although Blake had called last night and offered to go with her, she thought it best to tackle Shannon on her own. She would have welcomed the company and the help driving, but suspected Blake would have a hard time restraining his comments, and she didn't need to add any volatility to the situation with Shannon.

On the ferry, she looked through her notes. The case wasn't complicated. Getting Shannon out on bail would be a matter of paperwork. The complication would come when Izzy advised her on her plea options. The quickest and quietest way to dispose of the charges would be to plead guilty and take the punishment. She doubted Shannon would heed her advice.

She had booked Shannon on a flight leaving Seattle in the late afternoon, putting her back in the Tri-Cities an hour later, where their parents planned to meet her at the airport. Izzy had promised to call as soon as they were done with court.

When the ferry arrived in Anacortes, she stopped at a café for a bite to eat and a much needed latte. As promised, she texted Blake when she set out on the road for the city. She moved right along the freeway until she passed Everett and got closer to the suburbs outside of Seattle. It took her over three hours, but she finally pulled into the parking lot next to the Lewis County Courthouse.

Once inside, she found her way to the assigned courtroom and checked in, hoping to get a few minutes with Shannon prior to the hearing. The bailiff told Izzy Shannon was in a holding cell awaiting her turn in court, and he would arrange for them to speak in one of the attorney conference rooms. She also asked to meet with the prosecuting attorney assigned to the case, and he directed her to a building behind the ice center.

While Izzy waited, she tapped out a text to Mia, letting her know she was in the city for court and wondered if she had time to get together later in the afternoon. Her finger hesitated over the send button, not sure she wanted to further complicate her day by adding a visit with Mia on top of what she suspected would be a stressful day with Shannon, but hit the arrow anyway. She couldn't very well be so close to the campus and not call her own daughter, could she?

A few minutes later the receptionist addressed her. "Mr. Durham can see you now. He's only free for a few minutes." She led Izzy down the hallway.

Izzy found a middle-aged man sitting at a table with a cart of files at his feet and several case files stacked on the table.

She extended her hand. "Isabelle Griffin for Shannon Griffin." She glanced at her notes and gave him the case number.

He nodded and clicked the keys on his laptop. "Right, looks like Ms. Griffin," he looked up and said, "a relation, I presume?"

"Sister." Izzy slipped into the chair in front of the desk.

"Well, it looks like assault on a police officer and destruction of property are the most serious charges. What are you thinking?"

"I haven't talked with my client yet, but was hoping we might be able to negotiate some lesser charges in exchange for a guilty plea?"

He reviewed the file and Shannon's record, reiterating that the prosecuting attorney's office, as well as the new mayor and sheriff, were all taking a hard line on protestors assaulting the police. In addition, business owners were growing weary of the constant destruction of their property that seemed to be migrating from cities like Seattle and Portland. "Looks like she has a habit of protesting and so far, has dodged any real punishment. The best I can do is drop the resisting arrest and the theft, but I can't do much about the assault or the property damage."

Izzy nodded her understanding. "I'll chat with Shannon, and give you her decision when we get inside the courtroom." She thanked him for his time, and hurried back to the courtroom. She checked in with the bailiff, who ushered her into a conference room, where she found Shannon.

Her sister sat in her orange jumpsuit, her hair a complete mess, a sullen look on her face and anger in her eyes. As soon as Izzy set her things on the table, Shannon glared at her. "I can't believe you left me in that hell hole all weekend."

Izzy dug into her bag and handed Shannon a skirt and blouse she had packed for her. Shannon grimaced and shook her head. "I'm not wearing this costume. Where are my clothes?"

"All your personal belongings will be released to you once you're arraigned and bailed. You can either wear this or the orange jumpsuit. Your choice."

Shannon crossed her arms and huffed. "I'll wear this. You can't dress me up in some goody two-shoes outfit and make me something I'm not. I will not bow to the government."

Izzy said nothing, opened her notebook. "We need to concentrate on the next steps. How much do you have in your savings account that we can use for bail?"

The shock on Shannon's face was priceless. Her mouth hung open as her eyes clouded with confusion. "Why would I have any money? Mom and Dad will cover it."

Izzy pressed the issue to discover that Shannon only had one account and the last time she withdrew money from the ATM, she had about three hundred dollars.

"You're going to have the bail cost and also my fee, a greatly reduced fee, but nonetheless, you will need to cover the fees. You need to prepare yourself to find a job, so you can pay these bills."

Izzy ignored the grimace on Shannon's face, and continued. "Mom and Dad will be putting up the money to bail you and you'll need to enter a plea today. I talked to the prosecutor assigned to the case and he's willing to drop a couple of the charges, in exchange for you pleading guilty to the property damage and the assault on the officer. I advise you to plead guilty, and then you'll have one more court appearance after today for sentencing. If you plead not guilty, it means a trial, but with the evidence they have, including body camera footage of you, I see very little hope of getting you acquitted. All you'll be doing is wasting your time and money."

"I am not pleading guilty. That's crazy and you can't mean you're charging me for this horrible advice. I didn't ask you to come anyway."

Izzy took a long breath, thankful Blake hadn't come with her. "I'm here because of Mom and Dad. As a client, I'm charging you, albeit a fraction of my normal rate, as I said before. You are here, in jail, in court, because of the choices you made. If you would rather have a court appointed attorney, that's your choice." Izzy started packing her things back into her leather bag. "You're not going to get a better deal from the prosecutor's office and you'll be prolonging the process, as you'll have to be assigned an attorney and then reappear."

Izzy shoved the clothes into her bag and clicked the buckles. "It's up to you, but I'm not wasting my time if you'd rather have someone else. If you do as I advise, you'll be out of here and on the flight I booked for you, and home with Mom and Dad tonight. You'll stay there until your sentencing. That's the condition of them putting up your bail money. You will get a job, you will pay my fee, and you will pay them back. Take it or leave it."

She stood and reached for her bag, then continued in her calm tone. "I walk out the door, I'm not coming back. You can take your chances in there and make your own bail arrangements. I'll go back to the island and you're on your own. At some point, Shannon, you need to take responsibility for your actions, your life. Mom and Dad are getting too old for your shenanigans and this stress is really not good for them."

Shannon made a show of crossing her arms in front of her. "This is so stupid. You're controlling me, like the police and the government. You're part of the system. The system of oppression does nothing for the poor or the undocumented. Everything is skewed to favor the rich and powerful."

Izzy looked at her watch. "We've only got about two more minutes, so what's it going to be?"

Shannon slammed her hands on the table. "This isn't fair. Nobody cares about the little people, the powerless."

There was a knock on the door, and the bailiff stuck his head in. "Your case is up, Ms. Griffin."

Izzy nodded and made her way to the door. "Time's up, Shannon. You can go out by yourself or I can go with you."

Shannon shoved the chair and stood. She stomped toward the door. Izzy raised her brows. "If I represent you, I need to make it clear that you will not say a word or voice your opinions. You will be respectful of the judge, and only speak when asked to do so. Am I representing you?"

"Yes," Shannon snarled, and followed Izzy out the door.

"Okay, next question, do you agree to the plea deal or do you want to take your chances at trial and plead not guilty?"

"Not much of a choice, really." The two continued into the hallway. "I'll take the stupid plea deal, even if it is a complete farce." The bailiff took Shannon by the arm, and led her to the prisoner's entrance.

"Wonderful," said Izzy, making her way to the defendant's table, hoping her sister could keep her mouth shut for the next five minutes.

Chapter 13

S HANNON'S IGNORANCE OF court proceedings and the rush of the actual hearing process worked in Izzy's favor. Fear shone in Shannon's eyes as Izzy suspected the weight of the charges began to sink in, and the judge's stern manner was effective in quelling Shannon's argumentative nature. A quick word in the ear of Mr. Durham, seconds before they stepped forward to their respective tables, made for a speedy appearance, with the judge asking Shannon if she agreed to the plea deal outlined by the prosecuting attorney's office. When Izzy prompted her, Shannon answered that she did. The judge granted the reduced bail amount and set a date for sentencing next month, right before Thanksgiving.

Izzy completed the paperwork, and then collected Shannon from the county jail, conveniently located a block from the courthouse. No longer in the bright orange prisoner's outfit, Shannon wore patterned leggings and a long, wrinkled tunic with the words "People Not Profit" painted in angry black letters. The change of clothing had not improved her attitude.

As they walked to the parking lot, Izzy heard her phone chime and saw a text reply from Mia. She suggested meeting for a late lunch when she got out of classes for the day, at a place that was easy for her to get to and Izzy recognized from the few times she had appeared at the courthouse in Seattle. The hour she suggested would give Izzy enough time to drop Shannon at the airport and drive downtown. She hadn't expected a reply from Mia, much less for her to agree to meet.

As much as she hated the idea of navigating downtown, she texted Mia back and promised to meet her.

Izzy ignored Shannon's ranting about the justice system as she drove through the quiet streets. As she turned onto the freeway, Shannon started squealing and pointing. "No, no, you need to take me to my friend's place so I can pick up my things."

"Sorry, Shannon, no time for that. You'll have to call and arrange for them to be shipped back to Richland. I'm dropping you at the airport where you can eat and catch your flight."

"Why don't I get any say in what's happening. I'm not a child."

Izzy resisted the urge to tell Shannon her whining sounded like a child, as she pressed the accelerator down and kept her eye on the traffic. "Your alternative would have been to stay in jail. Since you don't have the means to solve your own problems and have to rely on Mom and Dad, you are, in essence, a child. I hope you are more grateful to them than you're acting at the moment."

Izzy kept her eyes on the road but felt the burning of Shannon's piercing glare. With traffic moving, it didn't take long to get to the airport exit. Izzy followed the signs for departures and pulled to the curb near the Alaska Airlines door. She handed Shannon a piece of paper with her flight confirmation number and some cash. "That should be all you need to get your boarding pass and get you something to eat. I'll be in touch about what to expect at your sentencing hearing. You'll need to make arrangements to fly back for it."

As Shannon opened the door, she stopped and turned toward her sister. "What happens if I don't come back for it?"

"They'll issue a warrant for your arrest, Mom and Dad will lose all their bail money, and I'll be happy to contact the court and tell them where to find you. Since I'm an officer of the court, I have a duty."

Shannon scowled at her, got out with a huff, and slammed the door so hard it shook the SUV. Izzy watched her walk through the glass doors, hoping she would actually check in and make her flight, but not feeling all that confident. She eased back into the airport traffic, and wound her way downtown.

She found a parking garage a few blocks from the sandwich shop Mia had suggested. The shop was nearly empty, and she chose a table and studied the menu written on the chalkboards behind the counter. She was a few minutes early and texted Blake and her parents an update, promising to talk to them later.

The savory aroma of soups permeated the air, and Izzy's stomach rumbled. She waited as the time Mia suggested passed by and the minutes kept ticking. Normally, she would keep waiting, but was starving and ordered soup and sandwich, vowing to apologize to Mia when she arrived.

Resisting the urge to text her, knowing Mia would perceive it as nagging, Izzy finished her lunch, albeit slowly, hoping to still be eating when her daughter arrived. After a full hour passed, she texted Mia and asked where she was, letting her know she had to get on the road soon to make the ferry.

The friendly waitress checked on her again and asked if she could get her anything else. Izzy put the huge chocolate chip cookie that came with her lunch in her handbag and asked for a latte to go. Her eyes darted from the door to the windows with a view of the street, but Mia was nowhere in sight.

After paying, she took her cup and reluctantly set out for the parking garage. The fleeting thought of something bad having happened to Mia filtered through her mind. If Mia hadn't stood her up so many times in the past, she would have dwelled on it much longer, but she suspected that her daughter had, like so many times before, simply blown her off.

Irritated, she picked up the pace and made it back to her SUV, where she tossed her bag on the seat and situated her coffee and cookie, so they'd be reachable. She could have already been at the ferry landing, if she hadn't come all the way back downtown, and wasted more than an hour on lunch.

As she put the gearshift in reverse, she heard the chime of her phone. She saw her daughter's name on the screen and slammed it into park. *Something came up, can't make lunch.*

"Really?" Izzy mumbled through gritted teeth, and shook her head. She didn't bother to reply and squealed the tires as she made her way to the exit. With the freeway already clogged, she spent the two-hour ride stressed as she yelled at inept drivers and seethed about her day surrounded by spoiled young women and their total lack of respect.

She shuddered when she thought about Shannon and how she would be treating their parents. Blake had talked with Lauren and Esther about making sure they planned to be at the family home to not let Shannon roll over them or pressure them into letting her leave. After witnessing her sister's attitude today, Izzy didn't envy their task.

By the time she drove onto the ferry, her head hurt and her neck and shoulders ached. She texted Blake and Jeff, so they'd know when she'd be home to collect Sunny. She checked to see if Mia had texted again and saw nothing, but smiled when she saw a text from Kate and a couple of photos of her new furnishings.

She couldn't wait to get home to see everything in person. She took her bag with her leftover cookie upstairs and nibbled on it while she read another text from Blake letting her know

Shannon had been collected at the airport, and Lauren and Esther were with their parents.

After getting a cup of hot tea, Izzy rested her head against the window and stretched her legs out across the booth seat. Exhaustion settled over her like a heavy, damp blanket. The mental anguish and disappointment she had held at bay, threatened to overtake her. Bites of the soft cookie, full of chocolate chunks and nuts, helped comfort her.

She thought moving to the island, starting a new chapter, would be exciting and wonderful. She thought it would remove her from some of the drama associated with Shannon and their parents. She hoped the distance would serve as a buffer between her and her daughter. Today was the latest punch in the gut from Mia. Now, all Izzy longed for was the comfort of her new home and a snuggle with Sunny.

Izzy sometimes wondered if Mia did things on purpose or if she was so self-absorbed she didn't even consider the impact her actions had on anyone else. Did she agree to meet Izzy so she could delight in ghosting her later? How many times had Izzy rearranged her plans for Mia, to accommodate her needs, and then suffered a disappointing outcome? Too many to count, was the sad answer.

Living on the island was supposed to be her protective bubble. Yet, here she was, the one who had to change her plans, sacrifice what should have been an exciting day in her new house, leave her new dog behind, and tackle the grueling traffic she loathed, while Mia and Shannon chose to play the victim card.

Mia was supposed to talk to John this week, and that could bring a whole new level of drama to the table. With John's focus on his fiancé and upcoming wedding, Mia wouldn't be his main concern. Izzy was also sure John would leave a path of destruction in his wake, and she'd be the one expected to pick up the broken pieces. She only hoped the distance across the water would insulate her from some of the blowback.

With the October days getting shorter, it was already dark by the time the harbor came into view. The warm glow of the streetlights along the waterfront and the shops still open on Front Street welcomed Izzy home. She drove away from the landing and was pulling into her garage in less than ten minutes. The stark and welcome contrast to Seattle's traffic freshened her mind.

When she unlocked the door leading into the house, the aroma of coffee greeted her. She walked by the utility room and into the main part of the house, where the lights had been left on to welcome her. She gasped when she saw her living room. The beige couches, with the gorgeous sea glass colored pillows and soft throws tossed across them, looked perfect. She loved the oversized chaise lounge chair that matched the couches, with its accompanying soft blue throw.

The rustic wooden coffee and end tables held some of the beach inspired items she and Kate had picked out in Driftwood Bay. Potted silk plants, glass vases, wooden framed mirrors, and beachy looking art completed the look. Everywhere Izzy looked, she noticed an added touch, evidence of Kate's hand in making her dream a reality.

She set her bag down and made her way into the master bedroom. The subtle blush color in the fabrics made for a cheerful haven. A comfy oversized chair, with an ottoman and table large enough to serve as a desk, made for the perfect reading corner. She saw a note in Kate's handwriting letting her know she had stashed coffee beans in all the drawers and they would absorb the chemical smell that so often accompanied new furniture.

The tufted headboard and matching upholstered bench with the rolled arms at the end of the bed were perfect. The dressers, tables, mirrors, and bookcases completed the room.

Sunny's dog bed was nestled next to Izzy's side of the bed, near a thick and soft rug atop the wooden flooring.

As she moved to test out the oversized chair, the doorbell rang. She opened it to find Blake, holding two tote bags. Sunny bolted over the threshold, her tail whipping back and forth as she hurried toward Izzy.

Blake held up one of the totes and said, "Ellie sent me with dinner, and I collected Sunny on my way." He handed her the other tote. "Jeff and Sam outfitted her with a bunch of new toys from the hardware store. They also wanted to let you know she loves the water. They had a hard time keeping her off the beach, and had to give her a bath after."

Izzy knelt to greet Sunny, who snuggled against her. "We'll have to take some of our walks along the beach." Izzy ran her fingers through the soft fur.

As Blake followed her into the kitchen, he whistled. "Wow, your furniture looks great."

Izzy unearthed several containers. "This all smells so yummy." She opened the container of beef barley soup, tore off a chunk of still warm bread, and sat down at the island counter. Blake finished unloading all of Sunny's toys into her new toybox in the corner of the living room, and joined her.

As she ate, she recounted her stressful day with Shannon and Mia. Blake shook his head and tossed a ball for Sunny. "I'm glad I didn't come with you. I would have lost it." He took the lid off a container and selected a chocolate chunk macadamia nut cookie. "Ellie did some stress cooking today and I did some stress eating."

"Hopefully, Shannon won't do anything rash and will go to her sentencing hearing without creating any more problems for Mom and Dad. In court, for a few minutes, I could tell she was scared, but as soon as the hearing was over, she was back to her feisty self."

Blake stood and reached for the ball Sunny had dropped at his feet. "Mom and Dad need to stick to the plan and not let her bamboozle them like she always has. We're probably going to have to call them each day between now and then to give them the moral support to withstand the pressure."

"Be gentle with them. They don't need more stress. I'm going to send them a copy of my bill to get to Shannon, so hopefully that will motivate them to keep her on task to find a job and pay my fees." She retrieved a bottle of red wine she had left in the fridge and poured herself a glass.

"Sounds like you deserve more than one glass tonight. Not only did you have to suffer through Shannon, but what's up with Mia?"

She shrugged. "I've given up trying to apply logic to her. I'm sure I'll hear from her if her plan to move in with John falls on deaf ears. Until then, I'm going to try and enjoy my new house." She glanced down at Sunny, who was leaning against her leg, her tongue hanging out, with what appeared to be a smile on her face. "And my sweet dog."

"Well, I'll let you get settled." He stood, snagged one more cookie, and wrapped Izzy in a tight hug. "Thanks for making the trip and handling the case. I know Mom and Dad are grateful."

She walked him to the door. "Thanks for the delicious dinner and cookies. Give Ellie my love."

She stashed the leftovers and tidied the counter, taking the time to unpack the gift bag Colin had delivered yesterday. Along with a sweatshirt, several golf accessories, discount coupons for meals at The Bistro, and the events calendar, she fingered his business card.

She smiled as she reached for her cell phone and scrolled to her contacts, adding his name and number. Sunny settled onto the floor and lifted her eyes upward to meet Izzy's.

"What? I'm not going to call him tonight. That would make me look too eager, don't you think?" She ran her hand over the business card. "I'll wait until tomorrow."

Chapter 14

IZZY ADDED EARRINGS and lipstick, glancing in the mirror to see Sunny lounging in her new favorite spot – across the soft blush colored bench at the end of her bed. She'd taken to sleeping there at night, and while Izzy didn't want her on the bed, she didn't have the heart to shoo the sweet dog from the comfy spot that was the perfect size for her.

After her hurried trip to the city, Izzy had heard from her realtor back in Richland who had a few offers on her house. She accepted the most advantageous one and set things in motion for closing within the next month. She'd be able to pay her parents back and even after buying new furnishings, would have a healthy sum to bank in her investment account. The sorrow, or maybe it was guilt she had felt about leaving the house and her life behind, evaporated as she spent more time in her new home, organizing it and situating all the things she loved, both old memories and new bits and bobs, blending them together to create the perfect haven. She felt lighter and confident surrounded not only by the objects she had chosen, but by the comfort and peace that the island brought her.

In addition to spending the week getting things organized and put away in the house, Izzy introduced Sunny to her new doggy door and fancy electronic collar that controlled it. Jeff had installed the door and built the dog run, and stained her deck in less than a day. Sunny went outside when Izzy told her and they practiced going back and forth, but the dog preferred to stick close to Izzy, following her around the house and resting near her.

They'd made several trips to the beach, and Izzy favored the view from Lime Kiln State Park, with its beautiful lighthouse, especially at sunset. There was nothing prettier than watching the sun sink into the sea or if the weather was a bit stormy, seeing the powerful waves crash into the rocks below the lighthouse. The view, the experience alone, was worth moving across the water.

Sunny romped and played along the edge of the water, sometimes diving under, and seemed to delight in shaking and spraying Izzy as she dried her fur. She loved to play fetch and if Izzy tossed a ball into the water, all the better. The cold water didn't seem to bother the dog and her thick fur never stayed wet for long, with the water never even penetrating to her undercoat.

Each time when they loaded up to leave the beach, Sunny gazed at Izzy, her tongue out, creating a happy smile. Sometimes, Izzy wondered if she still missed her previous owner. Izzy suspected she did, but Sunny seemed to be happy and adjusting to her new life.

With her plans tonight, Izzy didn't want Sunny to think she would leave and not come back, like her last owner had to. Tonight, would be the first time Sunny would be on her own for a few hours. She hoped her furry sidekick would behave and sleep while she was away. So far, she had been the model roommate, showing no interest in chewing on furniture or disturbing any of Izzy's things, but she hadn't been left alone.

Izzy hadn't been on a date in years and spent entirely too long choosing an outfit. When she took one last look in the mirror, she raised her brows, admiring the soft black sweater she had paired with a white shirt and a long lariat style silver and leather necklace. She and Colin were having dinner at

The Bistro, so the vibe was casual, but she worried about her choice of jeans. She added a soft, silky scarf in hues of blues, for a pop of color.

Telling her it made no sense to take two cars, Colin had offered to pick her up when they had walked the dogs together earlier in the day. Jethro was a large golden retriever, almost one hundred pounds, but was a gentle and sweet soul. He and Sunny took to each other immediately, their impressive feathered tails wagging in unison as they strolled the pathway with their owners. Sunny had been prancing with excitement to have a new friend and Izzy shared her enthusiasm.

As Izzy waited for Colin, she reflected on how much she had enjoyed their time together that morning. He was easy to chat with, and she could listen to his voice all day. His knowledge of golf communities came through as they walked and he pointed out houses and told Izzy the names of the people who lived in each one. Despite only being on the island for a month, he was well versed in the course itself, the entire community, and all the residents.

Izzy suspected he spent all his time at work, and she could relate. They had talked a bit about their families, and Izzy shared that Mia was going through a rough patch and they didn't always get along. She didn't share too much, but wanted him to know the situation was complicated. With it being such a small community, and him knowing several of her friends, he was bound to hear about it. She didn't want to seem like she was hiding anything.

She saw his car pull into the drive and bent down to tell Sunny goodbye. She left the television on a music channel that seemed to relax the dog and slipped out of the door. Colin was already out of his car and coming up the sidewalk.

He opened the passenger door for her before getting behind the wheel. "How was the rest of your day?" he asked, as he set out for the clubhouse.

"I've been rearranging drawers and shelves, trying to get settled, and Sunny and I spent some time outside this afternoon."

At The Bistro, he pulled into the parking spot reserved for the manager and hurried around the car to help Izzy out. She couldn't remember the last time she had encountered such chivalry. They made their way inside, with several staff members greeting Colin.

When they reached the hostess station, she led them to a corner table near the fireplace with a view out to the golf course. It was already dark, but the lights along the pathways and the firepits outside on the patio provided a cozy atmosphere.

Izzy ordered a glass of wine, and Colin opted for iced tea. As soon as the waitress left, he said, "I, uh, don't drink. Alcohol has caused problems in my family, specifically, my marriage, so after suffering through living with an addict, I pledged not to drink. It was a promise I made to my son, David. I don't want you think I was a recovering alcoholic, and I have no problem with other people drinking, but my ex-wife did so much damage to David and me, I can't go there. It was her responsibility, but I've always blamed the alcohol."

"That's admirable of you. I grew up at a winery, so needless to say, I have always drunk wine. But I've also witnessed the devastation alcoholism wages on families, so I understand completely. I had you pegged for a scotch or whiskey man, being from Scotland."

He smiled, and the flames from the fireplace reflected in his eyes. "Scotch was Phoebe's drink of choice. Well, one of them."

"I'm sorry, Colin, I wasn't trying to make light of it."

He shook his head, brushing away her worries. "Oh, no, it's been a long time. I've moved past all of it. She no longer occupies space in my mind." After they ordered, Colin clinked his glass with Izzy's. "Here's to your new job. You start on Monday?"

"Yes. I'm excited about it. It's always fun to have something new, sort of like the first day of school. I hope I'm not sorry I took it. I haven't changed anything in my life for fifteen years and it seems now I'm changing everything."

"Change can be a good thing. I know what it's like to leave home and chart a new course for yourself. It's not always easy, but can provide such satisfaction when you succeed at something new."

Their meals arrived and between bites of delicious risotto, roasted chicken, and vegetables, they chatted about the upcoming Halloween party at Sunset Bay. "I was actually planning a small housewarming party with a Halloween theme that same weekend."

"You could always have people over earlier in the day, and then move to the clubhouse when we kick off the events here. The more, the merrier. I'm happy to arrange tickets for all your friends."

"Oh, that's such a kind offer. I could also do the housewarming on a different weekend. I hadn't even really started planning it yet."

The conversation drifted to her friends, and as she suspected, Colin knew Nate from his delivery service and his dad's real estate business, Max and Linda through Max's golf membership, Jeff and Sam from visiting their businesses, and he had his hair cut at Jen's salon. He had heard about Kate's shop, but hadn't met her or Spence yet.

They finished dinner, and he asked if she would like to sit on the patio and enjoy the fire. He signed the tab for dinner and led the way through the restaurant, asking the waitress for hot tea delivered to the patio.

With it being a Friday night, the restaurant was bustling with activity, and Colin stopped at several tables to say hello and introduce Izzy as a new resident. The Bistro was open to anyone, but offered special rates for members and residents, so most of those dining lived in the community. All the couples were middle-aged or older, with some reminding Izzy of her parents and their friends. All of them were welcoming and friendly, inviting Izzy to get together at the clubhouse and pointing out all the activities.

Izzy thanked each of them, and as she wandered outside with Colin, her mood lightened. It may have been the wine, but she suspected it was the warmth she sensed and the feeling in her heart that moving here had been the right decision.

SATURDAY MORNING, IZZY called her parents to check on them and to see how things were going with Shannon. She had purposely stayed out of it all week, only emailing her invoice to her parents to pass on to her sister.

Blake had been checking in and reported Shannon was lounging around the house, not doing much, but their mom and dad were encouraging her to get a job. Izzy hadn't talked about sentencing with Shannon or their parents, but wanted them to face reality. It was likely Shannon would face some jail time. Not much, but if Mr. Durham was correct and they were cracking down on protestors, a month or two in jail would not be out of the realm of possibilities, along with a hefty fine.

Before calling, she had done a bit of research into jobs in Richland. Never having had a real job, Shannon wasn't qualified for much. Izzy found several retailers hiring extra help for the holidays, a stocker at a grocery chain, and an associate at a home improvement store. She wanted to make sure her parents were aware of the job opportunities, so Shannon didn't get away with saying she looked and couldn't find anything.

She chatted with her mom and talked about the house, and when her dad got on the line told them about Sunny and what a great dog she was. They talked a bit about the upcoming holidays and Izzy told them she planned to spend Thanksgiving with them, since she would have to make the trip over for Shannon's sentencing. Her parents would need all of the support they could get, and having all their children together would make them happy.

She pressed them about Shannon getting a job and the expenses she had to pay, and then told them she had found a few positions that might work. Her parents were worried because Shannon was so unhappy and depressed. "Having a job and a purpose will help her," said Izzy. "You need to make sure she applies for jobs and keeps up her end of the bargain. Chances are she'll have more expenses after sentencing, where she'll be facing some fines and maybe even some jail time."

Her mom's voice quaked when she spoke again and asked Izzy if there was any chance of keeping her sister out of jail. "I'll contact the attorney handling the case, but you need to be prepared."

She told them she loved them and promised to call next week, but reminded them she was starting her new job, so if she was tied up, she'd get back to them when she could. After she hung up, she felt drained and in need of a distraction.

It was a gorgeous mid-October morning, the perfect temperature for walking. She donned a jacket and attached Sunny's leash, and they set out for the main road to town. It was under three miles to the harbor and Izzy intended to reward herself with a latte, and stop by the bakery for a cookie treat for Sunny. She was in no hurry and set out at a leisurely pace.

They walked along the shoulder of the road, taking in the lush evergreen branches of the pines, firs, and cedars that stood tall above them, and admiring the stately oak trees and their bronze and orange leaves littering several driveways. The crisp air and the crunch of leaves signaled fall was in full swing, and on its heels would be the holidays. It would be the first time Izzy had been away from family for the season.

Spending Thanksgiving with her parents would be wonderful, but also stressful with Shannon's situation. As she thought further ahead, spending Christmas on the island appealed to her. She could already picture a tree in her new house. Christmas made her think of Mia. She still hadn't heard from her, so she wasn't sure if John had agreed to Mia's idea or if she hadn't yet talked to him.

Not knowing was killing her. She preferred to know if her life would be upended, but reasoned that asking Mia would only make her more inclined not to share. However, she wanted to tell her daughter she was spending Thanksgiving in Richland. When they reached town and had access to sidewalks and benches, she took the opportunity to tap out a quick text to Mia, letting her know the plan for the upcoming holiday. She winced when she hit the send button.

Izzy resented how hard she had to work to fabricate an excuse to contact her daughter or to navigate the tightrope she felt like she walked when it came to having an actual conversation. For so long, she had been waiting for the day when Mia would get her life together, and they could chat without the weight of the past hanging over them, but it seemed like that was never going to happen. She thought back to all the dreams she had for Mia and how they had fizzled, one by one. Now, all that existed was the desire for a text reply that wasn't rude. Her bar had fallen to new low level.

They walked into Harbor Coffee and Books, and found Sam behind the counter, with Zoe nestled into her bed by the bookcase. Sam smiled and waved, and Sunny darted over to Zoe. "I was about to call in a lunch order and Jeff is on his way over. Why don't you join us and we'll sit on the deck and enjoy this lovely day?"

Izzy's smile widened. *This*, this warmth and friendship was what had drawn her to the island. She put in her lunch request, and took Sunny and Zoe outside to a table on the deck, where she filled one of the oversized water bowls Sam kept for visiting furry patrons. The dogs settled in next to her chair, their heads resting against each other.

Jeff arrived with takeout from Dottie's Deli, and while they ate, Izzy asked what they thought about having a get-together at her new house followed by the Halloween party at the clubhouse. They encouraged her and thought it sounded like fun.

When they finished lunch, Jeff said he was heading home and would be glad to drop Izzy and Sunny off on the way if they'd rather not walk. Izzy was chilled from the breeze blowing in and noticed the sun had disappeared from the sky.

"I would welcome it. It looks like the weather is changing." She gathered Sunny's leash, said goodbye to Zoe and Sam, and followed Jeff to his truck parked behind the hardware store. They let Sunny and Bailey run around a bit before confining them to the truck, where they sat next to each other on the ride home.

Despite the protesting whine from Bailey, Jeff hung onto her while Izzy and Sunny got out of the truck and waved goodbye. Izzy settled into the oversized chaise lounge, her new favorite spot in the living room, and starting making a list for the party. Soon Sunny joined her, stretching out alongside her legs on top of the blanket Izzy had placed there. She hadn't intended to let Sunny on the furniture, but there was something quite comforting about feeling the weight of her furry friend against her legs.

She checked her phone several times, but still hadn't had a reply from Mia. After batting around ideas with Sam and Jeff, she had decided a casual brunch would be fun, and wouldn't stop people from enjoying snacks at the clubhouse later. She continued jotting down ideas on her notepad.

Knowing it was a longshot, she included Lily, Cyndy, and Mac in the invitation list, and hoped they might be able to come. She also invited Colin and made sure to include Nick's parents, Jack and Lulu, along with Lou and Andi. She suspected her sisters and parents wouldn't be able to swing the trip, but wanted to include them. She didn't have time to send formal invitations, so opted for electronic ones and pressed the button instead of using stamps and envelopes.

When she was finished, she settled in with a glass of wine, to watch more episodes of *Shetland*, marveling at how much she loved her new living space, especially the tiny white lights Kate had threaded through glass vases and trinkets on her shelves and tables. They provided the perfect warmth and light for the evenings and made every night feel like a special occasion.

As she listened to the accents of the characters in the series, her thoughts drifted to Colin. She couldn't deny her attraction to him, but she tempered her expectations. After all, he was new to the island, single, and hadn't yet had the opportunity to meet many other prospects. Not to mention, he was essentially a salesman for Sunset Bay, and from his interactions with the residents last night, it was clear he took his responsibilities seriously.

Her phone chimed with an alert and she saw her first response to the brunch invitation. It was Colin. She smiled as she read his note saying he was looking forward to it and to let him know how many tickets she would need for the Halloween party.

While she was reading it, a text message came through, also from Colin. He invited her to dinner tomorrow night and made a point of including Sunny. Before she could think too much, she typed in a reply and hit the send button, accepting his kind invitation.

"Looks like we have a date tomorrow night," she said to Sunny, who raised her eyebrows and gazed at Izzy with tired eyes. "It's probably not really a date, per se, dinner." She frowned as she contemplated it. "Do you think it's a real date?"

Sunny sighed, and closed her eyes.

Chapter 15

COLIN WAS MAKING a pot of tea to go with the chocolate cake he was serving for their dessert, when Izzy's cell phone rang. She apologized and glanced at the screen, where she was surprised to see her ex-husband's name. She tapped the button to ignore it, and slipped it back into the pocket on her purse.

"Take it if you need to," said Colin, carrying the tray with the tea and slices of cake into the living room.

She shook her head. "Oh, it's fine. It's my ex-husband and believe me, I'm in no hurry to chat with him."

"I never hear from Phoebe. When we first separated and then divorced, she would call constantly, usually in a drunken state, but it's been years since I've talked with her."

"I'm sure John is calling about our daughter, Mia." Izzy took her first bite of cake, which was delicious, and sipped her tea. She gave Colin a more in-depth version of Mia's situation, their longstanding difficult relationship, and the news of her unexpected pregnancy. "John is engaged to a young woman, emphasis on young, as in she could be his daughter. I'm sure he's calling to complain to me about Mia. I'm certain her idea of moving in with him is not going to fly."

Colin's eyebrows rose over the edge of his teacup. "I think sons must be easier. I'm not sure I could handle that kind of stress. I'm sorry you're having to deal with it now."

Izzy chuckled. "Truth be told, part of my reason for moving here was to be further removed from Mia's histrionics." She shook her head. "Actually, I thought she was on the right path, finally, going to school and interested in it. It worries me what the future holds for her."

"Those worries for our children, no matter their age, they never end do they?"

Izzy felt the burn of tears in her eyes and took another sip from her cup. "How old is David?"

"He's thirty-two, and we chatted today about him coming to visit for the holidays."

"Here I am longing for some distance between me and Mia, and it must be so hard to have him thousands of miles away from you. Is he married?"

"No, it seems people aren't getting married until much later in life these days." He finished his cake and added, "I think that's wise."

Izzy nodded and slipped another bite of the decadent dessert in her mouth. "I'm certain I married too young. I think young people are more focused on their careers than when we were that age. Marriage, I think, was the norm, or more expected. Now, it's not."

"My marriage turned out to be a disaster, but I wouldn't change my early decisions. Despite all the horribleness of my years with Phoebe, David is the best thing that has ever happened to me, so I'm thankful to her for him. I've always been one of those people who thinks life works out the way it's supposed to, even if at the time, it's hard."

Izzy pondered his words. "Sometimes, I try to control things too much. I think your outlook is healthier."

Her phone chimed again. She checked it and saw another call from John. "I'm so sorry. We should probably get home anyway. I've got to go into the office tomorrow."

He smiled and rose from the dark leather couch to collect her plate and cup. "Oh right, big first day at the new job. That's exciting."

She shrugged her shoulders, and smiled. "I'm looking forward to it." She collected her purse and he held her jacket for her.

"Thank you for the chili. It was delicious, as was the cornbread and dessert." She called for Sunny.

"I had a wonderful time and hope we can do it again soon." He stepped closer and hugged Izzy, brushing her cheek with an innocent kiss. "If you have any free time, let me know and we can meet for dinner or coffee."

The stubble from his cheek and chin sent a shiver through her and curled her toes inside her boots. She breathed in his scent and detected a peppery, citrus aroma followed by hints of figs and rum. Her decades of tasting wine had refined her sense of smell. She could always pick out the hints of various fruits and flowers, and was drawn to whatever Colin was wearing.

It had been years, far too many to count, since she had been close enough to a man to appreciate that musky aroma and sense whiskers against her cheek. It took all of her concentration to focus on making a coherent sentence. "I'll be in touch. I think I'll pass on walking tomorrow, but will know more about my schedule after I meet with Cliff, and then we can get on track with the dogs," she said, ushering Sunny out the door. Her stomach fluttered and the tingle from his sweet kiss made her shiver as she walked to her car. He opened the back door for Sunny, and then opened her door.

"Sweet dreams to you, Izzy," he said with his hand on the door frame. "If you need anything or need to talk, you know where to find me."

She nodded and gave him a little wave as he shut her door. When she pulled onto the road, she glanced in her rearview mirror and saw him and Jethro still standing at the edge of the driveway, waving to her.

SHE DUMPED HER purse and hung up her jacket, then got Sunny settled on the bench at the end of her bed before changing into her pajamas. Finally, she brewed a cup of tea, got a notepad, and took her cell phone in the bedroom.

After stacking the pillows behind her and slipping under the soft blanket, she inhaled deeply and tapped the screen to connect with John.

Instead of a normal greeting, he barked at her. "It's about time. Where have you been?"

"Not that it's any of your business, but I was at a friend's house for dinner."

"Mia told me you sold the house in Richland and moved to the San Juan Islands. I can't believe you would do something like that without telling me."

Conversations like this one reminded Izzy why she was divorced. "Did you have a reason to call or did you actually think I care about your opinion? News flash—I don't need to nor do I plan to inform you of my decisions and I'm not interested in your thoughts about where I live."

"Don't treat me like opposing counsel, Izzy. I have a right to know you sold our home and moved away. It's really upset Mia. Now she wants to move in with me, when she really belongs with you."

Izzy shook her head in disbelief. "I offered her a place to stay here when the time comes, and made it clear she and the baby could stay with me until she was back on her feet."

His voice got even louder. "She doesn't want to stay there. She would have stayed with you in Richland, I'm sure, but who would want to live on an island in the middle of nowhere? I don't blame her."

"She told me she had plans to move in with you, and go back to UCLA to finish college."

"I'm getting married in June. That's not going to work. Barbie is dead set against having Mia here and we don't need to start our marriage with a new baby in the mix."

Izzy smirked and shook her head. As she suspected, Mia's faith in her dad was ill placed. "How did Mia respond when you told her?"

There was no response. She heard him breathing, so knew the connection was still active. Instead of filling the silence, she waited.

"I didn't tell her. I told her to give me some time to talk to Barbie."

"I think it's important for her to complete the first two quarters of her program, so she can take the next quarter off for the baby, and then get back to it in the fall. Now, more than ever, she needs a good career."

"This wedding is costing a fortune and we really don't need Mia underfoot while we're in the middle of planning it and our honeymoon trip. Can you tell her it won't work?"

Izzy wanted to scream. He wanted her to be the bad guy for him. "No, I'm not telling her anything. If you can't have her there, you need to explain it to her. I've told her she can stay here, but made it clear she has to stay in school and return to school. As usual, Mia wants to control things and dictate the terms. You're going to have to have a tough conversation with her, John. I'm not doing it for you."

He continued whining about his hardships with the wedding and Barbie. Izzy moved down to the end of the bed where she could pet Sunny, while she ignored her ex-husband's complaints. She let him ramble on about how it wasn't fair that Izzy had moved and he had a right to his own life.

When he finally paused and took a breath, Izzy took her opportunity. "When you do decide to let Mia know she can't stay with you, I'd appreciate it if you'd let me know."

"Like you let me know you moved?" His tone was snarky. "I'm going to hold off as long as possible."

"Wonderful. As always, it was enlightening to chat with you. Have a good evening." She poked the button to disconnect before he could respond.

She blew out a breath, and Sunny turned her eyes toward Izzy. "Well, he ruined my plan for a quiet and early night." She ruffled the thick fur on Sunny's chest. "I'm going to try to go to sleep. Goodnight, my sweet girl."

Izzy tuned the television to another episode of *Shetland*, hoping it would take her mind off the call with John. If she could take him at his word, he wouldn't be telling Mia anything soon. In this instance, she believed him.

Chapter 16

MONDAY, IZZY WAS up early and took Sunny for a quick walk around her property. She had shoved John's conversation about Mia to the dark corner of her mind and was focused on making her first day at work a good one.

She felt a pang of guilt leaving Sunny on her own, but promised the gentle dog she'd be right back and stepped into the garage. Her phone chimed and she saw a group text from Sam inviting everyone to a barbeque on Saturday. Izzy tapped in a quick reply to say she would be there and asked what she could bring.

Bring Sunny and feel free to invite a friend, was the response from Sam. She followed it with a winking smile emoji.

Izzy chuckled as she made the trip into town, happy to have something to look forward to, and realizing she had a busier social life on this tiny island than she had ever had in all her years living in eastern Washington. She liked the idea of asking Colin, and as soon as she got to town and parked, she tapped in a message to him.

She made a quick stop at the bakery before continuing on to the court complex. She found Hazel at her desk. "Good morning, Ms. Griffin."

Izzy waved away the formality. "Please, call me Izzy." She handed her the box of pastries. "I thought I'd bring some treats for my first day."

Hazel grinned and rose from behind her desk, revealing a long floral print skirt. She slipped the reading glasses from her nose, leaving them to dangle on a chain around her neck. "That was thoughtful of you. I'll show you where the break room is, and we'll stash these in there." She led Izzy down the hallway leading to Cliff's office and pointed out the other attorney, Eric's office. In between his office and Cliff's were three paralegals, and across the hallway was the breakroom.

Hazel put the pastries on the counter, slipped one onto a plate, and gestured to the coffee pot and tea kettle. "Help yourself to anything. We rotate each month, and people take turns bringing in coffee and tea supplies." She pointed out the fridge and microwave, along with a collection of dishes, cutlery, and a stack of takeout menus.

"Let me show you to your office and you can get settled. Cliff had an early meeting, but he'll be here within the hour to get you started and introduce you to the rest of the staff."

Izzy had never worked in the government sector and realized how much she had taken the creature comforts for granted, like coffee and snacks, that were always provided by the firm. She followed Hazel down a short hallway in the opposite direction, passed by a small library, two conference rooms, and to the last door. Hazel opened the door and motioned her into the office. "It's not much, but at least you have a window. From what Cliff said, you'll probably do most of your work from home and only use this when you have to come in for meetings or to use the library or copier."

Izzy took in the wooden desk and sparsely furnished space, along with the bouquet of fresh flowers in the middle of her desk. "It's fine, and the flowers are lovely."

Hazel beamed. "I'm glad you like them. I love flowers." She showed Izzy how to work the phone system, gave her the password to login on her computer, and walked her through how to access their database program and email system. "If you need anything, give me a shout."

Hazel shut the door behind her, and Izzy put her purse in a drawer and hung up her coat. She was familiarizing herself with the computer systems when her door opened and Cliff greeted her with a friendly smile.

"Sorry, I wasn't here when you arrived. Hazel said she gave you a quick tour, but I want to introduce you to everyone, especially Kim, the paralegal I've assigned to you. I've gathered everyone in the conference room down the hall."

Izzy followed him to the open doorway where she found several smiling faces gathered around a large table, all with pastries in front of them. Cliff introduced her, citing her background and accomplishments, highlighting the glowing recommendations he had received from Izzy's references. He finished by saying again how thankful he was to have found someone of her caliber for contract work, especially so quickly.

He then introduced Eric, the other attorney on staff, Kim, Yvonne, and Dana, who were all paralegals. They each had their specialties. Dana handled all the family court and support issues. Yvonne worked for Eric, who handled most of the criminal work, and Kim focused on civil work.

Izzy's tasks would involve preparing briefs and cases for the civil side when needed, and relieving Cliff of the duties related to providing advice to local government entities. Once Izzy got her feet wet, he was hoping she could attend most of the meetings and provide advice to the elected officials, boards, and commissions the office supported with legal counsel.

Everyone welcomed Izzy, thanked her for the breakfast treats, and offered to help her with anything she needed. Kim made sure Izzy had her home phone and cell phone and told her she could call anytime. Her bubbly personality showed through her genuine smile and kind eyes behind her oversized glasses. "I'm used to calls at all hours, so don't hesitate to call or email me if you need anything."

As the group made their way back to their offices, Cliff took a long sip from his coffee cup. "I thought we'd get you started on a few meetings. Hazel will give you a calendar of them, so you can plan ahead. I'll take you around this week and introduce you to each of the chairpersons and all the elected officials, and give you a bit of background on them, so you know what you're up against. It's usually general questions related to liability and best practices. If you get in a position and you're not sure about what to say, tell them you'll do some research and get back to them. I do it all the time." He chuckled as he led her back to his office.

He handed her several binders and gave her a list of dozens of county boards and commissions, so she could familiarize herself. "All our previous opinions and guidance are in the database, so you can review them. You should familiarize yourself with the county codes and brush up on human resource laws, since many of the questions center around employee issues."

He smiled as he pointed to the thick county code book. "You have one in your office and they're available online as well." He glanced at his watch. "I've got us booked for meetings all week, except Friday. It seems nobody meets on Fridays. You can tag along with me and get a feel for everyone, and then you'll have a few weeks before they meet again. That means we'll probably eat up all your hours for the next two weeks this week. We have the leeway to use eighty hours per month and can use them all in one week, if necessary. Email me when you hit the eighty, so I know and be sure and submit your invoice."

Izzy nodded her understanding, and took the binders back to her office so she could gather her purse and a notepad before heading out to the first meeting. She hadn't expected to be tied up all week, but welcomed the opportunity to focus on work instead of Mia. On her way to meet Cliff, she took a quick look at her phone and saw a reply from Colin saying he would love to accompany her to Sam and Jeff's party. She smiled, slid the phone back into her purse, and hurried to catch Cliff for the walk across the complex to meet the sheriff.

BY THE TIME Saturday rolled around, Izzy was exhausted. After learning about her crazy schedule from Cliff, she had begged off walking the dogs with Colin until next week. Her introduction to all the boards and commissions had her running almost nonstop, attending back to back meetings and learning about topics from libraries and safety to solid waste and county fairs. She didn't know how Cliff had managed to keep up with all of these meetings and do his regular case work.

Sunny was happy to have Izzy home for the day and clung to her everywhere she went. Izzy felt so guilty for missing their morning walk, that after her second cup of coffee, she grabbed the leash and headed outside. Sunny, filled with excitement, danced in circles, as they headed toward the walking trail.

It had rained earlier in the week, but today was gorgeous, as was the forecast for the entire weekend and Sam's party. As she walked, Izzy's mind wandered to Mia. She still hadn't heard anything from her daughter about Thanksgiving. Also, after talking to John, she was convinced he wouldn't bother giving her a heads up when he told Mia the bad news. She had to get used to the idea of what she assumed would be major fallout, hanging over her head. John would probably string Mia along for a few weeks.

The section of the trail that went through the woods was mostly shaded, offering only brief moments of dappled sunlight peeking through the trees. The rich smell of the earth mingled with the leaves and needles scattered across the pathway. A slight breeze carried a trace of salt and seaweed from the nearby beach, and Izzy took in a long, cleansing breath.

Living all her years in the drier, warmer part of Washington, she loved the way her skin felt now with a bit of moisture in the air. The humidity also added volume to her hair. With each step, she felt more relaxed, and took delight in watching Sunny romp through the bushes, sniffing at the traces of squirrels and rabbits.

As they left the canopy of trees, the sun warmed Izzy's shoulders. Several groups were taking advantage of the day and were out golfing, and all of them waved hello as she and Sunny made their way back to her house.

Sunny settled in for a nap, while Izzy took a shower and worked on finalizing the last two recommendations she had to write for work. She emailed them off to Cliff and told him she would be available next week by phone or video chat, but had no plans to go into the office, unless he needed her for something.

She turned her attention to the brunch she had planned. Instead of worrying about trying to make everything herself, she ordered all the pastries from the bakery, a huge fruit salad from Soup D'Jour, and a platter of breakfast meats from the Front Street Café. That left a couple of egg casseroles and a cheesy potato dish for her to make. Blake would bring wine and champagne for mimosas, and she'd already stocked up on juice, coffee, and tea.

She hoped the weather would hold so they could eat outside on the patio, but made a backup plan for using the dining room and kitchen. Jeff was going to loan her an extra outdoor table and let her borrow a few patio chairs.

After a snack for lunch, she and Sunny made a quick trip to the hardware store to get a few spare keys made. She had already given Blake his, but intended to give Jeff and Sam one, as well as Kate and Spence, in case she ever needed them to take care of Sunny.

While at the store, she ran into several people she had met at the various meetings she had attended and exchanged small talk, doing her best to place them. She remembered most of them, but needed to brush up on each of the board members, especially those who sat on the more obscure ones. Although the meetings were a bit tedious, it was nice to feel connected and so much a part of the community.

She had always been involved in fundraising, events, and local government, and this position presented her with a chance to contribute to her new community, not to mention she would soon know every person in town.

She hated going to Sam's party empty handed, and stopped by Linda's floral shop to pick up a bouquet of beautiful fall flowers. By the time she got home, it was time to get ready, and then pick up Colin and Jethro.

Sunny could barely contain her excitement when they pulled into Colin's driveway and Jethro came bounding to the side of the SUV. Izzy laughed when she saw he was carrying a bouquet of flowers. He loaded Jethro into the backseat with Sunny, and climbed into the passenger seat.

She glanced at the flowers and raised her brows. "Great minds, huh? I picked up an almost identical bunch because I hate showing up with nothing."

"Same here, although I figured you would bring wine."

She pulled onto the road, and chuckled. "I'm counting on the guy with a barn stacked with cases of wine to keep us supplied."

As they drove, Colin took in the scenery, remarking that he hadn't had much time to explore the island. Izzy pointed out the turn off for Jeff's family's resort on Mitchell Bay. "Jeff and Linda are both great resources, since they grew up here. His family owns a fabulous resort, right on the water."

"David loves the outdoors, fishing, that sort of thing, so I told him he'll have to plan another trip in the summer or fall, so he can fish for salmon."

"Nate, who I'm sure will be at the party, and Jeff can tell you everything you need to know about fishing. They would love an excuse to plan a trip, I'm sure."

She turned off the road and drove down the driveway to Sam and Jeff's beautiful home. They led the dogs around to the backyard and huge deck with its flawless view of the water. They were the first to arrive, and found Jeff on the deck behind the grill and Sam attending to the tables.

Sam accepted both bundles of flowers, and hugged Colin and Izzy before taking them inside to put them in water. Jeff gravitated to Colin and led him off the deck to show him the rest of the yard.

Soon, the others began to arrive, and while Izzy helped Sam in the kitchen, Jeff made sure Colin was introduced to everyone.

The afternoon was filled with laughter and non-stop visiting, as they enjoyed the wonderful meal and company. As Izzy had suggested, Nate and Jeff were excited to plan a fishing trip around David's visit, and the men bonded over plans for that, as well as a golf outing Max proposed.

Each time Izzy glanced his way, Colin was laughing or smiling, fitting in with her friends like he'd known them forever. As it got dark, Jeff led everyone to the huge stone firepit, closer to the water. Izzy helped carry the supplies for making s'mores to go with the hot chocolate, coffee, and tea that Nate and Max carried.

Jeff had strung festive globe lights across the area, and outdoor pillows in the jewel tones of fallen leaves had been placed on stone and concrete benches ringing the huge fire pit.

The bright stars sprinkled across the inky canvas above, combined with the golden flames from the fire, providing the perfect ambience for the evening. Jeff had long metal sticks at the ready for toasting marshmallows, and everyone competed to get the perfect toasty golden shell and to slip it off the skewer without leaving any of the melted and sticky middle behind.

Izzy huddled close to Colin, their legs touching, as they waited for their marshmallows to cook. She hadn't had so much fun in a long time. By the time she finished her treat, her hands were sticky and covered in chocolate. She reached for another napkin and turned toward Colin, who grinned and then laughed.

"You've got marshmallow and chocolate all over your face, like a little girl who got caught in the candy jar." With gentle fingers and a fresh napkin, he wiped at her cheeks and lips, lingering as he ran his thumb across them.

He was close enough for her to smell the alluring scent of his aftershave, and as she looked into his eyes, the urge to kiss him overwhelmed her. She suspected it wasn't the heat of the flames that caused the warmth surging through her body.

Chapter 17

Sunday afternoon Izzy's phone rang, and she smiled when she saw Kate's name. Since she didn't know when John would talk to Mia, she was halfway expecting every call to be her daughter, and whenever the phone rang, a ripple of uncertainty flew through her. She knew the day was coming when all hell would break loose, and she didn't want it to be today.

She tapped the button to connect with Kate. They visited for a few minutes, talking about how much they had enjoyed their time at Sam and Jeff's last night.

"Cyndy called and said Mac and Lily are planning a quick trip over here next weekend to come to your party, but she can't get away."

"Oh, it's too bad she can't make it, but I'm glad that Mac and Lily can come. I'll make sure Colin gets two more tickets for the Halloween party. If they need a place to stay, I'm happy to have them here."

"That might be best, since you have two guest rooms available. We only have one, and I'm not actually certain they are a couple in that sense of the word."

Izzy laughed. "Well, I'm not asking. How about you let Cyndy know the options, with two rooms here and one room at your house and they can choose. I'd love to have them and they're welcome to bring the dogs. Sunny would be over the moon."

Izzy spent the rest of the afternoon finishing a couple of opinions for work and taking a walk with Sunny. As she was settling in for what had become her nightly routine of watching a few episodes of a series, her phone chimed.

Lily's name popped onto the screen with a message thanking her for her kind invitation and confirming she and Mac would like to stay with her, as they needed two bedrooms—and they would bring all three dogs, if Izzy was absolutely sure.

Izzy texted back and forth a few times, trading particulars with Lily, since they would be arriving on Friday and leaving on Monday. Lily insisted she and Mac treat Izzy to meals out while they were there, and they discussed the Halloween party, where costumes were encouraged.

After their volley of texts, Izzy snuggled under the blankets, with Sunny snoring softly in her place at the end of the bed. The thought of having her first guests at her new house gave her even more to look forward to for the weekend.

IZZY'S ROUTINE AT her new house was developing, and each morning started with a walk, which was Sunny's favorite part of the day. They met up with Colin and Jethro on the trail and, depending on how much time she needed to allocate to work, would either take the shorter loop or the longer one. Some mornings, they would stop for tea and coffee at The Bistro, sitting outside with the dogs, chatting about nothing...and everything.

Other mornings, she and Sunny would head back home and she'd have coffee at her desk. She had a few public meetings to attend this week, but was feeling more confident as she learned more about each of the agencies and boards. She was a quick study, and Cliff had been pleased with the work she had submitted. Each morning, when she sat down to check her work email, she was happy she had taken the job. She couldn't imagine trying to keep herself occupied all day without it. Without the distraction, she would have been sitting around worrying about things she couldn't control, like Mia's situation.

She wanted to get all of her work done by Thursday night, so she could relax and enjoy visiting with Lily and Mac and get ready for her brunch on Saturday, without any interruptions. She had stayed up late this week, completing the tasks related to each of the meetings she attended during the week, cranking out the necessary opinions and research the boards had requested.

On days she wasn't expected at meetings in town or bogged down with work, she and Sunny also took an afternoon walk. On the days she was working in town, she made lunch plans with one of her friends, and this week, she'd organized lunch with Kate, Sam, and Linda at Soup D'Jour on Thursday. The lunch topic had been Halloween costumes and with the exception of Linda, who was so creative, the rest of them were trying to get away with adding only a mask or hat, instead of a full-blown costume.

Linda shared her idea for a group theme or two, and everyone jumped aboard. Izzy had been toying with her own idea, chatting with Colin about it. She collected some things from her closet, then stopped by the thrift store after lunch to look for a couple items to complete their costumes. While she was there, she bought some extra pieces, in case Lily and Mac needed something to go with the group themes Linda had suggested.

Friday brought another sunshine filled morning, and despite the chill in the air, the day was pleasant. Colin had an early morning meeting and couldn't make their usual walk. She and Sunny made their usual trek, but it wasn't quite the same without Colin and Jethro. Despite knowing Colin for only a few weeks, she felt like they had been friends forever.

Though she remembered Mac and Lily had offered to treat her to meals, she thought after a day of traveling with three dogs, they would appreciate the opportunity to sit and relax and let the dogs acclimate. After getting ready for the day, she made a quick trip to Dottie's Deli and picked up sandwiches and salads that would work for a late lunch.

While she waited for them to arrive, she finished her cleaning chores, making sure the house was spotless and ready for brunch on Saturday. She double checked her list and organized her serving dishes, setting the plates, silverware, and napkins she'd need on the kitchen island. As soon as she finished adding a selection of teas to the beverage station by the coffee maker, Sunny took off for the door. Her early warning system was in action to announce the arrival of their houseguests.

Sunny couldn't quit spinning in circles when she saw Sherlock, Fritz, and Bodie. The four of them chased each other around the yard, leaping and running, as Mac unloaded his SUV. Lily greeted Izzy with a warm hug. "It's so kind of you to let us invade." She rolled her eyes as she watched the dogs, "Especially, with all these furry houseguests."

"It will be fun, and they're all such well-behaved dogs. Once they settle down, it'll be fine. Sam and Jeff, they're friends of mine that you'll meet tomorrow, offered to let us bring all the dogs to their place. They have two, and a huge enclosed area where the dogs will be safe during the brunch and party. If you're interested, we can take a visit out to see them later."

Mac nodded as he wheeled their suitcases to the front door. "I think that sounds like a good idea. You don't need them underfoot with a houseful of guests and they'd be happier outside than locked away somewhere in the house."

Izzy led the way inside. After setting the suitcases in the entryway, Mac herded the dogs around to the backyard, where Izzy kept some old towels to wipe Sunny's feet before she came inside. While he took care of cleaning up the dogs, Izzy showed Lily the two guestrooms upstairs and where they could find extra towels in the bathroom.

"Your home is lovely. You and Kate did a fabulous job of decorating." Lily gestured to the glass lamp on the nightstand. "I recognized that from Cyndy's shop. I love the aqua color."

"Kate gets all the credit. I loved all her suggestions, and she seems to put things together effortlessly. I'm not creative." Izzy pointed out her study, saying she didn't think she would use it while they were here, so they'd have the entire upstairs to themselves.

Lily smiled. "Mac and I are sort of trying to figure out what it is we have. We're wonderful friends and have really bonded over our love of dogs and our shared losses. It's hard to explain. I haven't actually dated in years, so it's not over the top romantic, but there's something special between us. At this stage, we're both more comfortable with our own rooms, but please don't feel like you need to grant us privacy."

Izzy sat in one of the chairs in her office, and gestured to Lily, offering her the other one. "It's complicated at this age, isn't it? I married so young and haven't really dated since my divorce. It's actually not something that's been at the top of my list, but after spending some time with Colin, I've realized I've missed having that sense of companionship, of the male variety."

Lily nodded. "I know exactly what you mean. Gary was my rock, my everything, really. I'm not sure I'll ever feel that heart-stopping kind of attraction again or if that's something that only happens when you're young and your hormones are surging. With Mac, it's different, it's not the same, but it's good. That huge chunk of my heart that's missing and I thought I'd never fill, is less empty. We get along so well, and he's so kind and thoughtful. It feels good to have a partner again, to not feel so alone."

Izzy gazed out the window. "Over all these years, I think I've substituted my work and family for John. When we divorced, I was sad to see my marriage fail and felt like a loser for failing at it, but I wasn't sorry to see him go. He had caused me so much pain, it was a relief not to have to see him. The romance had fizzled long ago in our marriage, and like you said, I think love and romance are a bit different in your fifties than in your twenties. I know I can be a lot choosier than I was with John. I'm not going to let physical attraction be the gauge for love."

Lily eyes twinkled with a faraway look. "Gary and I were lucky. We had it all." She turned her gaze back toward Izzy. "Not to say I don't find Mac attractive, it's just that there is so much more to him than that."

"I pride myself on being a good judge of character, my ex-husband notwithstanding. I've honed that skill over time, and I think Mac is wonderful. You two make a lovely pair. I know what you mean about the idea of more. I want something deeper, a best friend, a partner, a soulmate, someone who I can count on, always. Someone who can handle my crazy big family and my train wreck of a daughter." She laughed and added, "That's not too much to ask, is it?"

The sound of a couple of barks turned their attention to getting back downstairs. As they made their way to the kitchen, they spied Mac sitting on the patio with the dogs lounging at his feet. Izzy opened the door and said, "I picked up some stuff for lunch, so come on in whenever you're ready. We can eat here, and then I'll let you treat me to dinner in town tonight."

Mac delivered their suitcases upstairs and then retrieved the dog paraphernalia, situating their food in the laundry room and adding their dog beds to each of the guest rooms.

Once he washed up, he joined Lily and Izzy at the dining room table, where a selection of yummy food waited.

"This was so kind of you," said Lily, filling her plate. "I would have hated to leave these three hooligans in your house so soon after arriving today."

Izzy nodded as she added Dottie's homemade potato salad to her plate. "We can take them on a long walk later and tire them out before we go to dinner. I thought we could go up to The Bistro here at the golf course. It's close by and quite good. Also, I've got some free rounds of golf coming, so if either of you golf, you're welcome to use them tomorrow or Sunday."

Mac's eyebrows rose. "I wouldn't mind a game, and like Lily said, I appreciate this wonderful lunch. The idea of hanging around here for a few hours is perfect."

"I'll get in touch with Max, he's a friend and married to the local florist, Linda. He loves to golf and has a membership here. I'll see if he's available." Izzy poked at her phone and tapped in a message.

Once they finished lunch, Izzy encouraged them to get settled in their rooms and suggested some options for the Halloween costumes. They both liked the ideas she shared, and she showed them the items she had found at the thrift shop.

After, she tidied the kitchen, the dogs watching her avidly as she put the leftovers in the fridge. Her cell phone chimed with a message from Max saying he had reserved an early morning tee time and asked Nate and Sean to join in, saying they would pick up Mac on their way to the clubhouse. He assured her they would be done in plenty of time for her brunch party at noon.

After they relaxed, Izzy encouraged Lily and Mac to take a drive into town and do some sightseeing while she made reservations at The Bistro for dinner. While they were gone,

Izzy worked on her costume and talked to the dogs. Once she finished, she took the dogs outside and played catch. As the afternoon slipped away, so did the sunshine, and after wiping everyone's paws, she herded them indoors, where she brewed a pot of tea.

The dogs snuggled together on Sunny's bed and napped while they waited for Lily and Mac to return. Izzy finished her tea and shut her eyes with the television droning in the background.

The sound of a knock on the door woke her, and groggily she hurried to answer it. Expecting it to be Lily and Mac, she was surprised to find Colin. "Sorry to drop by without calling. I was on my way home and thought I'd pop in and see how you were doing, and ask if you needed anything for your party tomorrow."

"Come on in," she said, motioning him inside. The four dogs rushed to greet him, and he laughed as he petted all of them. "That's sweet of you to ask, but I think we're set. I've got to pick up a few things from the bakery in the morning and that should do it. My friends, Lily and Mac took a trip into town, but we're planning to have dinner at The Bistro tonight. Would you care to join us?"

Sherlock nudged Colin's hand, making sure it was on top of his head. "I would love to, thanks. I can't get over all these goldens. We'll have to introduce them to Jethro."

"They would love that. In fact, we're going to take the dogs out to Sam and Jeff's tomorrow, so they can play together in their yard during the brunch. Jethro could join them."

"Oh, he'd enjoy that. He doesn't get to play much. In fact, Sunny is his first friend, and he's so much happier now that we're walking together. If you're sure Jeff and Sam wouldn't mind?"

"I'll check, but I'm sure it's fine. What's one more dog, when they'll have six of them?" She gasped and added, "Oh, come and get those extra things for your costume and see what you think."

She led him into her bedroom and showed him what she had bought. He grinned his approval, and took the bagful of items. "Speaking of Jethro, I need to get home. I'll stop by and pick all of you up for dinner."

She followed him to the porch, where he turned and reached for her hand. "Sorry I couldn't make our walk this morning. I know I speak for Jethro when I say we missed you. Our mornings are better with you in them."

"We feel the same way," Izzy said, her heart beating a bit quicker as he squeezed her hand and bent to kiss her cheek.

As she waved goodbye, she thought she may have discounted the value of attraction a bit too soon. Maybe she could have it all.

Chapter 18

D ESPITE STAYING UP late and drinking too much wine, Izzy was up early on Saturday. Last night, the four of them had enjoyed a wonderful dinner, and despite Mac's objections, Colin had insisted on treating them. They had sat outside on the patio at The Bistro until late into the evening, sharing a huge warm brownie topped with vanilla ice cream and hot fudge sauce, sipping wines, teas, and coffees.

It was one of the most enjoyable evenings Izzy could remember of late. She had relaxed and laughed, listening to Mac's escapades with animals, Lily's adventures in innkeeping, and Colin's most memorable guests from the golf clubs he had managed. It had been a long time since she'd had friends, especially couple friends. In fact, until she came to visit Blake, she had never experienced the close-knit kind of friends she had met on the island.

Colin had driven them home and walked her to the door, lingering for a few minutes, long enough to wish her goodnight with a soft kiss on the lips. He had squeezed her elbow before waving goodbye, and after making sure everyone was settled in, she had slipped into bed, happier than she had been in years.

As she dressed in her exercise clothes, she willed herself to quit thinking about Colin and last night, and focus on what she had to get done for brunch. The house was still quiet when she poured a cup of coffee and made sure Sunny's breakfast was dispensed. She glanced at the list on the counter and opened the fridge to make sure she had everything she needed, then grabbed her keys and whispered to Sunny, "I'll be right back."

It didn't take long to pick up the boxes of pastries, and the café had her platters ready to go. Soup D'Jour wasn't open yet, but Izzy had made arrangements to pick up the fruit salad early and after a quick knock on the back door, had it situated in the cargo area.

When she got home, Mac and Lily and all the dogs were up and about. Max was due to arrive in a few minutes to pick up Mac for golfing, and Colin had volunteered to transport all the dogs out to Jeff and Sam's house to give Izzy time to get ready for her party.

Izzy felt guilty about not walking Sunny, but knew Jeff would let them all romp and play along the beach, so she wouldn't miss out on any exercise. When Max arrived, she introduced him to Lily and Mac. With both of the men having medical backgrounds and loving golf, they hit it off.

Soon after they left, Colin arrived, and between Lily and Izzy, they herded the dogs into his SUV. Lily added a box with bags of their individual servings of food, labeled and ready. She started to retrieve some toys when Izzy stopped her. "Jeff and Sam have every dog toy known to man, so they'll have plenty of stuff to play with, not to mention a huge section of beach to run along and acres of land to explore."

Once the dogs were gone, Izzy set about getting her potato dish ready while Lily offered to do some touch up vacuuming to get rid of any lingering dog hair. After prepping the food, Izzy took some cleaning products and rags outside to wipe down the patio furniture. The weather was cooperating for the moment, and though chilly, it was sunny and pleasant.

As a reward for all their hard work, Izzy suggested she and Lily split one of the decadent pastries she was placing on a serving tray. She brewed a pot of tea and they took a break outside. Lily sat back in her chair and sighed, taking in the view.

"This is my first real break from the cottages. It's lovely here, I see why you chose it." They chatted as they sipped tea and watched a few golfers go by, waving from their carts.

Izzy glanced at her watch. "I better get changed. I'll be a few minutes."

Lily elected to stay on the patio while Izzy changed into jeans and a double-layer shirt in black over white. She layered several necklaces in silver and black, added earrings that matched the pendant on the shorter necklace, and slipped into her black heeled boots. After touching up her hair and makeup, she took one more look in the mirror, satisfied and even thought her silver streaks in her hair looked nice with her shirt.

She put the casseroles in the oven to bake and set the timer, so she could add the breakfast meats for the last twenty minutes. Lily descended the stairs, having gone to her room to freshen up after her time outside.

Izzy filled her electric kettle and set the coffee to brew, as the doorbell rang. Lily had offered to handle the door and hurried to answer it, while Izzy selected an instrumental playlist and turned the volume to a low setting. She turned and saw Colin was her first guest. He presented her with a vase of gorgeous dahlias in deep purples and oranges, handed her a card, and greeted her with a kiss to the cheek.

"I came early in case you needed any help." He sighed and added, "And, I'm missing Jethro. My house is too quiet."

"These are absolutely stunning," said Izzy. "You must not have read the part of the invitation that said no gifts." She winked and added, "But I do love them. Come get something to drink while we wait for the others."

It didn't take long for the rest of the guests to arrive, and soon Izzy's new home was filled with laughter and warm conversation. Mac's new golf buddies introduced him and Lily to their better halves, and Kate made sure Spence got to know Mac and Lily. Izzy watched over the oven while she visited with everyone. When Linda linked her arm in Izzy's and led her toward the front door, Ellie and Regi offered to keep an eye on the cooking food.

Izzy stepped onto the porch to see several new pots of chrysanthemums in gorgeous fall colors. Linda said, "I put mini lights in them. They're solar and will come on automatically at dusk."

Izzy slipped her arm around Linda and hugged her. "You really shouldn't have, but they are gorgeous."

She and Linda lingered over the flowers, and then Linda led her around to the back of the house. "There's one more surprise for you, and it's from everyone."

When Izzy came around the corner to the patio, she saw Jeff and Spence standing behind a new glider bench, grinning. "Oh, it's beyond perfect. The pillows even match my furniture."

Jeff motioned her toward it. "Take it for a spin."

Izzy sat down and began to rock, then noticed the small fountain nestled in the shrubbery at the edge of the patio. She pointed and gasped. "And a fountain. You guys are too generous. I can't believe you did this. I really meant no gifts when I put that on the invitation." She continued to glide. "This is quite lovely."

Jeff smiled. "We know how much you like this view and we had this in stock taking up room at the hardware store, so we thought it would be perfect on your patio."

Tears burned in Izzy's eyes as she relinquished the glider, then made her way around the patio, hugging everyone and thanking them again. By the time she went inside to find Ellie and Sam and squeeze both of them in an embrace, they had the casseroles out and on the island. "We thought it probably best to keep the food in here, and then people can fill their plates and wander to the patio or the dining area," said Ellie. "That way the hot food will stay warm."

"Smart thinking. Thank you for handling it. I'll go let everyone know it's ready."

The next few hours flew by as Izzy visited and everyone enjoyed the delicious brunch. She and Colin, along with Mac and Lily viewed camera footage from Jeff's phone, showing the dogs running around in the fenced area of the yard, having fun and enjoying their playtime, despite being alone.

The four golfers had enjoyed a great time on the course, and were already urging Mac to plan another trip so they could golf again. The group lingered late into the afternoon, nibbling on leftovers and coffees.

Rather than have to trek out to Jeff's to pick up the dogs after the party that night, Colin volunteered to retrieve them. Mac agreed and thought because they'd been playing all day and would be tired, they could be trusted to hang out alone in the house. They would most likely sleep while everyone was at the clubhouse.

As the guests began to leave, showering Izzy with good wishes for her new home and new life on the island, Mac and Colin set out together to follow Jeff and Sam. Ellie and Regi had tidied the kitchen and everything was put away and spotless, save for a few coffee cups.

Izzy and Lily took care of those and then sat on the patio on her new bench, gliding together, enjoying the soft trickling sound of the water in her new fountain. Izzy sighed and said, "This was such a lovely day. I'm so glad you and Mac were here and a part of it."

"It was wonderful and I can see why you decided to move to the island. What a terrific group of friends you have."

Izzy shut her eyes and continued to sway with the motion of the bench, letting the love and friendship she felt warm her heart, knowing she was right where she should be.

COLIN AND IZZY were a hit as Maxwell Smart and Agent 99, but the others didn't disappoint, dressed as characters from *Gilligan's Island* and *Cheers*. It was a night filled with fun and laughter, scavenger hunts, and karaoke.

Her busy week caught up with her, and Izzy felt her eyes getting heavier as the night went on. She wandered out to the patio, and found Colin saying goodnight to a couple she didn't know. When they were gone, he turned and met her eyes. "There you are. I'm sorry I've been such a horrible escort tonight. I'm afraid I never really get to enjoy myself at these parties."

"Oh, not at all. I appreciate you getting all the tickets for us. Everyone is having a great time."

"Don't tell me you're worn out from your big day."

She smiled. "I'm just tired. Too much excitement packed into one day, I guess."

With a serious look, he said, "I asked you not to tell me that." She chuckled, recalling the phrase Maxwell Smart always said to Agent 99.

"You nailed that line. All that watching of the classic television channel paid off." She arched her brows at him.

"I'm glad you suggested it. It's hilarious." He grinned back at her and checked his watch. Izzy laughed when she spotted his extra shoe, the prop Colin used to simulate making a phone call and elicit laughs from the residents, sticking out of his jacket pocket. "It's getting late," he said. "Are Mac and Lily ready to head home?"

She looked through the windows, spying Mac in his captain's hat and Lily's feather boa on the dance floor. "Looks like they're still raring to go."

"I'm sure Jeff or Max could drop them by if you'd like to go home."

Her brow wrinkled and she shook her head. "I don't want to make you leave your party."

"Oh, I've had my fill. Let's go." He linked his arm with hers. Once inside they spotted Jeff and he agreed to drop Lily and Mac by the house. Izzy waited for the dance number to end and sought out Lily to tell her the plan, while Colin said goodbye to his staff stationed near the entrance.

Izzy had given him her housekeys, since she had no pockets in her outfit, and Colin led the way to her door and unlocked it for her. "You're welcome to come in for some tea, if you'd like."

He smiled, and said, "For a few minutes. I need to get home and check on Jethro."

She filled the kettle, and excused herself to quickly change out of her vintage clothes. A minute later, she emerged in a hooded cardigan over comfortable lounge pants and a t-shirt. She poured two cups of tea and found Colin on the couch with all four dogs begging for attention at his feet.

"Here you go," she said, settling into her oversized chaise, where Sunny hurried to plop beside her.

She saw the light blinking on her cell phone; she'd left it at home, since she hadn't wanted to take her purse to the clubhouse. She picked it up and saw a string of text messages and missed calls from Mia.

"Oh, that can't be good." She frowned as she scanned them.

"What's wrong?" he asked, petting Sherlock and Bodie as Fritz sprawled at his feet.

She sighed. "It's Mia." Her eyes swept over the screen. "Exactly what I don't need right now."

He gave her a quizzical look, and took a sip from his mug.

"It seems Mia got tired of waiting for John to decide about letting her move in with him in LA. She called and instead of John answering, Barbie, the bride-to-be, took the call and told her in no uncertain terms she would not be welcome to live with them. Now, Mia is having a meltdown." She tossed the phone on the cushion. "Of course, she's angry with me because she couldn't get in touch with me tonight."

"I'm sorry, Izzy. Is there anything I can do to help? Or, I'll get out of your hair so you can deal with it."

Tears burned in her eyes and throat. Colin's kind offer to help was unexpected and touched her heart. "I don't want to deal with it all," she said, shaking her head. "I don't need her using this for an excuse to quit school."

"I don't have much advice, as I've not dealt with what you're facing. But I can tell you're a good mom, and I think you're being pretty hard on yourself. The only thing I can offer is to be gentle, with yourself and with Mia. I'm sure she's scared and if this is the first time her dad hasn't come to her rescue, she'll be lost."

Izzy nodded. "I'm tired, and don't feel like arguing or being blamed. I've had such a lovely day and this ruins it."

"Perhaps you can tell her your phone died, and you didn't notice until morning because you were at a raucous Halloween party and were out all night with a man who finds you very attractive." He wiggled his brows, grinning with mischief.

She laughed and said, "I like that idea. I might use it."

Colin stood and walked to her, then bent to kiss her. A long, slow kiss. A kiss that made her wonder what it would be like to stay up all night with him. "Get some rest, and things will look better in the morning. I promise."

Izzy felt his hand over hers, and gripped it in a tight squeeze. "Thank you for today. It was wonderful."

"I'll see myself out. And I'll see you at breakfast tomorrow."

She watched him leave, so handsome, even in a thrift-shop suit and tie. Sam had suggested they all meet up for breakfast at the Front Street Café, but Izzy wasn't sure she could wait that long to see him again.

Chapter 19

IZZY TOOK COLIN'S advice and instead of calling Mia, had gotten a good night's sleep. Early Sunday morning, she texted to let Mia know she was sorry, but she had been at a party until late and had left her phone behind. She told her the offer to stay still stood, and she'd be happy to have her there in March once the quarter ended at school. She also reminded her about Thanksgiving in Richland and offered to buy her a plane ticket.

She didn't get an immediate response, which was nothing new, and went about her day, enjoying breakfast with her friends and afterward taking the dogs for a long walk. Lily and Mac set out to explore the island and offered to take Sunny along so she could play with her dog friends on the beach. They wouldn't be home until late afternoon, when they hoped to take Izzy to dinner at the Cliff House to thank her for her hospitality. They also urged her to invite Colin.

She watched them leave and slipped back into the house. It was so quiet and she already missed Sunny. She had the whole day to herself and wasn't quite sure what to do. She made a cup of tea, texted Colin who accepted the dinner invitation, and was settling in to read a book when her cell phone rang.

She smiled when she saw her mom's photo on the screen. She had sent her some photos of her house and told her about the brunch party this weekend. Izzy wished her parents could have been there to share in the celebration. She chatted with her mom for a few minutes, and then her face fell.

"Oh, I'm sorry, Mom. Don't call her back. Let me take care of it. The last thing you need is more drama. If Mia calls again, tell her to call me."

She reassured her mom that everything would be okay, and promised to send her photos of her new glider bench and flowerpots.

As soon as she hung up, she poked the button for Mia. It rang and rang, but her daughter didn't answer. Izzy left a voicemail and followed up with a text asking Mia to get in touch, letting her know she had already talked to Grandma and staying with her was not an option.

She shook her head, disgusted Mia would try to guilt her grandparents into letting her live with them. There was no reason she couldn't stay in school until March. As usual, she couldn't accept no for an answer.

After, Izzy couldn't concentrate on her book and went upstairs to her office to check on work emails. Despite the quiet and knowing she would have heard her phone chime, she couldn't resist checking it every thirty minutes, to make sure she hadn't missed a text from Mia. She hadn't.

Before long, it was mid-afternoon. She had completed a couple of work assignments and checked on flights for Thanksgiving for Mia. She made her way downstairs for more tea and carried it out to the patio, where she tried to glide away her worries, listening to the soft trickle of water from her new fountain.

MONDAY, IZZY AWOKE to find a text from Mia that had come in around two o'clock in the morning. A tactic Mia had perfected, knowing Izzy wouldn't be awake to reply. Mia ranted on about how Izzy was trying to control her life and was sure she had turned her dad against her and was to blame for him not allowing Mia to move in with him. She made it clear she would not be living with Izzy on the stupid island and would figure it out herself.

Izzy chuckled at that notion, but instead of replying with her actual thoughts, sent a text letting Mia know she supported her desire to figure things out herself. She assured Mia if she changed her mind, she was welcome and that Max said there were three capable obstetricians at the new hospital. She asked Mia to let her know if she wanted airline tickets for Thanksgiving and listed some flight options. She signed off telling Mia she loved her. How she wished Mia would engage in an actual phone call instead of all these texts.

After visiting over coffee, Izzy wished Mac and Lily a safe trip home, giving all the dogs lots of cuddles, and comforting Sunny, who whined a bit when they drove away. She distracted the dog with a game of fetch before she left for a meeting downtown.

She didn't hear back from Mia on Monday, and pushed her from her mind, concentrating on her work week and making sure she was prepared for Shannon's upcoming sentencing.

She and Colin got back into their normal routine of walking the dogs and visiting, as they greeted the first light of the day. She had work commitments all week, except Friday, and they agreed to celebrate the end of the week with dinner at The Bistro.

Izzy didn't hear from Mia until Thursday when her daughter texted which flight she wanted booked for Thanksgiving. She didn't mention anything else. Izzy booked the flights and sent her the confirmation number, telling her she was looking forward to seeing her soon.

She spent part of Friday in town, getting a haircut at Jen's salon, splurging on a pedicure, and doing some shopping. When she got home, she hung her new fall wreath on the door, and added the cute glass pumpkins and faux leaves to her entry table. She bought a few sets of the mini lights Kate had used in the living room, and wove a string through the decorations, then took the other sets and strung them around the mirror of her dresser and in the leaves of a plant near the bathtub.

With the days growing dark earlier and the rainy weather they'd had all week, she craved the warmth of the festive lights that made everything happier, and wanted to make sure she had some everywhere in the house. In addition to providing a cozy atmosphere, they made for gentle nightlights.

When she was done, she spent some time playing with Sunny before she had to get ready for dinner. Colin was bringing Jethro to stay with Sunny, since the two of them had proven they could behave quite well together. With it so wet outside, Izzy locked the doggy door, knowing they wouldn't be gone more than a couple of hours.

She didn't need to touch her hair since Jen had styled it. As she glanced in the mirror, adding silver earrings that matched the silver threads throughout her hair, she smiled, thinking her hair actually looked quite nice. Maybe she was getting used to it. She added a pretty red silk scarf with subtle black flowers over her black sweater, and grabbed her leather jacket when she heard Colin arrive. Seeing it was drizzling, she plucked an umbrella from the slender oak wine barrel in the entry that Blake and Ellie had given her, restored with gleaming copper bands and made from one of the family barrels.

She and Colin enjoyed a delicious meal, split a sinfully delicious chocolate dessert, and she savored two glasses of her favorite red wine while they sat by the fire. It was still sprinkling when they left, and Colin offered to take the dogs out, keeping them on their leashes, so they couldn't get muddy.

Izzy filled the kettle and brewed two mugs of tea, helping Colin dry the dogs' paws when they returned. The two of them settled onto the couch, the dogs lounging near the patio door. They chatted a bit about Izzy's upcoming trip to spend Thanksgiving with her parents.

She took a sip from her mug, and met Colin's eyes. "I've been embarrassed to mention this, but need to tell you, we're going over early in the week on Tuesday because I'm due in court to represent my sister, Shannon. She's the reason I had to travel to Olympia, actually a small town outside of it, for court earlier, when I first met you."

She shared the details of Shannon's escapades, including her sister's past involvement in the protest movement and lack of direction. The more she explained and contrasted Shannon with her other sisters, Colin's eyes widened. "I know my parents are going to be heartbroken," she added, "but I think Shannon is going to be facing some jail time."

"Sounds to me like she might deserve it." He brought his hand to his mouth. "Sorry, I shouldn't have said that."

Izzy laughed. "No, I agree. I think she needs to face the music. I didn't want to keep the situation from you. It's obviously not something Blake or I am proud of, and our whole family is embarrassed by the entire situation."

"I understand, believe me. I'm sorry you've had such a rough go of it with this and your daughter. That can't be easy."

"Thanksgiving is usually a time I look forward to and enjoy, but this year, I think it is going to be difficult. I'm fairly certain the judge will allow Shannon to spend it with family and report the following week, but I know Mom and Dad will be so upset. Then, of course, there's Mia. She's sure to add some unnecessary drama to the mix." Izzy chuckled, and said, "I'm spending Christmas here. I can't deal with any more craziness, and am looking forward to having my first celebration in my new house."

"Well, as you might guess, Thanksgiving isn't a thing in Scotland, although since living here, I have gotten used to enjoying the traditional meal. I normally offer to work, so will be keeping an eye on things at the office. In Scotland, we celebrate St. Andrew's Day on November thirtieth. Here it's not even recognized, but back home, it's a huge feast and celebration."

They chatted a bit more as he explained some of the other traditional Scottish holidays, usually involving saints or wars. "David is coming in mid-December and will be here until the new year, so I'm excited for his visit and will be taking some time off to spend with him. I'd love to introduce you."

"Of course. We'll have to have dinner or something while he's here. We're going to do Christmas Day here, and Ellie and Blake will come. Mia is invited, but who knows what she'll be doing. I asked Kate and Spence to come and I think her son, Mitch, will be here visiting. I'd love to have you and David, if you're up to it."

He nodded. "That would be wonderful. Sounds like much more fun than the two of us."

"Once I get through Thanksgiving and whatever it brings, maybe we can think of a few more fun things to do while your son is here. I'm sure Jeff and Nate will figure out a way to go fishing, no matter the weather."

"Already counting on it," he said with a wink.

She made more tea and they kept talking, long into the night. She learned Colin's parents had passed away before he came to the United States. He also had one older brother, Stephen, who still lived in Scotland, but they were not especially close.

He went on to recount one of Phoebe's many drunken rampages, one where she had made a pass at Stephen and he hadn't resisted. "We had never been close, but that drove a wedge between us. So, when you talk about feeling shame and being embarrassed, I get it. Not only did our entire town know about Phoebe's issues, but then they got a front row seat to the fallout of her sleeping with my brother."

"Oh, that had to be torturous. I'm so sorry you and poor David had to endure such a heartbreaking situation. Knock on wood, Shannon hasn't gone too far afield back in Richland. Most of her shenanigans take place in Seattle or Portland. I'm not sure our business could survive it, if her antics were plastered all over the papers in our hometown."

"Yes, small towns are lovely until you're the talk of them. Not long after that, I took David and moved, only going back home to visit my mom and dad. It's been a relief to live across the ocean from all of those memories."

As THEY SHARED stories, the talking and the tea ended the week's fatigue that Izzy had felt earlier in the evening, and before she knew it, it was almost two o'clock in the morning.

"Oh my gosh, it's late," she said. "It feels like we've only been talking for an hour."

Colin stood and said, "The old proverb is true. When you're spending it doing things you enjoy, time does fly. Hours seem like mere minutes and you long for a few more of them. On the other hand, when you're doing something you loathe, each minute seems like a long and excruciating hour."

He roused Jethro from a deep sleep. "Come on, boy, we need to get home." Sunny stood and followed Jethro, with Izzy bringing up the rear.

He opened the door to the stillness of the dark night. The fresh scent of rain greeted them, and although it had stopped raining, Izzy heard the quiet patter of drops falling from the bushes along her driveway. She also heard her heart pounding when Colin turned and leaned closer to her.

"That was by the far the best night I've had in years. The more time I spend with you, the more I like you." He brushed his lips against hers. "I'm afraid this could become a habit."

She chuckled as she watched him drive away, and like any addict, was already craving the next opportunity to spend time with him.

Chapter 20

IZZY WAS UP early, stuffing her toiletries into her suitcase for the trip home, with a detour to the courthouse outside of Olympia. Instead of thinking about Shannon and court, she let her mind wander to last night and the lovely dinner Colin had treated her to at his house.

The last few weeks, she and Colin had spent more and more time together. In addition to their morning walks with the dogs, they had a new habit of having dinner on Friday night, and squeezing in a few lunches together when Izzy was working from home. Saturdays, they went to Lou's and Sundays met for brunch in town. The Bistro did a delicious Sunday Brunch, but Colin preferred to socialize away from work on the weekends. She was going to miss him and Sunny while she was away this week.

She saw headlights flash across the front windows, and doublechecked to make sure she had everything. While Izzy wrapped her scarf closer to her neck and slipped behind the wheel, Blake loaded his and Ellie's suitcases into the back of Izzy's SUV. Izzy glanced at Ellie in the backseat. "Did you get Oreo situated at Linda's?"

"Yes, she's in heaven. She loves playing with Lucy. I doubt she'll know I'm gone, and Max and Linda will take great care of her."

"I feel bad leaving Sunny, but she's with Zoe and Bailey. Colin offered to watch over her too, but I think she'll have more fun being around Jeff and the other two dogs. I hate to leave her on her own all day."

"I know what you mean. She'll enjoy all the action with Jeff and the dogs. He's always loading them in the truck and going somewhere."

Blake slammed the cargo door shut and slid into the passenger seat. "All set."

Izzy tapped the screen on her phone. "Sam's at the shop and is asking what we want. She'll have our drinks ready so we can grab them on our way to the ferry." She keyed in their requests and hit the send button before backing out of the garage.

In no time they were at the harbor, where Izzy got in line for the ferry and Blake offered to retrieve their drink order.

Izzy watched her brother hurry across the street, and turned to face Ellie. "Is he ready for the day?"

Ellie's brows rose and she pursed her lips. "I hope so. He's not looking forward to spending time with Shannon, especially the ride from Olympia to Richland."

"I'm dreading it already. If my gut is right, I'm sure Shannon will get some jail time. The prosecutor is not willing to budge, so it will be up to the judge. Honestly, I think it could do her some good, but worry about Mom and Dad."

Ellie nodded. "Right. Blake is concerned about them too."

Moments later, Blake was at the door with a drink carrier and a bag. "Sam sent some brownies and muffins in case we get hungry on the road."

As soon as Izzy had taken her first sip of the chai tea latte that always reminded her of pumpkin pie, the vehicle line started to move onto the ferry. Once Izzy parked, they went upstairs and sat at a table. The soft light of dawn was appearing across the water, giving them the first glimpse of the islands.

Blake opened the bag of pastries and bit into a muffin. "If Shannon gets jail time, do you think they'll take her into custody right there, or will she have to report later?"

"It could go either way. I'm prepared to ask the judge to allow her to spend Thanksgiving with her family, and figure we could drop her off when we head back on Monday." Izzy shrugged and took another sip.

"Two long car rides with Shannon is not my idea of a holiday." Blake rolled his eyes. "I guess we'll do whatever we have to do."

When the ferry docked in Anacortes, Blake offered to drive and Izzy was happy to let him take the wheel. Shannon wasn't communicating much with Izzy or Blake, but still responded to Ellie, so she had been elected the point of contact.

Izzy wanted to pick her up from the airport, rather than rely on Shannon to get to the courthouse on her own. There was still part of her that expected Shannon to do a runner, meet up with one of her friends, and disappear.

They were due in court at three o'clock, and Shannon's flight landed before noon. In their last video chat, Izzy had brought up the importance of dressing more professionally to make a good impression on the court. Luckily, her mom had been there, nodding along in agreement, so she hoped Shannon would show up in something other than one of her protestor t-shirts.

Traffic was heavy, but at least it was the Tuesday of Thanksgiving week and not Wednesday. When they had made plans for the trip, Blake had pointed out that staying until the Monday after Thanksgiving would make for lighter traffic than on Sunday.

Izzy was tracking Shannon's flight and saw it had landed a few minutes before she helped Blake navigate to the exit. They couldn't linger at the curb for long, but it took some time to get through the congestion that always seemed to plague the airport. Blake steered to the arrival concourse, while Ellie texted Shannon to let her know they would meet her outside of the baggage claim area.

Ellie and Izzy kept their eyes focused on the crowds standing outside, searching for Shannon as Blake crept along the loop, hoping not to have to exit and return. Ellie shouted, "There she is, one more set of doors down, keep going."

Izzy spotted her sister, in a loose skirt, in a gauzy material with a camouflage pattern. She paired it with her black combat-style boots and an oversized olive-green sweater that hung on her, drooping over her shoulders. The outfit was an improvement over her normal t-shirts, but what stood out was her hair. Her naturally wavy hair, which was usually a mass of messy braids all over her head, was cut a bit shorter, but was a shocking bright red.

Blake turned his head as he wedged the SUV into a tight opening at the curb. "Oh, my gosh. Look at her hair."

Izzy took a deep breath. "Let's not say anything. I think part of the reason she does the things she does is for attention and the shock value. There's nothing that can be done about it at this point. Let's ignore it."

Ellie popped open the rear passenger door closest to the curb. Blake jumped out to help Shannon with her backpack and loaded it into the cargo area. "How was your flight?" asked Ellie, as she scooted across the backseat.

"Fine," mumbled Shannon.

"We should have time to stop and have lunch near the courthouse," said Izzy, giving Blake directions, as he left the airport and followed the signs for Olympia.

Ellie filled the awkward silence with chatter about Thanksgiving and her favorite dishes, and told Shannon about Sunny. Shannon barely responded, focusing instead on looking out of her window.

Izzy took out her notebook. "Just to confirm, you're still working at the fabric and craft store, Shannon?"

"Yes," she snapped.

"Did you get the name of the manager and a contact number for me? The court may want to confirm it."

"The manager is a cow named Audra. I have the number to the store in my phone."

It didn't take long for Blake to find a parking spot, and they walked down the street to a sandwich shop. Shannon perused the menu behind the counter and rolled her eyes. "I hate small towns. I can't wait to be back in a real city, where they have vegan options. I'm so sick of living with Mom and Dad."

Izzy held her breath, hoping Blake wouldn't say what they were all thinking – Shannon's wish to get out of a small town would probably not be granted today. Izzy ordered last, paid for everyone, and took their number to their table.

It didn't take long for their meal to be delivered, and as they ate, Izzy tried to gently prepare Shannon for a jail sentence. With a smug look on her face, Shannon waved aside the notion. "There's no way I'll get jail time. We do these protests all the time and nobody ends up getting in any real trouble. You're trying to scare me."

"This time you and your friends chose a small town. One that is not going to put up with what you all get away with in the cities. I've talked to the prosecutor at length, and they are not taking this lightly. I want you to know it is a strong possibility."

Shannon slammed her spoon onto the table. "You have got to be the worst lawyer ever. I still can't believe you're charging me anything for this shitty advice. A good lawyer would make sure I don't get in any trouble."

Izzy counted to ten. "Like I've told you many times, you are free to seek out new representation. All lawyers charge a fee, unless you ask for a public defender and submit your finances, like I told you that first time we met at the courthouse."

Shannon pushed her bottom lip out. "I should have done it. And I should have never said I was guilty."

Blake cleared his throat. "Here's the thing. You are guilty. You are a complete loser, who is nothing but an embarrassment to our entire family. You do nothing productive, just run around with your dirtball friends, destroying things people, who actually work for a living, built. You hit a police officer, you damaged businesses and stole things. You are more than guilty, and you deserve anything you get and more. Your choices are taking a toll on everyone, and it's high time you finally paid a price." He stood and stormed out of the deli, leaving Izzy and Ellie staring at his back, both wide-eyed.

Shannon's mouth hung open. Izzy checked her watch, and said, "We need to get going." As she collected her purse, she turned toward Shannon. "Every lawyer knows it's never a good idea to represent family. I knew that going into this, but Mom and Dad insisted I represent you instead of letting you get stuck with an overworked public defender, who wouldn't have the time to dedicate to your case. Trust me, I'll never allow my heart to overrule my brain again."

Once they were outside on the sidewalk, Izzy stormed off in the direction of the courthouse, leaving Ellie and Shannon to rush to catch up with her. Blake was nowhere to be seen, and Izzy suspected he went for a walk and would meet up with them later at the car.

Izzy checked in with the clerk's office, and waited on a wooden bench outside the courtroom. Shannon and Ellie took a seat next to her, neither of them saying a word. They watched a dribble of attorneys and defendants go into and out of the courtroom. After about thirty minutes, Izzy stood when she heard their case called.

She motioned to Shannon to follow her and told Ellie she could take a seat in the audience or wait in the hallway. Izzy made her way to the defendant's table, nodded at Mr. Durham, then listened as the judge reviewed the case.

Mr. Durham recommended three months in jail, a fine, and restitution to the business owners. Izzy sought no jail time and countered with community service, a fine, and restitution, citing Shannon's job and her ability to work out a payment plan.

The judge looked down at his paperwork, and then addressed Shannon. "I've had a look at your record and it would appear you've been involved in several protests, including the destruction of property. Each time, you've been warned and promised to keep your protesting to non-violent activities. It seems all you've done is take advantage of the leniency you've been granted. I am hopeful my sentence today will impress upon you the need to do exactly what you've pledged the last five times you've been in court. I hereby sentence you to ninety days in jail, a ten thousand dollar fine, and your portion of restitution to the business owners as stated in the prosecution's request. I would strongly suggest you change your ways, as a repeat of this offence will get you one to five years in prison."

Shannon stood at Izzy's side, unmoving and quiet. Izzy turned toward the judge. "Your honor, my client would like to request that she be able to spend a few days with her family and report for her sentence on Monday, after Thanksgiving."

He nodded, but before he could speak, Shannon flung her hands in the air. "Like I would want to spend time with my family. Who are you kidding? You're all against me. This is an injustice. I demand a new trial and a new lawyer." Her shrill voice echoed throughout the courtroom.

The judge banged his gavel, and said, "Motion denied. Counselor, get your client under control. Bailiff, please remand the defendant into custody now."

Izzy's heart sank as she watched two bailiffs approach Shannon, both of them keeping their hands near their tasers, signaling they were not going to put up with any nonsense.

Izzy reached for Shannon's arm. "I'll come with you."

"Don't bother. Why would I need you now? You're the one who got me into this mess." She practically spat the words at her sister.

Before Izzy could say anything else, the two bailiffs had Shannon across the courtroom and through the doors they used for prisoners. Izzy let out the breath she had been holding, and shakily gathered her things. She shrugged at Mr. Durham and made her way down the aisle, where Ellie was waiting for her at the door.

Izzy looked into Ellie's huge eyes, full of shock and disbelief, and gestured for her to follow her into the hallway. Once they were away from the crowd, Izzy turned to her. "Have you heard from Blake?"

Ellie nodded, and pointed to her phone. "He texted and said he was walking around. He'll meet us at the car."

"I need to stop by the clerk's office here, and then I'll run over to the jail and put some money on her account, so she can buy anything she needs. This is going to kill Mom and Dad. Do you want to go back to the car, and I'll meet you both there?"

Ellie nodded. "I'll let Blake know what happened, and that will give him time to process it and calm down." She shook her head. "I can't believe she would act out like that in court."

"Sadly, I can." Izzy set off to take care of the paperwork, her shoulders sagging as she wondered how in the world she would explain this to her parents.

Chapter 21

As soon as Izzy arrived at the car, Blake started the ignition and headed for the highway. Izzy pulled her phone from her purse. "I'm going to let them know we're on our way."

"They're going to ask what happened," Blake said, maneuvering through the heavy traffic.

"I'll say we'll explain it all when we get there and tell them to eat without us. It's going to be too late when we get there and we won't be able to get them to eat after they hear the news."

He smacked his palms against the steering wheel. "This is going to be a horrible Thanksgiving. Why can't Shannon ever keep her mouth shut?"

Izzy shook her head as she hit the button on her phone. She made the call short and dodged any specific questions about Shannon, giving her mother vague answers, using the word *we* often, but not making it clear Shannon wasn't with them.

Next, she called Lauren and Esther and explained what had happened. Neither had plans to be at their parents' house, but were willing to drive over and be there when Izzy and Blake arrived, so they could help provide emotional support.

With the four-hour ride ahead of them, Izzy suggested they stop and grab something quick for dinner on the way, then she leaned her head back against the headrest and shut her eyes for several minutes, hoping to calm her mind.

Ellie and Blake talked back and forth, with Blake quizzing his wife on what she thought of Shannon's outburst. Ellie had never really seen Shannon in action, so she was stunned and still couldn't believe it. Izzy blocked out their conversation and concentrated on what to say to her parents. Although she had predicted the outcome, she hated defeat. Even more, she hated what this would do to her parents. She felt as if she had failed them.

Blake spied a sign for a small café and took the exit. After a drama-free meal, they all were in better spirits. However, the closer they got to her parents' home, the larger the lump in Izzy's throat felt.

Blake pulled into the driveway after nine o'clock. He retrieved their luggage, along with Shannon's backpack and the three of them stood at the end of the driveway, reluctant to enter the house and bring their parents' world crashing down on them.

Izzy inhaled a deep breath. "I guess we better get this over with." She pulled her suitcase behind her and lugged it up the steps. Blake didn't bother knocking and opened the door.

They found their parents and their sisters in the large great room. When Helen saw them, she sprang from her chair. "Oh, thank goodness." Her eyes darted to each of them, and then her face fell. "Where's Shannon?"

Izzy took her mom by the hand, and led her back to her chair. "I'll explain everything." Ellie and Blake sat on the couch beside Izzy, and for a moment, the only sound was the soft ticking of the grandfather clock.

Then, with a gentle voice, Izzy explained everything that had happened. Gene shook his head, as Izzy described Shannon's outburst and the judge's response, and Helen softly cried when Izzy mentioned they could visit Shannon through video, until her release in late February.

Helen sobbed and seemed to shrink into her chair. "Izzy, you promised you would make sure Shannon could be here for Thanksgiving, even if she did get sentenced to some jail time."

Before Izzy could explain it again, Blake approached their parents. "Izzy did ask for exactly that, and the judge was about to say yes. He was nodding and about to grant the request, when Shannon opened her big mouth and sealed her own fate. This, like everything else, is her own fault. It's not on Izzy."

Helen hung her head and her shoulders shook as she wept, her hands holding a mass of sodden tissues. Gene didn't say much, but rubbed his fingers together and chewed on his bottom lip. Esther and Lauren moved to comfort their mother, murmuring to her, but their words didn't seem to have any effect.

Izzy leaned against the cushion, deflated, but glad the worst was over. Her body was heavy with exhaustion. She had been running on pure adrenaline since picking up Shannon at the airport, and now having delivered the horrible blow to her parents, she wasn't sure she had the strength to get into her pajamas.

She hated seeing her parents so distraught, and while everyone was focused on them, she stood and slipped away, collected her suitcase, and carried it to the guest room she always used.

She didn't bother unpacking, but dug in her bag for her soft pajamas and fell into the bed. The fresh bouquet of flowers and the smattering of pumpkins and leaves around the room wasn't lost on her. Her mother always enjoyed decorating for the holidays and loved having her children home and celebrating with them.

This was going to be so hard on her. Tomorrow, Mia was due to fly in. Dread coursed through Izzy as she thought about facing her daughter. She willed it away, then rested her head against the pillow, shut her eyes, and succumbed to the fatigue.

A LOUD CLATTER startled Izzy awake. She opened her eyes, unsure where she was for a few moments, and then remembered as yesterday came rushing back at her. She wasn't sure what the noise was that interrupted her sleep. It was still dark outside, and she checked the clock to learn it was five-thirty in the morning.

She stuffed her feet into her slippers and made her way down the hall, following the soft glow of lights coming from the kitchen. When she walked in, she didn't see anyone and took a quick look in the great room. It, too, was empty.

She made her way further into the kitchen and around the end of the long granite topped island and stopped short. Her mother was on the floor, along with several metal baking sheets, gasping for breath.

"Mom, Mom!" Izzy knelt and shook her mother's shoulders. Helen's eyes fluttered, she moaned, and clutched her chest, still struggling to breathe. Izzy hollered for Blake, and reached for the phone on the counter. While she held her mom's hand, she gave her address to the emergency operator and requested an ambulance.

Seconds later, Blake rushed into the kitchen, followed by Ellie. "What's happened?"

"A loud noise woke me up. I came in and found her on the floor."

Blake put his mouth next to his mom's head. "Are you in pain, Mom? Where does it hurt?" She mumbled something and Blake straightened.

Izzy was already rummaging in the cabinet where her mom kept some over the counter medications, looking for aspirin. She found a bottle and popped the lid, meeting Blake's eyes.

He nodded. "She says her back and chest hurt."

Izzy reached for a glass and filled it with water, while Blake propped his mom's head up and put the aspirin in her mouth.

Helen grimaced at the bitter taste, and he offered her the glass of water, sloshing it all over her, as he helped her drink from it.

"I'll go get Dad," offered Izzy. She hurried to the other side of the house, where the master bedroom was and tapped on the door. She got no response, but her dad's hearing wasn't the best.

She opened it and found him still asleep, oblivious to all that was happening. Part of her hated to wake him, hated to be the one to deliver more bad news, fearful of what it might do to him. She steeled herself and tapped him on the shoulder.

When he opened his eyes, he looked bewildered, and then smiled. As he focused on her, the smile slipped away and worry filled his eyes. "Izzy, what's wrong?"

She rested her hand on his shoulder. "It's Mom. She's collapsed in the kitchen. I think it might be a heart attack."

He threw the blankets and sheets off, his hands shaking as he gripped the edge of the bed. Izzy sat down beside him. "An ambulance is on the way, and we've given her an aspirin."

He nodded as he reached for his robe and followed Izzy to the kitchen, arriving as the sound of a siren wailed outside.

Blake still kneeled beside their mom, talking to her, and she was responding, though her eyes were closed. Gene knelt on the other side of her and grabbed her hand, still over her chest. "Sweetheart, it's going to be okay." Tears speckled his cheeks as he did his best to reassure her.

Ellie led the paramedics in through the front door and the family moved to give them access to their beloved matriarch. They asked several questions related to allergies, current medications, her primary care physician, and known conditions. Gene answered as best he could, and went to a drawer where they kept their prescriptions. He trembled as he collected the bottles, so Ellie offered to make a list.

After several minutes, they loaded Helen onto a gurney, and said they were taking her to the main hospital, a couple of miles away. Blake tried to question them, but they hurried from the house, saying the doctors would know more once they got Helen to the hospital.

Everyone scurried to put on clothes, and while she was still getting dressed, Blake rapped on her bedroom door. "I'm going to take Dad and get going. I'll call with any news."

"I'll be there in a few," she said, tugging on her jeans.

Izzy's stomach lurched as she brushed her teeth, almost gagging on the toothpaste. What if she lost her mom? And how was her dad bearing up under the terrible strain? She'd always thought of him as tough and strong, but he'd seemed to wilt when he saw his wife on the kitchen floor. She loved them both so much, and guilt washed over her as she thought about what she had been forced to tell them last night. She couldn't help but think her mom's condition was due to it.

She emerged, dressed, and with her hair tamed, but not feeling at all put-together. The smell of coffee greeted her and she found Ellie in the kitchen. Her sweet sister-in-law didn't say anything, just poured Izzy a cup and delivered it with a long hug.

She took her first sip and sighed. "Mia's flight arrives this morning."

Ellie nodded. "I can handle picking her up. I need to borrow a car."

"That would be wonderful. I'd rather not leave the hospital, if I don't have to." She spied her mom's purse on a kitchen chair. She always kept her keys in the outer pocket, and Izzy found them easily. "Here you go," she said, handing them to Ellie. "I'll text you her flight information."

"We'll probably head straight to the hospital and see how things are going." Ellie's brows arched, looking for affirmation.

"Sure, that's great. Whatever Mia wants to do. I don't need to add any stress to the situation." Izzy gasped and said, "I need to call Lauren and Esther and let them know."

She sipped on the warm coffee as she explained what had happened. Both of her sisters thought it might be better if they came over to the house, got started on the Thanksgiving preparations, and waited for information from Blake or Izzy.

Izzy agreed and promised to call them with any news or if she thought they should come to the hospital. She rinsed her cup and turned to Ellie. "Thank you for always being there for us, for putting up with this crazy family. We're so lucky to have you."

Ellie smiled. "I feel the same way about all of you." As Izzy was gathering her purse, Ellie suggested she not bring Mia to the hospital and instead they could help Lauren and Esther with the meal preparations, which would also give Mia a chance to see Sabina.

"That's probably a good idea," said Izzy. "But if Mia gets obstinate, bring her. I don't need you to have to deal with her moods. Hopefully, the baby and everyone will distract her. It's not like packing the waiting room is going to do any good, and there's no sense in all of us sitting there. Blake and I can handle it."

Izzy retrieved her coat and set out for the hospital. She found Blake and her dad in the waiting area outside of the emergency room. When she met Blake's eyes with a questioning look, he shook his head and shrugged. No news.

She explained everyone was going to stay at the house and wait for an update, and offered to get them some coffees. As soon as she slipped into the chair on the other side of her dad, a nurse emerged and asked for the Griffin family.

Gene bolted from his chair, and they all made their way to her. "Helen is resting, and the doctor is still waiting for some tests. I can let one of you back to sit with her, if you'd like."

Gene nodded. "I'll come get you when the doctor has the results, and is ready to go over them," the nurse said to Izzy and Blake. She took Gene by the arm, led him down the corridor and through a locked door she had to open with her keycard.

Izzy sank into a chair and stared up at Blake. "How's Dad doing?

He wiggled his hand from side to side. "He's worried, but he's trying to be strong."

"Does Mom have any heart problems that he knows of?" she asked, taking a sip from the water bottle she opted for instead of coffee.

Blake shook his head. "She takes medication for high blood pressure, but no heart issues that she's mentioned."

Izzy nodded and stared at the paintings on the wall. "I knew she had high blood pressure, but I think it's controlled with her medication. She's normally quite healthy."

Blake paced the wall of windows looking out to a small courtyard. "You know, this is all Shannon's fault. All of this." His steps quickened as he walked back and forth, mumbling.

She could almost see the waves of anger spreading from him. He slid into the chair next to Izzy, tears in his eyes, and said, "If Shannon kills Mom, I'll never forgive her."

Izzy gripped his hand in hers and squeezed it. Shannon had put their parents through so much grief, but this topped everything. There was nothing anyone could do. Her mom and dad were used to fixing things for Shannon, and while this whole set of circumstances made Izzy angry with her sister, she knew her mother's heart had to be breaking.

Why did children make life so difficult for their parents? You would think at forty, the nonsense would be over and Shannon would have found her way, but based on how she behaved in court, Izzy wasn't sure she ever would. Her thoughts drifted to Mia. While she didn't have the anarchist streak that seemed to drive Shannon, she was also past the age of needing to be bailed out by her parents.

Izzy was always steadfast in her approach to Mia, but adding a baby to the mix would change things. While she would never admit it to her daughter, since it would only give her more ammunition, Izzy would never let her grandchild suffer or go without because of Mia's choices. She hoped it wouldn't come to that.

She glanced at her watch, confirming they had been there for hours. Ellie had texted her that she and Mia were heading back to the house and would wait to hear how Helen was, but they would come to the hospital if they were needed.

Izzy nodded and tapped in a response, let Blake know, and confirmed there was no need for more people to sit in the waiting room. Blake stood again. "How blasted long does it take to get these tests done? This is ridiculous."

A few minutes later, the door opened and the same nurse approached them. "The doctor is on his way to see your mom, and would like you to come back so he can tell you the results."

She wasn't smiling and the knot in Izzy's stomach tightened as she took Blake's hand and they followed her through the heavy door.

Chapter 22

THE NURSE LED them into a room, where Gene was sitting next to their mother's bed, holding her hand. They gathered around Helen's bed, looking with worry at the oxygen mask over her face.

"Are you feeling better, Mom?" she asked, studying all the monitors and their cords attached to parts of her mother's body.

Helen nodded and tried to say something, but Izzy shook her head. "Don't talk, relax. The doctor is coming in to tell us the results."

Seconds later, a young man in blue scrubs with a white coat overtop hurried into the room. "Sorry to keep you waiting so long. I wanted to rule out everything."

He stood next to Gene and consulted his tablet, nodding as he tapped the buttons on it. "Okay, we've checked for cardiac and pulmonary issues, and I even had a neuro consult to rule out any possibility of stroke. Helen's blood pressure was very high, but I actually think it was a panic attack. I don't see anything to indicate a serious issue."

He turned to Izzy and Blake. "Your dad tells me you've experienced some recent family stress. Quite often a stressful event can bring on a panic attack, and patients feel like they are having some type of cardiac event, often experiencing an extreme shortness of breath. I would recommend we increase her blood pressure medication until this period of stress is over, but outside of that, I don't think we'll need to do much."

Izzy and Blake both let out the breath they had been holding. "So, she can go home today?" asked Izzy, looking at her mom, whose eyes were filled with tears.

"I don't see why not. It will take a bit to get her discharge orders done, but I'm confident she'll be fine. Maybe do some meditating, take a walk, something to relieve the stress she's under." He smiled at Helen. "Does that sound good?"

She nodded, and reached for his hand and squeezed it. He asked if they had further questions, and when they didn't, wished them all a Happy Thanksgiving and told Helen she was excused from any and all kitchen duties for the weekend, before leaving.

Blake reached for his mom's foot and squeezed it. "I'm so glad you're okay, Mom."

Tears leaked from her eyes as she bobbed her head. The nurse came in and suggested they all wander down to the cafeteria to give her a few minutes to get Helen ready to go, then removed her oxygen mask.

Helen whispered, "I'm so sorry."

Izzy shook her head and bent to hug her mom. "Don't worry. We're glad you're okay. You gave us a scare."

She patted Izzy's back. "I scared myself, believe me."

Gene chuckled, back to his old self. "Some people will do anything to get out of cooking a big meal, huh?" He kissed his wife's cheek. "We'll be outside waiting for you, dear."

Blake led the way to the small cafeteria. "I'm starving," he said. "Does anybody want to eat?"

"Hot tea sounds good to me," said Izzy. "I'm not much for hospital food."

Gene and Blake looked at the offerings, and decided on pie and coffee. "I'll call Ellie while you guys order," said Izzy, moving down the line to a table by the window.

She passed on the doctor's update to Ellie, and let her know they would be bringing Helen home. "How's Mia?"

"She's okay. Worried about her grandma. Mostly she's been visiting with Lauren and playing with the baby. I decided to get started on the pies. Your mom had her menu sitting on the counter."

"Aww, that's wonderful. Mom needs to rest and relax, so we'll all have to pitch in and handle dinner."

"Esther and I are already working on it, so tell her not to worry. I have a pot of chicken soup on the stove right now, for her." Ellie's words filled Izzy's heart. She was so skilled in the kitchen and everything she baked was delicious. Blake had struck gold when he married her, and Izzy loved her like her real sisters, maybe even more.

"You guys are the best. We'll be home as soon as we can. Do you need anything from the store?" Ellie promised she'd do a quick inventory and text if they needed anything. "I think I'll stop by the deli on the way home and pick up sandwiches to go with your soup and then we'll figure out something for dinner tonight."

Izzy disconnected as Blake arrived, carrying a tray of pie slices, coffees, and Izzy's pot of hot water with a tea bag. Gene dug into the apple pie. His spirits lifted as he and Blake talked about Ellie's pies that were sure to be the highlight of the feast tomorrow.

It took more time than they thought, but they were finally on their way home about an hour later. Izzy detoured to Dockside Deli, while Blake drove their parents' home.

As she waited for the takeout order, her phone chimed. She smiled when she saw a text from Colin asking how things were going. She pursed her lips as she tried to figure out how to recap the last couple of days in a concise text. *Stressful and eventful. I'll call you tonight.*

He sent her a hugging emoticon and a heart, which made her smile. She also noticed an earlier text from Jeff that she hadn't seen. It was a photo of Sunny playing with her two friends and a note saying she was having fun and all was well.

Izzy hated to admit it, but she couldn't wait to get back to the island, to Sunny…to Colin. Knowing her mom wasn't seriously ill was a huge relief, and as she stacked the containers of food in the back of her SUV, she felt suddenly weary. Like the rush of adrenaline that had been coursing through her from the moment she found her mom this morning had finally worn off and left her completely drained.

When she pulled into the driveway, Lauren and Blake came out to help her carry in the lunch provisions. She found Mia sitting on Helen's bed, chatting with her. Izzy walked into the room, smiled at her mom, and put a hand on her daughter's shoulder. "How are you feeling, Mom?"

"Happy to be home and feeling rather foolish for causing all the fuss."

"We're all glad it wasn't serious. Ellie's made some soup, if you'd like some, or I picked up a bunch of stuff from the deli and can make you a plate?"

"Soup sounds wonderful. Then, I think I'll have a nap."

Izzy nodded, and turned toward Mia. "How have you been? I love your outfit." Izzy admired the pretty floral kimono in burgundy Mia wore over jeans and a pink shirt, where her baby bump was finally visible.

She shrugged. "Okay, I guess. Busy with school." She had a sad expression on her face, begging to be asked what was wrong, but Izzy didn't feel like going there. She was tired and hungry.

"I want to invite you for Christmas. I'm looking forward to having it at my new home and hope you'll come." She turned toward her mom and added, "With Lauren hosting Christmas this year, I'm sure you and dad will want to be there for Beanie, but you're also welcome."

Helen smiled, and said, "Oh, yes. We're looking forward to Christmas at Lauren's, but would love to see your house.

We're talking about a summer trip to the island to visit you and Blake."

"Oh, that would be great. Dad could golf and we could find some things to do." Izzy smiled and raised her brows at Mia. "What do you think about Christmas?"

"I had planned to spend it at Dad's." She shrugged. "Now, who knows?"

"Well, I'd love to have you. Think about it, okay?"

Mia didn't answer her, and turned toward Helen. "I'll bring your soup, Grandma," she said, and followed Izzy out of the bedroom.

The kitchen was bustling with activity, and everyone was filling their plates. Izzy found a tray and set it on the counter while Mia ladled the soup into a bowl. She added a fresh pumpkin cookie and a few napkins to the tray, and let Mia take over the delivery, knowing how much she loved her grandma. Being her first grandchild, they had always shared a special bond.

Izzy's mind was foggy, and she felt like she wasn't really there, watching all the action from the sidelines. Her loud, boisterous family laughed and talked over each other, while they ate and celebrated the return of their matriarch. She took a plate and filled it, poured herself a cup of tea, and quietly left to make her way to her bedroom.

She devoured her lunch, sipped her tea, and collapsed on the bed, shuddering as the image of her mom lying on the kitchen floor flashed in her mind. She took a deep breath, blew it out, and closed her eyes.

SHE WOKE TO a soft tap on her shoulder. Ellie smiled down at her. "Are you feeling okay, Izzy? We're about to have dinner, so I wanted to check on you. It's almost eight o'clock."

Izzy blinked several times, realizing it was dark outside. "I'm sorry. I was so tired, and meant to take a short nap."

Ellie shook her head. "Not to worry. Your mom is going to join us in the dining room. She and your dad said they want to tell everyone something. She seems better after resting this afternoon."

Izzy sat on the edge of the bed. "I'll be right there."

Ellie nodded. "Mia's been dropping some pretty strong hints that she could come and stay here and keep an eye on Helen. She told everyone that John, well actually it was Barbie, told her she couldn't move in with them, so she thinks moving back here with Grandma and Grandpa is the perfect solution."

Izzy rolled her eyes. "She already tried it, and I shot it down. Mom and Dad don't need her problems or one more thing to worry about right now." She checked the mirror and unearthed a brush, trying to perk up the side of her hair that was flat.

She finally gave up, found a hair tie in her bag and pulled it into a ponytail. She gathered her plate and mug, and followed Ellie into the kitchen, where the smell of garlic and her mom's marinara sauce greeted her.

Blake was putting the garlic bread in a basket, and smiled when he saw Ellie, darting toward her and kissing her. "Thank you for making dinner for us." He handed Izzy the basket. "I'll carry the lasagna."

Ellie followed with a huge salad and added it to the table. Gene was in his usual spot at the head of the table, with Helen next to him, holding onto his hand.

Blake set the bubbling pan of lasagna on the trivets in the middle of the sturdy wooden table, where the family had enjoyed thousands of meals, and took a seat next to his mom. He raised his glass of wine and said, "To Ellie, for pitching in and making sure we had this delicious meal tonight." He glanced toward his mom and added, "And to Mom. We're so thankful you're home with us and we all love you so very much."

Tears leaked down Helen's face as she nodded and clinked her glass with Blake's. "Thank you so much. I'm so sorry I caused such a commotion today. I'm ...overwhelmed."

Gene gripped her hand tighter and kissed her forehead. "Your mom and I have something we want, we need, to tell you. It has to do with Shannon. We know she's done some things nobody understands and she's caused so many hard feelings in the family. While we don't excuse them, we think it's time you all know something that may or may not make a difference in how you judge her."

He looked at his wife who bobbed her head.

Gene cleared his throat. "Blake, you've always said you thought the hospital messed up and sent us home with the wrong baby, because Shannon is so different, so difficult at times, and has caused so much turmoil. As much as we know you were joking, the truth of the matter is, Shannon is not our biological daughter."

There were collective gasps around the table, and Izzy's brow furrowed as she tried to remember the circumstances surrounding Shannon's birth. She had been ten years old and didn't really remember much, except her mom bringing home a newborn baby all bundled up in a pink blanket and telling her she had a new sister.

Her mom had four other children, and most of Izzy's childhood memories were of her mom being pregnant or juggling babies and toddlers. She was five when Esther had been born and from then on, a new sibling arrived every couple of years. Shannon's birth had been between Lauren's and Blake's, and despite her trying to remember anything out of the ordinary, nothing came to Izzy's mind.

Gene took a sip of wine. "Your mom had a close friend, Charlotte. She found herself in trouble, and in those days, it wasn't acceptable to be a single mother. Your mother and I discussed it and decided to take Shannon, as our own daughter, and raise her with our other children. We used a lawyer in the city to handle the adoption. At the time, your mom was between pregnancies and hadn't ever lost all her baby weight, so we made out like she was pregnant again. She spent most of her time at home, so it was easy for everyone to believe the fabrication. We made Charlotte a promise, and we never told another soul, until now."

Izzy stared at her parents in disbelief. Shannon's middle name was Charlotte, and when she really studied her sisters, Shannon didn't resemble them in any significant ways. She couldn't believe her parents had kept such a secret for over forty years. "So, Shannon doesn't know this?"

Gene shook his head. "We never wanted her to feel different or out of place."

"No, she accomplished that one all on her own." Blake shook his head. "Sorry, I'm surprised, but then again, not really. She is so different from all of us."

Helen spoke in a soft voice. "We didn't tell you this to excuse what Shannon's done, but with the hope you might understand more about her and why we have seemed reluctant to hold her to the same standards as the rest of you."

Blake began passing the serving dishes and cut up the lasagna, dishing it onto plates. Unlike their usually loud and disorderly meals with lots of conversations, the sound of cutlery against plates was the only noise to be heard.

Izzy took another swallow of wine, and asked, "What happened to Charlotte, Mom?"

Helen's eyes grew sadder. "She died soon after Blake was born. She came to visit a few times a year. She had moved to Idaho, and died there in a car crash when Shannon was two."

"I'm not sure Shannon needs to hear this news while she's, uh, away. She'll need some support to process all of it. She won't be in a good position to handle it in jail." Izzy met her mother's eyes and noticed them fill with fresh tears. "I'm sorry to bring it up, but I don't want anyone to slip and say anything to her. I know you'll all be visiting with her via the video system."

"You're right, Izzy," said Gene. "We had no intention of ever telling her or any of you. We didn't want her to feel different or for any of you to think of her as anything less than your sister. We know you resent her, and we understand why. Believe me, we've gone the rounds over how to deal with her and we've obviously failed. We probably made far too many allowances for her long ago, and we shouldn't have. For all our efforts to make her feel accepted, like one of you, we've accomplished almost the opposite."

As they ate, the conversation drifted to Charlotte and her mannerisms. Someone asked if they knew who Shannon's biological father had been, but Charlotte had never said. She had been living in Spokane at the time of the pregnancy, and all Helen knew was Charlotte had had an affair with a married man. She would never divulge his name and didn't list a father on the birth certificate or legal papers. She said she'd never told the man about the pregnancy, and had moved to Seattle for the duration and the birth of her baby.

Charlotte had wanted her little girl to be called Shannon, which also explained the lack of any Griffin family history associated with her name. All the other sisters were named for relatives, but there had been no such story for the choice of Shannon's name. There were no Shannon's or Charlotte's in their lineage.

As Izzy thought back to all the memories of her past, she realized now, why her parents had been so distraught when everyone had insisted Shannon be left out of the trust set up to manage the business and finances. None of the siblings wanted to have her associated with the business, citing her demonstrated lack of judgement, lack of interest in the success of the business, and the fear her activities could adversely impact it by marring their reputation or leaving them liable for monetary damages.

Now, Izzy was sure she had succeeded in breaking their parents' hearts as she explained the legalese and business sense it made to simply compensate Shannon, but leave her out of all the official corporate paperwork and trust documents. Everything they had strived to do, to make Shannon a part of the family, to treat her as an equal, had been for naught.

Her heart ached, knowing their parents had lived with this secret for so long, and realizing their best intentions had led to such a dysfunctional situation. Now, they'd have to face telling Shannon the truth, but thankfully, not for a few months. Perhaps while Shannon was away, the rest of them could come to terms with the news and approach her with more grace and understanding.

Izzy turned her attention to Mia, who had been quiet throughout the dinner conversation, her pale face still looking shocked at the revelation.

They finished dinner in relative silence. Gene helped Helen up from her chair, and said they were going to turn in early and would see everyone in the morning. They hugged each of their children, and Izzy gave her mom an extra tight squeeze as she whispered, "Love you, Mom," in her ear.

Maybe this news, as disturbing as it was, would provide an opportunity for her to have a calm conversation with Mia. A real conversation about her future and her plans. Izzy began to clear the table and set about doing the dishes, giving Ellie a much-deserved break from her kitchen duties. She tapped Mia on the shoulder. "How about helping me with the dishes?"

Before she could answer, Lauren started stacking plates, and said, "Oh, I'll help. It's late and I'm sure Mia is beat."

Mia hugged her aunt, and then surprised Izzy by putting an arm around her shoulder. She said she would see them in the morning, filled a glass with water, and toddled off to her bedroom.

Izzy watched her go, hoping the gap between her and Mia had inched a bit closer.

Chapter 23

IZZY HAD GONE to her room early, settled into bed, called Colin, and told him about the court case and her mom's hospitalization, and shared her disappointment in not being able to talk much with Mia. Having not had time to fully process the impact of the secret her parents had divulged, she chose not to share it. Instead, they chatted about the dogs, and that Sam and Jeff had invited him and Jethro to join them for Thanksgiving dinner after he finished work at the clubhouse.

Talking to him, hearing his calm voice, his reassurance, not to mention his Scottish accent that never failed to make her knees weak, listening to him laugh about the dogs, calmed Izzy and by the time she disconnected, she was feeling better. It had been far too many years since she had experienced the comfort of having someone to chat with about her day, someone to share some of her burdens with, someone who could make her laugh and melt away the tension.

The conversation with him made for a peaceful night, and Thanksgiving morning welcomed Izzy with the tempting aroma of pies baking. Feeling rested, she climbed out of bed, wrapped herself in her soft hooded cardigan, and made her way to the kitchen. She found Ellie sipping coffee, keeping an eye on her pies. Izzy washed her hands and got busy cutting up celery and onions for the stuffing.

Soon Esther arrived. Blake went out to the extra refrigerator and carried the huge turkey into the kitchen, where Esther got to work, slathering it with butter and herbs before letting him put it in the roaster. Ellie fixed a breakfast tray to take to Gene and Helen, so they could lounge and take their time.

As the siblings prepped for the holiday meal, and Lauren and Sabina showed up, they talked quietly, still reeling from the news of Shannon's birth mother and the forty-year old secret. None of them had had an inkling that Shannon's arrival was anything but legitimate. They had a long conversation about the age-old nurture versus nature argument, and wondered what Charlotte had really been like. Maybe more of a rebel than their mother suspected.

Shannon would be eligible for video visitation starting on Monday, and Lauren and Esther planned to be on hand to help their parents and offer their emotional support, since none of them could predict how Shannon would respond.

Izzy suggested Esther and Lauren connect with Shannon first and explain about their mother's hospital trip and the need for her to keep her blood pressure down, hoping their sister would curb her outbursts and her tendency to blame everyone but herself. Her mom, especially, didn't need to be goaded into accepting the guilt for Shannon's situation.

Izzy had no intention of visiting Shannon, unless she requested it. As her attorney, she had a right to speak with her sister without it counting against her family visits, but she wasn't going to waste her time arguing. She had endured her fill of Shannon's blame games. There was nothing more she could do at this point. Shannon would just have to suck it up and serve her time.

Izzy knew she was still reacting angrily toward Shannon, though she wasn't without sympathy for her sister. She just hoped this ordeal would help Shannon change her ways and give her life some direction. Their parents would need help when they told Shannon about her biological mother, and

Izzy agreed with her siblings that they should all be together when that happened.

Once they had the side dishes done, Izzy went to take a shower and get ready for the day. When she emerged, her dad had the football game on, and her brother and brothers-in-law had arrived and were camped out around the television, munching on snacks.

She found Mia sitting in the sunroom, holding a sleeping baby Beanie. Everyone else was in the kitchen, visiting and getting the table set for the special meal, with Helen supervising from a chair. Izzy sat in the chair next to Mia's, and smiled at her beautiful niece. "She's such a sweet girl, isn't she?"

Mia nodded, and Izzy saw the streaks of tears on her cheeks. "What's wrong?"

She shrugged. "I don't know if I can do this. I'm not sure. I had it all figured out that I would move in with Dad and I wouldn't be alone."

"You don't have to be alone. You can come to my house."

"I don't want to move to the island. I want to live in a real city. You basically ruined everything when you sold our house. I could have lived here, but there's no way I'm living in that place. There is nothing there."

"Coming to stay while you have the baby doesn't mean that's where you have to stay forever. If you want to live in Seattle, those are choices you'll have to make, depending on what's best for you and the baby. I can help you look for quality childcare. As you'll learn, when you're a mother, you rarely get everything you want and end up doing what you think is best for your child. I don't want to see you quit school and throw away such a great future."

"You don't even care if I'm happy." Mia handed Izzy the baby, and stormed out of the room.

Izzy jiggled Beanie and whispered, "I hope you grow up to love your mommy and are always kind to her, sweet girl."

IZZY TRIED, WITHOUT success to engage Mia in conversation after dinner on Thursday and again on Friday. Mia ignored her, even going so far as to get up and change seats so she was further away from her mother and initiated a conversation with someone else. It hurt Izzy, but she tried not to let it bother her and chalked it up to Mia blaming her again for John's shortcomings and everything else that was wrong with her life. She suggested lunch at one of Mia's favorite restaurants, but even that didn't get her to budge.

Somehow, Izzy made it through the weekend, with Mia steering clear of her and making herself scarce whenever she was in the vicinity. Izzy tried to push the pain she felt at not having a conversation with Mia to the side, and concentrated on enjoying the time she had with her parents and siblings. She took a ride to Yakima with her dad when he wanted to check on something at the winery, and did some Christmas shopping at some of her favorite stores downtown and at the mall. She even bought some baby clothes, taking care to pick neutral colors since Mia didn't yet know the gender.

She even found a beautiful dress at one of the boutiques downtown, for the upcoming winery celebration. She was drawn to the simple silk sheath, the color of merlot, with a gauzy jacket, embellished with beads and subtle sequins that gave it the perfect amount of pizzazz. When she tried it on, she knew it was the one.

The family chatted about the anniversary celebration at the winery, marking fifty years of business. Blake and Ellie were handling most of the arrangements, and the whole family would be there to honor Gene and Helen, their vision, and the successful business they had built. In addition to the public anniversary party, they planned a private dinner for a few select friends and guests the night before.

Ellie and Blake had honed their skills in event planning, and were talking about the decorations and menu options with Helen for much of Saturday. Izzy had already marked her calendar and told Cliff she'd be out of town for the event. She would come over with Blake and Ellie early to help with all the preparations leading up to the party.

They already had tickets reserved for their platinum wine club members, and Ellie had activated the ticket sales to the public and had been posting on social media. Like other years, it was sure to sell out. By the end of the weekend, the catering had been finalized, and Helen had approved of all of Ellie's suggestions.

On Sunday morning, Lauren and Ken took Mia to the airport, and Izzy breathed a sigh of relief. She and Ellie spent the day preparing some meals to put in the freezer for Gene and Helen. After dinner, Izzy made sure her mother's follow up doctor appointment was on the calendar, and reminded her to stop by and get her blood pressure checked each week.

Her mom and dad thanked her again for helping Shannon, and reassured her they understood it wasn't her lack of skills that had landed Shannon in jail. As Izzy listened to them talk about her sister, she felt such sorrow. "It's not your fault, either. Shannon's behavior and actions are her own doing. I'm hoping after spending some time in there, where she truly has no freedom, she'll be ready to make some positive changes." Helen and Gene both nodded their heads. "Let me know how the visit goes tomorrow," Izzy continued. "And if she acts inappropriately or starts to upset you, I hope you will tell her. If she is unkind, disconnect the call." Izzy took a sip from the mug of tea she was holding.

Her mother patted her hand. "Don't worry about us, dear. You have enough without that. I truly hope things are better between you and Mia soon. Izzy, your dad and I talked about it and we could let her stay here, if it will help."

Izzy shook her head. "I don't think it's a good idea. I appreciate your willingness, but you don't need any more upheaval. She can stay with me or make other arrangements."

She hugged them both goodnight, thanking them for the weekend, and telling them how much she loved them before turning in early. They planned to get on the road by four o'clock in the morning. "Don't get up tomorrow to see us off. We'll be quiet and slip out. We'll call you from the ferry landing."

BLAKE DROVE THEM through the dark of morning, skirting around the worst of the traffic and getting them to Anacortes in time to catch the last ferry of the morning. Izzy checked in with her mom to let her know they had made it and were safe and sound. Not knowing what the traffic would be, they hadn't dared stop for fear of missing the sailing, so were starving when they got on board. After surveying the offerings in the snack bar, they opted to tough it out and have breakfast when they arrived.

As soon as they sat down at a table, Izzy's phone chimed. Jeff messaged letting her know he had Sunny with him at the hardware store and she could stop by and pick her up when her ferry arrived. The thought of seeing her sweet girl lightened her heart.

She texted a reply, and her phone chimed again. This time it was Colin asking her to dinner. He suggested he pick up something and bring it to her house, guessing she would be tired and want to relax. She had been looking forward to getting home, but now she couldn't wait. She tapped in a reply, and added a heart to her message.

She smiled as she tucked her phone back into her purse. These twinges of excitement she felt were new and a welcome change from the drudgery of her normal routine. Without Sunny and Colin, the only things on her mind would have been Mia and Shannon. Blake and Ellie arrived with coffees, and while they sipped, the three of them chatted about Helen and how relieved they were to know her health condition wasn't serious.

"I'm glad we have some time to deal with the news of Shannon's adoption before they tell her. I think it might tip her over the edge," said Blake. "She has such dramatic reactions to the most mundane issues, I can only imagine what she'll do. I'm sure it will involve lashing out at Mom and Dad, and I'm not sure they can handle it."

Izzy nodded and added, "I've decided not to think about it until after the holidays. Dealing with Mia these next few months is probably about all the chaos I can manage. She wasn't too keen on the idea of coming for Christmas and had planned to spend it with John. Hopefully, for Mia's sake, he'll invite her." Her voice caught and she took another sip from her cup.

Blake reached across the table and put his hand on her arm. "She can always go to Lauren's, if she doesn't end up going to John's. You've invited her, Izz. It's up to her now. You can't fix everything."

Tears stung her eyes. "I know. I'm so tired of feeling like a failure, and each time I see her, it's like she delights in twisting me in knots. I love her, but sometimes I can't stand being around her." She dabbed at her eyes. "I'm looking forward to getting home."

Ellie's brows rose. "Speaking of home, Colin sure seems like a nice guy. He seems quite smitten with you."

Izzy felt the heat rise in her cheeks. "Do you think?" She fiddled with the napkin under her cup. "It's been so long since

I've dated or even had an interest in anyone, but I have to admit, I'm looking forward to seeing him." She went on to tell them he was bringing dinner tonight.

Blake grinned. "You've been the one to take care of everyone and everything for so long, Izz. I think Colin is great and you deserve to have some happiness in your life, and someone to look after you for a change."

Izzy leaned across the table and kissed him on the cheek, touched by his heartfelt words. She let them sink in as the ferry pulled into the harbor, and her pulse quickened at the thought of seeing Colin in a few hours.

Chapter 24

THE WEEKS LEADING up to Christmas were busy. Izzy was working extra, so she could take time off during the holidays. Izzy and Colin attended the annual music festival at the community theatre, went to a Christmas party at Max and Linda's, and enjoyed their first ever tree lighting in the park adjacent to the harbor, followed by a lovely group dinner with everyone.

The whole town was decked out in festive lights and decorations. Izzy made a point of chatting with her parents at least once a week, and they reported Shannon was still bitter about being in jail, but had thanked them for taking the time to visit via video.

Helen had been feeling better, and her doctor had recommended she stick with a higher dose of her medication to keep her blood pressure in check. She and Gene were busy getting ready for Christmas and had a few of the staff from the winery come and put up all their lights and decorations, which Helen loved.

All of Izzy's weekly calls to Mia had gone unanswered, but she'd tried texting her again that morning. Colin's son would be arriving the next weekend, and Izzy still hoped Mia would come to the island for Christmas, since her finals were done and she would be on a break until early January. As she was about to call it a day and go downstairs, her cell phone vibrated against the top of her desk. Mia had texted her reply about Izzy's invitation for Christmas, saying her dad had sent her a ticket to spend it with him.

Of course, he had. He probably felt guilty about Barbie spilling the beans, and was trying to placate Mia. Izzy could already see a new car in Mia's future. Her dad gave her a car from one of his dealerships to drive on a regular basis, but whenever he did something hurtful or shameful, he chose to fix it by buying expensive gifts. Once the baby arrived, Mia would need a more practical vehicle than the sporty little car she had been driving, anyway.

Although Mia had made it clear she had no interest in staying on the island with the baby, Izzy opted to prepare the room anyway, and Nate had delivered Emma's old crib to the house, helping to set it up in the guest room upstairs. Izzy didn't see that Mia had many options when it came to a place to recuperate and have some help. It certainly wasn't going to be at John and Barbie's house.

She had been going through all the things Regi and Nate had given her, and had decorated the room with a neutral theme of bunnies and llamas, with a few fluffy sheep thrown in for good measure. Even if Mia and the baby may not spend much time there, she wanted to be ready. Thinking back to those early days when Mia had been a newborn, Izzy knew she would need help, even if Mia was too naïve, or perhaps too stubborn, to admit it.

Izzy shuddered at how chaotic her life had become. It was probably a good thing she moved before Mia's news and Shannon's mess. She would have felt guilty and irresponsible to leave in the midst of all of it. Now, with the mass of water cushioning her from it, she took solace in her house, thankful for the beautiful refuge Kate had helped her create. As if to remind her how lucky she was, Sunny scooted closer to Izzy and rested her chin on Izzy's foot.

She gazed out the window, smiling as the Christmas lights glowed in the shrubbery surrounding the patio. Like her mom, the lights and the tree were her favorite things about the season. She had paid some high school boys, who worked through the hardware store, to put up lights on the house and decorate the shrubs and bushes. She loved pulling into the driveway and seeing the house looking so festive.

She and Sunny made their way downstairs, where she stopped to admire the beautiful tree in the corner of the living room. She had been enjoying her evenings and the early mornings when the lights from the tree provided a warm glow in the house. She didn't have many gifts under it, as she had already mailed everything to her family in Richland. Mia always wanted cash, so that was easy enough to put in her account in a matter of minutes. *Ho Ho Ho.* She would have preferred to send her daughter a gift, but years ago she learned that Mia always returned whatever Izzy bought her for a refund, so she had quit taking the time to select anything special. She had sent her a care package of fruits, nuts, and cookies to cheer Mia on through final exams, but she'd never heard from her.

Izzy took her mug to the sink and filled Sunny's dinner bowl. Tonight, there was an office Christmas party to attend. She wasn't really in the mood for it, but didn't want to hurt Hazel's feelings, as she had organized the event. Thankfully, it was casual and was at the office. Izzy planned to make an appearance, but wouldn't be staying long. She and Colin had dinner plans later, and then David would be arriving tomorrow night.

She changed out of her walking clothes and into a red sweater and black pants, then added a long black vest over the top and some pretty silver jewelry. After giving Sunny a pat on the head and a cookie, she told her furry friend she'd see her soon.

She loaded a tote with a few bottles of wine to contribute to the Christmas party, and was thankful she didn't have to worry about a gift exchange. Hazel had taken care of adopting several seniors in the community and the staff had pitched in to purchase gifts, which amounted to socks, blankets, puzzles, books, and a few treats for those who could eat them. It broke Izzy's heart that they asked for so little and were so appreciative.

Izzy made the rounds, wishing everyone a Merry Christmas and nibbling on a few appetizers and delicious homemade cookies, courtesy of Hazel. The sweet receptionist, dressed in a fancy red dress and a string of pearls, along with a Christmas tree pin that lit up, beamed as the staff complimented her on the food and decorations, and asked for cookie recipes.

As she made small talk, Izzy kept her eye on the time and after a couple of hours, said her goodbyes, letting Cliff know she would be in the office next week for a few meetings and then would be taking the holidays off until the first week in January. She gave Hazel a hug and slipped her a bottle of wine to thank her for all her efforts.

She drove the few blocks to the Jade Garden, where she found Colin already at a table waiting. He greeted her with a kiss on the cheek and helped her with her coat, letting her slide into the booth seat before he joined her.

"How was the party?" he asked, pouring her a cup of tea.

"It was nice and Hazel was thrilled." She stole a glance at the menu. "Have you heard from David?"

He checked his watch. "He'll be getting to the airport soon, and will be here in under twenty-four hours." He grinned, reminding her of an excited young boy, anxious for Christmas. They placed their orders and chatted about David while they waited.

Colin was picking David up at the airport in Friday Harbor. After the long flight from Edinburgh to Seattle, he didn't want his son having to make the drive up to Anacortes, and had paid for him to take a small plane, using a service that flew to the island airport and marina. David was sure to be exhausted after all the travel, and Colin was organizing takeout from The Bistro for them at home.

Colin rested his fingers atop her hand. "I thought I'd let him settle in, but if he's up to it, how about we get together on Sunday?"

The waiter delivered their plates, and the inviting spicy smell from her garlic chicken made Izzy's mouth water. "That sounds great. He's okay with coming to my house for Christmas Eve dinner?"

Colin nodded as he heaped rice onto his plate. "He's excited to meet you."

Izzy sighed. "I haven't mentioned you to Mia, well to anyone really. With all the uproar at Thanksgiving, it didn't seem like the right time. I was hoping to introduce you if she came for Christmas, but I finally received a text and she's going to John's." She felt her heart pounding in her throat thinking about introducing Colin to Mia and the carnage that was sure to follow. She wasn't exactly sure what she and Colin had, but the slight flutters in her stomach each time she saw him or heard his voice on the phone were leading her to understand it was more than friendship.

Relationships, dating, it had all changed since Izzy was young. It seemed more black and white back then. When she thought back to those early days with John, they were full of fun and action, not to mention the hormones surging through both of them. Then, she had been swept away and selfish, with no concerns other than her own desires. It had been natural to go steady with John, to call him her boyfriend. Young love was different. Actually, she wasn't sure if it had really been love but when you're young you believe it is, you trust it, you think it will last forever.

Now, things were murkier. It wasn't as simple or easy to say Colin was her boyfriend. *Boyfriend.* The word alone made her cringe. She was too old to have a boyfriend. She had girlfriends, who were friends who happen to be female, so why couldn't she have boyfriends, as in male friends? That concept had always mystified her.

Izzy had always been of the mindset men and women could be friends and have a platonic relationship. She had many friends and colleagues who were men, and had only suffered one bad experience when a fellow attorney had come onto her. She made it clear she wasn't interested and that had been the end of it. She had regularly met with male friends for lunch and coffee, to discuss career decisions, cases, and share advice. She actually had more male friends than female friends, but they were all related to her work.

What she felt for Colin was different. She couldn't remember a time when a male friend or colleague's voice had made her palms sweaty or heart pound. She wasn't sure how to navigate these new feelings and all it would mean if she actually labeled them. Was Colin her beau, her companion, or the dreaded life partner? She hated that phrase more than boyfriend.

If things did get more serious with Colin, her parents would be thrilled, as would her sisters. Well, maybe not Shannon, but that was a whole other story. As she focused on the flickering candle on their table, she recalled their Friday night dinner last week. She had finally shared the secret of Shannon's parentage with Colin and the worry it brought her when she anticipated them telling Shannon.

Despite only knowing Colin for a few months, Izzy felt like she had known him forever. She had debated about disclosing one more weird family secret involving Shannon, but also longed to have someone to talk to about it. She only hoped he wouldn't run for the hills when he learned how dysfunctional her family was. The sad thing was, she never thought of her family as anything but normal, except for

Shannon's activities, which were not widely known, and outside of some legal work, didn't impact Izzy's daily life. Her relationship with Mia bothered her much more than Shannon, but saying it aloud to someone else, it all had sounded worse.

Although shocked at the news, Colin had been calm and supportive. He had cringed and told her he didn't envy her parents having to break that news to her. He couldn't imagine it going smoothly. Sincerity had shown in his kind eyes, as he brewed another pot of tea and let her ramble late into the night.

He talked about a friend of his, Graham and his wife, who had adopted a baby and welcomed her into their family with their other two children. Despite what he described as them treating the child like their other kids and being raised in what he considered an ordinary family, Graham and his wife struggled with the girl throughout her childhood. She suffered from behavioral issues and ended up getting in trouble for some criminal acts, even spending some time in jail. He said it had broken his friend, who didn't understand what they had done wrong.

They spent hours talking about the difficulties of parenting and those challenges being compounded for adoptive parents. The decision of whether or not to tell the child would be heart wrenching, and when to share that information had to weigh heavily on the parents too. Izzy understood, especially given the time period when her parents adopted Shannon. They would have been inclined to keep it quiet, but she thought they would have told her when she was older, even in her twenties.

With Shannon tending to be volatile, Izzy was sure that played into their decision and after not saying anything for so long, it would have been easier to never tell. She imagined how difficult it must have been for her parents to keep quiet during the reorganization of the business and the development of the trust. That would have been an opportune time to speak up, but she understood the fear of Shannon's reaction held them back and kept them silent.

Her parents feared they risked losing Shannon forever, once she learned of the adoption and the secrecy. Izzy hoped it didn't happen and suspected her parents wouldn't survive such a strife. Thinking about parents losing children brought her thoughts back to Mia.

Her family would love Colin and be happy for Izzy, but Mia would be the one to throw a wrench into it all. After the divorce, Izzy had dated a handful of times, and had a vivid memory of Mia, who had stopped by unexpectedly and found Izzy leaving for dinner with a man, becoming enraged. It had caused an even deeper fracture in their already fragile relationship.

Colin reached across the table and put his hand on her arm, dragging her from her thoughts. "Don't stress about it. I want you to meet David because it will be your only opportunity until next year. I've been chatting about you so much, he's anxious to get the chance to meet you."

The compassion in his eyes and the way he rubbed his thumb against the back of her hand, conveyed he sensed Izzy's trepidation. She nodded and took a sip of water. "My family will adore you. Mia is my only concern. She has a way of extinguishing the slightest glimmer of happiness I might be experiencing." She sighed and pushed the rice around on her plate. "It's not that I care that much about what she thinks. Over all these years, I've come to understand she likes to fight with me. It's just exhausting."

"I wonder if it might change, with her being unhappy about the situation with her dad now." Colin raised his brows at Izzy.

"Time will tell. John always comes out on top in these things. She's already decided it's my fault she can't move to

John's. I sold the house, so that took away an option for her to stay there. She always has a way of bending reality to make me the problem."

He moved his hand over hers. "I don't want to be the cause of a problem for you. That's the last thing I'm looking to do."

Izzy grinned and turned her hand to hold his. "Trust me, you're not the problem. In fact, our... friendship has made me the happiest I've been in such a long time. Since my divorce, I haven't had anything close to a lasting relationship, and to be honest, barely even a handful of dates."

"I feel the same way," he said leaning toward her and kissing her. "I'm not sure what we have either, but I know the best part of my day is seeing you. When we're apart, I'm counting the hours until I see you again. In Scotland, I would say you're my jo."

She loved the feel of his soft lips against hers, gentle and reassuring. "Well, my middle name is actually Josephine, but I don't think that's what you mean. What is jo?"

He grinned. "It's a variant of joy, and is the equivalent of sweetheart or darling. It's gender neutral."

She chuckled. "I was thinking of how to introduce you to my family. Mi amor was all I could think of that sounded less fussy than all the American words. I like the idea of jo meaning joy."

"You're definitely my jo. This whole dating thing is much more complicated at our age, isn't it? You're going to love David, and he has been hoping I would find a lovely woman for years, so he'll be thrilled to spend time with you."

"I'm looking forward to meeting him and agree about things being a bit tricky." She smiled and added, "Actually, in some respects it's easier at our age. I'm more confident now, I'm not beholden to anyone's expectations or moods. I can simply take delight in the happiness we bring each other and enjoy spending time with you. The whole idea of building a life together, having a family, starting a career...it's all done, so there is nothing but us."

His grin deepened. "I like that analysis. Like you, I think there are some wonderful things about finding each other at our age. We're free to relax and enjoy each other's company without having to have a clear plan for our future hanging over our heads. Honestly, I never imagined myself getting married again, because of the first disaster. I think nowadays it's much more accepted to be in a relationship, even a long-term one, without the pressure of marriage."

Izzy nodded. "Oh, yes. I'm not sure anyone even notices. Look at Kate and Spence. Honestly, I don't give it a thought. They're so perfect together and everyone can sense the love and adoration they have for each other. I thought they were married until I found out they weren't."

"I like the idea of no pressure and we enjoy what we have, learn about each other, make each other happy, and not worry about what anybody thinks, or anyone's expectations except our own. For me, meeting you was a fantastic surprise and at the moment, I see no reason why we can't spend all our remaining days enjoying life and each other, but I'm also not so naïve that I don't realize the future holds lots of unknowns. I say we live in the present and be thankful for what we have, whether it is to be for a short time or forever." He brought her hand to his lips and kissed her palm.

She held his gorgeous eyes, sparkling with a hint of mischief, and realized how lucky she was to have discovered this new chapter of her life.

Chapter 25

ALONG WITH ENJOYING the holidays with Colin, Izzy fell in love with David. He was much like Colin: tall, handsome, with a wonderful sense of humor, and an appealing accent. He and Colin had a close relationship, sharing inside jokes and grins, catching up on stories and David's life.

Izzy hosted Christmas Eve dinner and Christmas brunch, enjoying cooking alongside of Ellie. She was so thankful to have Ellie and Blake there, and sharing the holiday with them, Colin, and David, along with Spence, Kate, and Mitch, made for a relaxing and fun time. Mitch and David were of similar age and got along well, both lamenting their busy jobs and missing time with their family.

Izzy, Blake, and Ellie gathered around her office computer to video chat with everyone at Lauren's house on Christmas Day. Their mom and dad looked great and were enjoying all the fun and traditions with baby Sabina. Izzy didn't mention Shannon and neither did anyone else. It pained her parents to know Shannon was spending Christmas in jail, but yammering on about it wouldn't do anyone any good. It warmed her heart to see them both relaxed and enjoying themselves.

She tried to call Mia several times, but it always went to voicemail. She left her a message and also texted her to wish her a Merry Christmas and ask how she was feeling. Texting was not her forte, and Izzy disliked having to carry on a conversation via a tiny keyboard, but wanted to make sure Mia knew she was thinking about her.

She even braved texting Mia a couple of photos of the spare bedroom she had decorated with the crib and all the cute animal motif items she had added. The rooms upstairs were both large, and by arranging the bed on a different wall, it left plenty of room for a baby nursery in half of the space. She loved the miniature fuzzy llama that was the Camelids answer to the rocking horse and the beautiful rocking chair Kate had found.

As much as Izzy dreaded having Mia live with her, she wanted her daughter to know she had a place to stay, and wanted her to feel welcome. Being a new mom was hard enough, and being a new mom on her own was not something she wanted for Mia.

She was sure Mia would have something negative to say about the room or the décor, but she vowed to let it roll off of her. She could take whatever insult was hurled at her, but she could never forgive herself if she didn't help Mia and the baby. If Mia rejected her, it wouldn't be the first time and sadly, she knew it wouldn't be the last. Despite how her daughter treated her, Izzy wasn't going to let it keep her from doing what was right and offering her help.

Jethro and Sunny were getting used to spending their days together and were always next to each other, whether outside playing or inside huddled together in a mass of fur. They stuck so close, they sometimes looked like one giant dog sprawled on the floor. Jethro stayed at Izzy's when David and Colin went golfing and during the fishing trip Jeff and Nate had organized.

Colin hosted dinner at his house several nights and always included Izzy. They played board games, watched movies, ate way too much, and visited. It was the perfect way to spend the holidays. While Izzy enjoyed watching Colin and David and their easy way with each other, it also made the sad reality of her broken relationship with Mia painfully clear.

By the time New Year's Eve rolled around, she still hadn't heard from Mia. She had finally broken down and texted John to make sure Mia was okay and he let her know she was and they were busy with parties and activities. While she was glad Mia wasn't suffering through a horrible holiday or in an emergency room somewhere, she winced at the callous way her daughter could ignore her and let her think the worst.

The only silver lining to her unanswered texts was that Mia hadn't belittled her efforts to decorate the nursery. Maybe she was reconsidering her quick dismissal of Izzy's offer. After spending almost three weeks with Barbie, Izzy might be looking more appealing. The thought made Izzy chuckle, and Jethro and Sunny both raised their heads to look at her.

Colin and David were squeezing in another round of golf and then they would all be attending the huge New Year's Eve bash at the firehouse, with the friends Izzy had come to think of as family. She dug around in her closet and chose a fancy pair of pants in a foil printed medallion pattern, and paired them with a black sweater with metallic threads and a shimmery scarf in black and silver.

Being a volunteer fireman, Jeff had the inside scoop, and had promised to reserve enough tables to make sure they could all sit near each other.

When she opened the door to Colin, who had arrived with David to pick her up, her breath caught in her throat. He was wearing jeans and a jacket that looked like it had been tailored for him. The shirt, an almost iridescent material the same brilliant color of his eyes, made her heartbeat accelerate.

He took a step back, and said, "Wow, you look gorgeous." He leaned in and kissed her, his thumb gliding under her jaw and down her neck. His touch sent tingles down her spine.

"I could say the same about you. I love your shirt."

Jethro and Sunny nosed their way next to Izzy, opening the door wider. He bent down and gave them both several scratches and pets, and then told them to go lay down. He helped Izzy into her beautiful faux fur-trimmed wrap, a rich merlot color, that he had given her for Christmas, and took her arm in his.

They ended up parking several blocks away, but the walk amid the beautiful Christmas lights decorating the storefronts and wrapped in the branches of the trees made for a magical stroll.

They walked inside the firehouse, which had been transformed with twinkly lights and decorations and found their table, where they took chairs next to Kate and Spence. Jeff's favorite local band was playing and delivered a mixture of country, rock, oldies, and even a bit of jazz. Between Mitch and David, they made sure the women at their two tables never missed a dance.

Izzy had grown up dancing at family events and winery dinners and could hold her own when it came to traditional dancing, but David was a talented dancer. He could dance to anything, fast, slow, and anything in between. While she was trying to keep up with him and the upbeat country rhythm of "You Look Good", he told her how happy he was his dad had met her. "I've been hoping he would meet someone special who could make him smile again."

Izzy chuckled. "Well, I think you're responsible for the perpetual grin on his face. He adores you and was so excited for your visit. But I appreciate you saying such nice things. He is a wonderful man, friend, neighbor, and as he taught me, jo."

David laughed as he twirled her. "You are definitely his jo. I've never seen him so relaxed and content. With me being so far away, I worry about him. Always imagining him working nonstop and alone, like all the other times I've visited him. The twinkle in his eyes, the new happiness in him, it's all due to you. You're good for him, so please don't break his heart."

Izzy swallowed the lump in her throat. She inched closer to David and hugged him tightly against her, whispering in his ear. "Never. He is lucky to have such a lovely young man for a son."

Tears stung her eyes as she finished the dance, wishing with all her heart Mia cared for her as much as David did his father.

The next few dances were slow ones, and Izzy savored every moment wrapped in Colin's arms as they swayed to "She's Everything" and "My Best Friend". She closed her eyes, let the scent of Colin wash over her as she rested against his cheek, listening intently, perhaps for the first time, to the lyrics of both of the songs that spoke of finding love.

Years ago, fresh from her divorce and feeling lonely, she had longed to find love, but disheartened and a bit fearful, she tossed out the hope of a risky dream, instead choosing safer options and throwing herself into her career and the family business. Now, for the first time, something stirred deep inside her, something that surprised her, something she had thought died long ago.

She didn't know how long the two of them had been on the dance floor without any music, still clinging to each other, but the loud voice of the emcee broke the magic as he urged them all outside before midnight.

Colin helped her with her wrap and they followed the group outside where they had a view of the harbor and watched the fireworks light up the dark sky. Izzy had never seen anything more beautiful, and as the countdown began, her eyes widened as the heavens lit up with a roar of magnificent explosions of color. As the lights faded and the last shimmers of glitter fell into the sea, her lips met his and promised the new year was going to be a magical one.

Chapter 26

AFTER A LOVELY meal at the Cliff House on David's last night, and seeing him off at the airport, the holidays were over, and a dreary January was upon the island. Izzy's life returned to normal, filled with morning walks, work, and as much time as she could spend with Colin crammed into her schedule.

As predicted, Mia texted Izzy a photo of a brand-new SUV John had given her for Christmas. It was a vivid blue, and would serve her well when she had to cart around all the items babies seemed to need. She was back at the university now and all Izzy could do was wait and see what Mia decided when the quarter ended in March.

January had always been Izzy's least favorite time of the year. After the excitement of the holidays, the cheerful lights and decorations, it was a bit of a let-down. This year was the first time she hadn't felt the melancholy that the short and dark days of winter, absent the soft glow of colored lights, brought with them.

In addition to kicking off the year with what had become their customary Friday dinner, she and Colin decided to attend some of the events at the clubhouse, where they played cards, and took in a few movie nights. Izzy enjoyed all those things, but more than anything she loved it when Colin dropped her at home, came in for a cup of tea, and they chatted for hours.

Despite being married to John and dating in high school, she felt much closer to Colin than to the man she had married. They explored all sorts of topics, from political points of view, to Colin's dual nationality status in the UK and US, to the surge in the use of technology, to their favorite books and movies.

As she listened to Colin and they shared their likes and dislikes, views and thoughts, it became clear why she and John had divorced. They had literally grown up together, married far too young, then were saddled with an unexpected baby, giving them no room to become themselves. She and John never talked about important topics, and looking back she understood he had assumed she would share his views and interests. When it became clear she didn't and wouldn't, he drifted elsewhere.

Granted, she had been more compliant at the beginning of their relationship. Once she found her own way, and began to pursue the law, developing her own sense of self and her own ideas, which often diverged from John's, things began to get rocky. He admired and frankly used her for her expertise when it came to contracts and business, but dismissed her ideas. He wasn't looking for an independent woman, one with her own thoughts, one who could be his equal.

Colin was different. He listened when she talked, expressed an interest in her thoughts, and was willing to see a different point of view. Patience and tolerance often came with age, and while Izzy wasn't naïve enough to think they would never disagree or argue, it was a refreshing change from all the years she felt stifled or dismissed by John.

She had made the decision long ago, that marriage wasn't something she planned to revisit. She didn't want a do-over. Once had been more than enough. She had come to love her independence, and suspected she would resent having to check in with anyone or make decisions based on someone else. As the years went by and she relied on herself, she vowed never to make the same mistake again and had come to value her solitude. As she spent more time with Colin, her heart softened, and while she still wasn't eager to ever be married again, she treasured the time she spent with him. The thought of having Colin in her life comforted her.

In late January, on a weekend that coincided with one of the football playoffs, Jeff posed an idea for a chili cookoff. He didn't have to twist Colin's arm to get him excited. Max, Spence, Nate, Blake, and Colin all took a crack at making chili, as the women handled side dishes and desserts.

The men and all the dogs took over Sam's house and created their masterpieces while they watched the game. The women gathered at Linda's, where they visited, drank wine, and cooked together.

Ellie coached Izzy in making fluffy dinner rolls and honey cornbread, while the mouth-watering smell of pies baking in the oven filled the house. Izzy had never had so much fun with a group of women who weren't her relatives. Focused for so long on her career, she never had time to cultivate close friendships, nor did she have the time to fritter away like she did now.

Back at Sam's house, the women found the chilis in stockpots and slow cookers, spread across the huge granite island. They were labeled only with numbers, to give the ladies, along with Sean, Jen, Lou, and Andi, who arrived later, the opportunity for a taste test to choose the winning chili.

It was an evening filled with laughter and fun. Colin edged out Jeff taking the top prize for his chili, which included Guinness beer and a bit of dark chocolate. As they gathered around the fire, eating warm apple pie, Izzy took in the smiling faces, the camaraderie, the love this group had for one another and sighed with contentment. No matter what happened with Mia or Shannon or anything else, she knew this was where she belonged. This was home.

THE DAYS SLIPPED by, and the week of the anniversary celebration at Griffin Winery was upon them. Ellie and Blake headed across the water on Sunday, determined to get a head start on the Friday night dinner and Saturday celebration. Izzy had planned to accompany them, but Colin had accepted her invitation, and had an important meeting on Wednesday morning, so they were taking an afternoon ferry.

Jeff and Sam had volunteered to take all three of their dogs, and Izzy promised a lifetime supply of wine in return. After dropping Jethro and Sunny at Jeff's, she went back home to collect her suitcase and brew a cup of tea to settle her nerves. This trip would be the first time Mia would meet Colin. She had told her parents she would be bringing him, and they were both thrilled and excited to meet him, but she wasn't so sure about Mia's reaction.

Their communications over the last two months hadn't been exactly conducive to Izzy letting her daughter know she had met a special man and would be bringing him home to meet her family. She shut her eyes and hoped Mia wouldn't cause a scene. Her parents were so excited about the party, about everyone being together, and she didn't want it ruined. She also didn't want Colin to think poorly of her family or Mia. When he was over Saturday night, she had warned him that she had no idea how Mia would react to their relationship.

He assured her, with a wink, and several kisses, that it didn't matter and he could handle it. She was confident he would, but she wanted to enjoy her time and not have to deal with an uproar. Her mother had suggested she and Colin stay in the casita next to the main house. That would make the sleeping arrangements far less complicated and give them a bit of privacy and a place to escape to, should Mia get out of hand.

Her mom had been feeling well since her spell in the hospital, and had been diligent about checking her blood pressure and her doctor visits. Their visits with Shannon had been taking place each week, and while her parents didn't say much about them, she got the feeling things were still a bit frosty between them. Shannon's release date was in about three weeks, and with it loomed the day her parents would have to disclose the secret they hid from her.

She tried to push her concern and worry from her mind, as she hoped her parents would, so they could all enjoy the company of all their many friends and business associates, who would be on hand to celebrate their milestone. She checked her watch, slipped into her coat, and drove down the road to Colin's.

He opened the door as she drove onto the driveway. He hopped into the passenger seat and greeted her with a smile, followed by a gentle kiss on the lips. "You're a sight for sore eyes."

On the ferry, they took a seat at a window table to take in the beauty of the surrounding islands on their way to Anacortes. The ferry wouldn't arrive until five o'clock, which meant they wouldn't get to her parents until sometime close to ten o'clock, which was another reason the casita made sense.

Colin offered to drive from Anacortes and suggested they have dinner at a restaurant he had found with rave reviews. She agreed, and he drove them downtown, where they found the restaurant inside a historic boutique hotel.

"This is lovely," said Izzy, as they walked inside. Over a delicious dinner, including crab cakes that rivaled Lou's, they visited and talked about returning when the weather was nicer and they could take advantage of the rooftop bar and lounge where firepits and couches promised stunning sunsets and breathtaking views of the islands.

With them due to arrive so late, they didn't rush and savored the ambience of the historic building and the well-appointed furnishings, along with a sinful dessert. Back on the road, Colin took the wheel and Izzy navigated, guiding him to the cut off that would avoid the worst of the traffic and take them to Richland.

The evening was drizzling and gloomy as they drove along. They listened to an audiobook for a while, then stopped for coffee at a café in Ellensburg. Finally, well after ten o'clock, they arrived at her parents' house. The porch light was on, but Izzy knew her parents would be fast asleep. She punched in the keycode to get them through the back gate and led Colin along the lighted pathway toward the casita. The door was unlocked and the heat had been turned on, so it was warm and toasty inside.

They walked into an open area with a niche carved out on the right for a kitchen and tiny table, and a larger space on the left, consisting of a bedroom suite and sitting area with a television, couch, and recliner. All the furnishings were old pieces that had once been in the main house.

Izzy watched as Colin lugged their suitcases over the threshold. The large bed that dominated the space loomed as she took a few tentative steps toward it. She hadn't given much thought to the actual sleeping accommodations. She and Colin had not taken their relationship to that level, and she wasn't ready to tackle that discussion, especially in her parents' backyard.

He shut the door and said, "This is nice." He surveyed the space and said, "That couch looks like a sleeper. I can take it."

Izzy's shoulders relaxed. Relieved she wouldn't have to face the awkwardness of moving from what she and Colin had, however wonderful it was, to the seriousness of an actual intimate relationship this weekend. It was going to be enough to introduce him to Mia; she couldn't handle the thought of explaining they were sleeping together.

"I'll get some sheets and help you make it up." She wandered to the large bathroom and collected what she needed from the linen closet. Together, they made quick work of getting the bed set up and made. After changing into her pajamas, Izzy brewed a pot of tea, and offered Colin a cup, when he emerged in sweats and a T-shirt.

The television was situated on a chest of drawers atop a turntable that allowed it to be viewed from the couch or the bed. "I don't think I can go to sleep quite yet. Do you want to see if there's something to watch?"

"Sure." He picked up the remote and turned on the television. "Your place or mine?" He laughed and arched his brows.

She laughed and said, "I think mine is more comfortable." He turned the screen to face the bed and followed her.

There was a quilt her mother had made at the foot of the bed, and she pulled it up and over them. As a decades old movie flickered on the screen, he reached for her hand. "Are you okay? You seem quiet."

She smiled and squeezed his hand. "I'm fine, tired, and find myself nervous with this being our first night together. I hadn't thought this through and am so out of practice with dating, men, well...all of it." Heat radiated from the back of her neck and she felt sweat form at her hairline.

He chuckled. "There's no need to be nervous. I'm all for taking things slowly. Trust me, I'm far from an expert. I haven't dated in years and after Phoebe, honestly, haven't been too excited to dip my toe into the water." He turned and gently kissed her. "Relax. There are no expectations. I came with you because I enjoy spending time with you and I want to meet your family and support you. It's also a nice getaway."

She breathed a sigh of relief. "Oh, good. That makes me feel so much better. There are so many expectations and when I walked in here, it all hits me at once. All that, and I'm worrying about Mia and how she'll react to learning you're in my life." She felt the burn of tears in her throat. "I have a hunch she won't be welcoming and lovely like David was. I don't want you to be hurt by her."

He brought her hand to his lips and kissed it. "Don't you worry about it. I'm not that fragile, trust me. I'm here only for you and not to make you more stressed. Whatever happens, we'll deal with it. Together."

She rested her head against his shoulder and finally relaxed. It was hard to adjust to having someone supportive, someone who would be there for her. That was the role she usually played. She tried to focus on the movie, but her eyes wouldn't stay open. She snuggled closer, thinking she could get used to the idea of having someone to lean on, someone like Colin.

Chapter 27

THE SOFT LIGHT of dawn woke Izzy Thursday morning. She blinked a few times, orienting herself, and was startled when she moved her hand and felt Colin next to her. She looked over at him, sleeping soundly, atop the comforter with the quilt still covering both of them.

She hated to disturb him and grinned when she realized they had literally slept together. Although poking fun at their predicament, a bit of guilt washed over her. She didn't want to disappoint her parents and didn't want them thinking poorly of Colin. Although over fifty now, she still felt like a child when it came to those values her parents appreciated. They hadn't indicated any concerns about her bringing Colin—quite the opposite. Her mother, especially, was beaming with excitement when Izzy chatted with her on video and asked if Colin could join her.

There was that familiar twinge, deep inside, nestled there since she was a small girl, that always served to remind her of right and wrong, and the values instilled in her for the last five decades didn't involve sharing her bed with men. She was sure her parents had evolved, and learning about their willingness to adopt Shannon, made her realize they may have been more open-minded than she ever thought, but the respect for them, for their home, had taken root long ago and wasn't something she could ignore.

Mia, on the other hand, despite being raised with similar values, obviously didn't take them to heart. Disappointing her parents, or at least her mother, was not a tenet with which she seemed to struggle. Izzy would have been mortified to be pregnant and without a husband or fiancé in the picture, but times had changed. She was still old-fashioned enough that it bothered her and it wasn't something she wished for Mia, but Izzy also understood most women younger than her, and even many in her peer group, would take exception with her views and think of her as outdated.

Despite being strong, intelligent, and independent, in her heart, she still believed a child needed a mother and father, and experienced firsthand how difficult it was to be a single parent. Lots of women succeeded and Izzy knew it was possible to have a fulfilling career and care for a child, but it was much easier with two parents. She often wondered if she had paid too much attention to her own career at the expense of Mia. Maybe if she had been a stay-at-home mom or more focused on her daughter, Mia would have had a different life.

Thoughts of Mia's future were depressing, so she pushed her worries away as she tiptoed to the bathroom. As she let the hot water work the knots out of her shoulders, she vowed to immerse herself in the fun of the celebration and enjoy time with her family. She would focus only on today and worry about Mia when she arrived tomorrow.

When she emerged, her hair in a towel, she smelled the rich aroma of coffee and found Colin in the kitchen, filling a cup. "Good morning," he said with a smile, handing her a cup. "First, I must apologize for falling asleep in your bed. I hope I didn't bother you."

She smiled, and took her first sip. "Not at all. I was surprised, but in a good way. Not to mention, it's way more comfortable than that old sofa bed." She took her coffee and sat down at the small table, opening the blinds on the window facing it.

"I didn't intend to stay there all night. You're right about it being comfortable. I slept like a rock." He finished his coffee and set the cup in the sink. "If you're done, I'll jump in the shower?"

She nodded. "I'll have to fix my hair, but other than that, it's all yours."

Once she heard the water running, she dashed to her suitcase, got dressed for the day, and hung up her clothes, which she'd been too tired to tackle last night. She eyed the sofa bed, mussed up the sheets and blanket a bit, and elected to leave it open in case prying eyes poked in to check on them.

She straightened the quilt and pillows on her bed and heard her phone chime. Blake texted to let her know breakfast would be ready in fifteen. The bathroom door opened and Colin glanced at the sofa bed, and smiled, but didn't say anything.

After fixing her hair, they walked across the huge patio to the back door. The smell of delicious baking greeted them. They found Blake and Ellie in the kitchen and her parents sitting at the island countertop. "Mom, Dad, this is Colin Sinclair." She turned to Colin and added, "My mom and dad, Gene and Helen Griffin."

Gene stood and shook Colin's extended hand. "Pleasure to meet you, sir," said Colin. He turned to Helen and took her hand. "Mrs. Griffin, thank you for your hospitality. Your home is lovely."

She smiled and waved her hand. "Oh, call me Helen." She pointed at her husband, "And Gene. We're not formal and we're delighted you're here. It's so nice of you to drive over with Izzy and spend your weekend with us."

"I'm looking forward to seeing the winery, and Izzy is always talking about her family, so I'm excited to meet everyone."

Ellie handed Blake two plates. "Your timing is perfect. We've got breakfast ready, so let's go in the dining room."

Over a cheesy egg dish and homemade pecan cinnamon rolls, they talked about plans for the day, which would culminate with a dinner outing in the evening. Izzy loved how Colin fit in, joking and chatting. It helped that Ellie and Blake already knew him, and she could tell her parents liked him.

They filled the day with a trip to the winery, where Gene and Blake took Colin for a ride on an ATV to show him the vineyards and operation. While they did that, Izzy and Ellie made sure things were set for the winemaker's dinner tomorrow.

After a busy, but wonderful day, Gene and Helen treated the two couples to dinner at one of their favorite restaurants. Colin made easy conversation with her parents, and with Gene's love of golf, he never tired of hearing about the courses Colin had managed and visited, especially some of the famous ones in Scotland. After dinner, they sat around the living room and chatted until late into the evening.

Izzy took Colin's hand as they walked to the casita. He drew her closer. "That was a great day. Your parents are wonderful."

"I can tell they like you. Dad never stays up late, so you should feel honored." She led the way through the door, feeling none of the unease and angst she had felt last night as they settled in for the evening.

Friday morning went by in a flurry of last-minute activities at the winery. Mia's plane was due to arrive in the early afternoon, with Izzy choosing to pick her up on her own. She waited in the large hallway near baggage claim and spotted her daughter, waving as Mia approached her.

Izzy greeted her with a hug. "How are you doing? Have you been feeling okay?"

"Yeah, tired. And fat." She pointed at her mid-section, which was much larger than it had been at Thanksgiving. Izzy helped her with her bag and loaded it into her SUV.

"We can stop and get something to eat, if you're hungry. Grandma also has a kitchen full of food, and Ellie's been cooking and baking."

Mia smiled at the mention of Ellie. "Grandma's house is fine. I'm tired and want to take a nap before dinner tonight."

"I don't want to take you off guard when we get to Grandma's, so you need to know that I brought a friend with me. His name is Colin Sinclair and he's actually my neighbor. We've become quite close and have been dating for several months. I hoped to introduce you at Christmas."

Mia's smile disappeared and she turned toward Izzy with a frown. "Well that explains why you moved to that stupid island. You've got a boyfriend? At your age?" She shook her head with disgust.

Izzy's pulse quickened and she took a deep breath. "Colin is not why I moved to the island. I didn't even meet him until after I moved into the house."

Mia glared at Izzy and turned her back to her, gazing out the passenger window as they pulled in the driveway. Izzy left the car running and the door locked. "I hope you can treat him with kindness, no matter what you think of me. This is an important weekend for your grandparents." She turned off the car, grabbed her purse, plucked Mia's bag from the back, and strode up the walkway.

She took several deep, cleansing breaths before opening the door. The last thing she wanted was to insert drama into the celebratory weekend. Her mom was the only one home, as everyone else was at the winery. Izzy deposited Mia's suitcase in the guestroom she always used, and went into the kitchen to brew a cup of tea. She found her mom at the sink, doing a few dishes.

"Where's Mia?" She smiled and wiped her hands on a dish towel.

"She's on her way in from the car." Izzy heard the front door close, and a moment later, Mia came into the kitchen and approached her grandma with a hug.

The kettle whistled. "Would you like some tea, Mia?" asked Izzy.

She shook her head. "No, I'm going to take a nap." She kept her arm around her grandma for a few moments and leaned her head into hers.

"How have you and the little one been feeling?" Helen asked, looking at Mia's midsection.

"Not bad. Tired. She's been moving much more."

Izzy gasped. "She? You had an ultrasound and learned it's a girl? How exciting."

Mia turned to her mother with a hint of a smirk on her face. "I told Dad about it weeks ago. I guess I forgot to tell you." She turned and made her way down the hallway.

Izzy passed her mom a cup of tea, and leaned across the counter. Her mother reached for her hand. "I take it things aren't any easier between you two?"

Izzy shook her head, but didn't trust her voice.

ONCE THEY WERE dressed for the dinner, Izzy introduced Colin to Mia. He was gracious and polite, and Mia, while not being overtly rude, was cool and disinterested, not answering Colin's inquiry about her studies, instead rushing off to greet Lauren after glaring at Izzy.

"That went well," Colin said with a chuckle, taking Izzy's arm as they made their way outside.

"I warned you." Filled with sorrow and a bit of embarrassment, she shook her head.

She was quiet on the ride to the winery, and Colin didn't fill the silence. She tried to push the heartache Mia caused aside, and concentrated on the lovely evening and the fabulous meal designed to honor her parents and all they had accomplished. Mia sat as far from Colin and Izzy as she could manage, in the last chair at the opposite end of the table.

Gene and Helen smiled and laughed with some of their best customers and most important distributors, who had also been invited to the exclusive affair. Blake and Ellie had organized the refurbishing of the barrel room over the last few months and the result was stunning. The huge rectangular family table was set up in front of the barrels, and additional guests were seated at round tables draped with white cloths. Twinkle lights and beautiful glass balls hung from the ceiling, while candles and flowers only added to the romantic and upscale feel.

The dinner, catered by a local restaurateur who carried the Griffin wines, was superb. Izzy did her best to enjoy the evening, but found it difficult since each time she met Mia's eyes, she was rewarded with a scowl. She had to find a way to get through to her daughter and have a meaningful conversation about the future. She was so tired of their inability to communicate.

SATURDAY, IZZY TOOK Colin on a tour of the Tri-Cities, stopping for lunch at one of her favorite spots with a view of the Columbia River. Despite it being winter, it still offered a lovely perspective of the river from Clover Island. Izzy gave him a bit of a geography lesson on the area as she pointed out the pathways to the three different cities that were so often treated as one, and the convergence of the Yakima and Snake Rivers with the wide water of the Columbia. It was a fisherman's paradise.

She promised to bring Colin back later in the year when they could explore more of the area. As they finished, Colin reached for her hand. "Are you okay?"

She smiled and nodded. "I'm sorry I haven't been the best company. I'm troubled about Mia and devising a way to talk to her before we leave tomorrow. She couldn't even be bothered to tell me she's having a girl. It hurts."

He rubbed a thumb over her hand. "What about tonight after the event? She has no way to leave and I could keep your parents busy. Give you two some privacy in the casita?"

She shrugged. "It's as good a plan as any. I'm willing to try. Her typical response is to leave. Get up and walk away whenever the conversation gets real."

"Maybe take her for a ride somewhere, so she can't leave."

"That might work. Maybe I can drive us home tonight and talk on the way. You could go with my parents?"

"Sure, anything you need." He squeezed her hand as they walked to the car, bolstering her confidence with that one small gesture.

THE OPEN HOUSE at the winery was well attended and by all accounts a success. The appetizer stations Ellie had arranged were a hit, and Gene and Helen enjoyed visiting with their customers and friends who had come to support them and take advantage of some fabulous deals on wines. Even Izzy and Blake took a few cases of their favorites to take back to the island.

As they were all getting ready to leave, the family made sure their cars were full to help Izzy orchestrate Mia having no choice but to ride back to Richland with her. As she drove the familiar route that would take them home, she glanced over at her daughter. Mia was doing her best to ignore Izzy by looking out the window.

"We haven't had much of a chance to talk. Have you given any more thought about coming to stay and let me help you when the baby comes?"

"It's not what I want to do, but I don't have many options."

"Why are you so reluctant?"

Mia shrugged. "I don't need you telling me what to do or pressuring me about school. I'm an adult and can figure things out on my own."

"I'd really like to get to a place where we aren't always adversaries. Speaking from experience, I think you'll need help after the baby is born. There's so much to do and you won't be getting much sleep. It can wear you out. I'd love to help with her. It's not a permanent arrangement, a few weeks or as long as you need."

"I don't know. I know I wouldn't be happy staying there. I had it all figured out. Staying at Dad's would have been perfect. He's got such a huge place, and it would be easier." She hung her head, pouting like she had when she was a child. "I guess it doesn't matter what I want. I don't have a choice."

"I've got plenty of room. That won't be a problem. Why don't you plan on coming over when the quarter ends? You'll have to find a new place to live anyway, right? The housing unit you're in isn't for students with families?"

"Right. That's another problem. I haven't even had time to do that."

"I can help. Do you want me to check into housing and apartments?"

Mia lifted her shoulders, and let out a loud breath. "I don't know. I'm not sure when I'll go back, so it might have to be a private apartment, not anything affiliated with the university. It's too hard to think that far ahead."

"We can do that while you're recuperating. You probably won't go back until fall, so you don't have to stress about it."

Mia sat up straighter. "I'm not staying with you until fall. A couple weeks at the most. I can't imagine staying much longer, and I don't want to cramp your style with your new boyfriend."

Izzy counted to ten, and decided to ignore the remark about Colin. "Okay, I wasn't trying to get you to stay that long. I'm sure we can find something that will work for you and the baby." Izzy took a deep breath. Talking to Mia was like tiptoeing through broken glass and then walking across salty potato chips. "Have you thought about names for her yet?"

"Not really. I think I need to see her before I know for sure. I thought I would use Helen for her middle name, after Grandma."

Tears burned in Izzy's throat. "That's a lovely idea. I can't wait to meet her."

She pulled into the driveway, and after parking, reached across and drew Mia close to her. "I love you, and I'm truly only trying to help."

She felt her daughter begin to relax against her, and although Mia didn't say anything, she tightened her grip around Izzy's shoulders. After, Izzy watched her walk into the house. Tonight, she would allow herself to bask in the glimmer of hope she saw through the crack in the wall that had always been between her and Mia.

Chapter 28

IZZY GOT UP early and visited with her parents before Colin was awake, leaving him under the blankets on the sofa bed. While her parents relived some of their favorite moments of the weekend, chattering on about how wonderful it was to see so many of their friends and longtime customers, Izzy listened and drank two cups of coffee.

At a lull in the conversation, she cleared her throat. "I hate to even bring this up, since it's been such a lovely weekend. But I want you to know I'm available if you need me to come back when Shannon is released, so we can all be here together when you tell her about her birth mother."

Helen reached for Gene's hand. He met his daughter's eyes. "We think it best it's only us. We expect she won't take the news well, and having everyone around may make it worse. We don't want her to feel any more embarrassed than necessary. She'll be lashing out, and there's no reason to subject all of you to it. It was our decision and we should have told her long ago."

Tears pooled in her mother's eyes, and Izzy stood to hug them both. "I'm so sorry. I know it won't be easy. Don't take what she says to heart, okay? She'll be angry. And call to let me know how it goes?"

Helen nodded. "Lauren said she'd help us arrange the transportation to the airport and a flight home."

"I want you to know I'm here if you need me." Izzy held both of their hands.

Gene smiled. "You've got yourself a good man there in Colin. I hope you'll bring him back to visit us again."

"We were talking about it yesterday. I explained about all the fishing opportunities and told him you have a boat." She grinned and winked at her dad.

"I'd love it."

"And we're coming over to visit this summer for sure. Maybe even spring, depending on Mia's situation and the baby," added Helen.

Blake and Ellie came around the corner, already dressed, dragging their suitcases. "Morning," said Blake. "We thought we'd get out of here right after breakfast, and try to beat the traffic."

Izzy took her empty cup to the sink. "Same with us. In fact, I need to get a move on. We can caravan together, if you can wait for me?"

Blake nodded as he filled a cup from the coffee pot. "Sure, take your time."

AFTER MORE HUGS and even a pleasant, but short exchange with Mia, the two couples were on the road before nine o'clock. Helen and Gene planned to treat Mia to lunch on their way to the airport.

Colin offered to drive and Izzy rested in the passenger seat, her mind reeling with ideas and a bit of excitement at the prospect of having a new granddaughter under her roof. She made a mental list of a few items she would need to make sure she was ready, and also promised to connect Mia with an obstetrician on the island.

Izzy texted Max while she was thinking about it, so he could arrange a consultation with the doctor and get things scheduled. Regi had a few more things to donate to outfitting the nursery, and Izzy added diapers and wipes to her list, along with some formula and bottles, in case it was needed.

She wondered how receptive Mia would be to a small baby shower. She thought it might be nice, but didn't want to push her luck. She'd let one of her friends suggest it, perhaps Ellie. Thank goodness she and Mia were close.

Colin reached across the console and squeezed Izzy's knee as he turned off the highway for the ferry landing. "I'm glad you and Mia talked. You seem so much more at ease now."

"I am, thank you. We have such a tumultuous relationship. Part of me is scared to have her under my roof, but the other part hopes our time together will mend a few tears in the fabric that connects us. She's not an easy child. Having her there will test my patience, but I'm looking forward to helping her with the baby. It's scary and exciting at the same time."

"There's a Welsh proverb about grandchildren that says perfect love doesn't come until your grandchildren are born."

"Oh, that's lovely. Perfect love. I like that idea." She squeezed his hand as he guided them onto the ferry deck, behind Blake and Ellie.

While Colin and Blake discussed fishing, Ellie and Izzy passed the hour-long journey talking about a baby shower and making Mia welcome, despite her misgivings about Friday Harbor.

Anxious to see their dogs, Izzy drove them directly to Sam and Jeff's where they picked up two excited golden retrievers, who wouldn't stop running in circles, and loaded them in the back of her SUV. After thanking Sam and Jeff for taking care of the dogs, and promising to treat them to dinner soon, Izzy dropped Jethro and Colin at his house. He left her with a sweet kiss and a wave, promising to see her in the morning for a walk.

Izzy settled into her warm pajamas and defrosted some soup for a quick dinner, then petted Sunny as she worked on her list for the baby and Mia. She placed an online order for most everything she needed and began searching for apartments close to the university.

She made a list of a few possibilities, noting the cost would be substantially more for something private instead of going through the university housing program. There were some family housing units that would work, but she wasn't sure what Mia would prefer. Chances are Mia wasn't sure, since she hadn't given it much thought.

Her eyes were struggling to stay focused, so she checked her work email, noting nothing of importance and no changes to the meetings scheduled for the week, before trudging to bed, where she snuggled under the covers and fell asleep listening to Sunny's soft snores.

THE NEXT FEW weeks were filled with work, adding more supplies to the baby's nursery, and dinners with Colin. Izzy texted Mia several times to check on her and give her some links to housing units and private apartments, but usually only received an annoying thumbs up symbol or nothing at all.

She talked to her mom and dad on video the evening after Shannon was released. As planned, Shannon had flown home and after giving her the day to rest, they broke the news they had been hiding all these years. Not to anyone's surprise, Shannon was livid and outraged.

Helen and Gene were visibly upset, their voices trembling, but they held it together as they said Shannon had stormed out after calling a friend to pick her up. She didn't tell them where she was going, she wasn't answering any of their calls, and they were worried about her.

"Shannon's a free spirit and I doubt you usually know where she is, so try not to worry. She has a large network of friends and I'm sure she's staying with some of them. She's hurt, so it's understandable she would want to get away to think." Izzy's calm voice and reasoning seemed to soothe them.

"She told us she always knew she didn't belong, and now she understood why. It breaks my heart," said Helen, her voice cracking. "We thought we were doing the right thing, but we should have told her long ago. We hope this doesn't get in the way of her turning her life around and taking positive steps." Helen used a tissue to blot her cheeks.

"All you can do is move forward, Mom. It's done, and now she knows, and you don't have to live with the secret. It's going to take some time for her to come to grips with all of it, so be patient. I'm happy to try to call her too. I don't know if it will do much good, but at least she'll know I'm thinking of her."

Izzy shifted the conversation to Mia's arrival in a couple of weeks, and how excited she was to spend some time with her and the baby. "Maybe you can make a trip a little earlier than summer and come over in April or May to see the baby and spend some time here?"

They both agreed it would be a welcome distraction from their current worries. Helen had already crocheted a gorgeous baby blanket for the new arrival. They discussed the idea of a baby shower, and Helen suggested it might be better to wait until after the baby arrived, adding she would talk to Lauren and Esther and see if they could make the visit to the island with them to celebrate.

When Izzy disconnected, her parents were in better spirits, focusing on the excitement of their first great grandchild. Izzy was getting caught up in the thrill of it all too, and spent some time sitting in the beautiful room she had decorated, rocking in the comfy chair and soaking in the sweet animals that decorated the space. She hoped Mia would feel as happy as she did.

THE DAY OF Mia's arrival, Izzy fussed over every detail in her room, making sure she picked up some fresh flowers from Linda's shop, and stocked the fridge and pantry with everything she could think of in the way of comfort foods and childhood favorites, along with lots of healthy options.

While she waited for the ferry to arrive, she sipped a chai tea latte at Sam's shop, and reflected on her conversation with Colin last night. After their customary Friday night dinner to celebrate the end of another work week, he came back to her place and they talked over several pots of tea.

They had grown closer in the last month, after their trip to her parents, and he and Jethro had stayed overnight a few times. They had talked about Izzy's disappointment when the only response she received from Shannon was a profanity-laced message, and he sympathized with her concern for her parents over how the whole situation was impacting them.

She had felt for Shannon when her sister was in jail, knowing it wasn't a pleasant place to be, but the update from her parents brought more sympathy for her sister than anything else. She didn't want Shannon to feel alone or lost; she wanted her to change her life and grow up.

They talked about Mia, and what having her and the baby would mean. Izzy never anticipated wanting to share her life with anyone, but Colin had changed her feelings—and while she didn't want to upset Mia, she also wasn't willing to let Mia destroy her own happiness while she was there. Manipulation was Mia's weapon of choice and she was a master. That, along with a helping of passive-aggression, and a sprinkling of guilt usually got her what she wanted, especially with John. Izzy, however, was determined, no matter how badly she wanted a loving relationship with her daughter, not to let Mia dictate her life or spoil the peaceful existence she had created.

With that in mind, she invited Colin to join them for dinner and had soup simmering in the slow cooker, waiting for Mia. Colin didn't want to be the source of any discord and had offered to make himself scarce for a few weeks, giving Mia time to adjust, but Izzy wouldn't hear of it and wanted to set the tone with her daughter early. She was done walking on eggshells and Mia was a guest in *her* house.

Being a mom was hard, and Izzy had imagined it would be much easier by now. In her heart, she knew Mia was smart and capable enough to manage her own life, and had just been rewarded for being lazy and dependent. Now, with a baby, she hoped her daughter would rise to the occasion.

She spotted the ferry, said goodbye to Sam, and headed down the street. Mia's car would have navigation and finding her house was simple, but she wanted to meet her when she arrived.

It didn't take long for Izzy to spot the pretty blue SUV, and she waved and pointed to a parking spot down from her own car. Mia's car was packed to the roof and the harried expression on her face didn't give Izzy much confidence as she approached her with a smile. "I wasn't sure if you wanted to stop and get a snack or something to drink, or just head back to the house?"

Mia blew out a breath and shook her head. "The house. I'm worn out. Getting here is a real treat." Her words were heavy with sarcasm.

"Okay, follow me." Izzy walked back to her vehicle, breathing deeply and letting the salty sea air calm her.

When they arrived, Izzy gave Mia a house key and invited her in to sit and relax, offering to unload her car for her. At the door, Izzy introduced her to Sunny, who greeted her with several excited swishes of her tail, bringing a hint of a smile to Mia's face. Sunny followed her as she toddled into the house and plopped onto the couch. Izzy brought her a glass of cold water, and noticed how much more her daughter's stomach was protruding. The weariness on her face prompted Izzy to brush a strand of hair from her daughter's cheek. "You relax."

Mia nodded, and rested her head against the plump cushion, while Sunny nestled at her feet. Izzy started unloading and had returned from depositing the second pile of clothes upstairs, when Colin arrived with Jethro.

He greeted Izzy with a kiss, and took a stack of boxes from Mia's car. Jethro followed them inside and rushed to play with Sunny, but not before giving Mia a through sniffing. Izzy watched as Mia petted both of them, talking softly to them.

While Colin hurried up the stairs, Izzy wandered into the great room. "This is Jethro, Sunny's best friend and Colin's dog. Mia's eyebrows rose. "Colin's joining us for dinner tonight?"

He came around the corner and slipped an arm around Izzy's shoulders. "Hello, Mia. Nice to see you again. Your mom is so excited to have you here and can't wait to meet her granddaughter. She's been working nonstop on your room and nursery."

"I'm glad this whole ordeal is almost over," said Mia, placing a hand atop her significant middle. "I can't take much more of this." Her voice faltered.

Colin gestured to the front door. "I'll finish unloading." He hurried away, while Izzy rushed across the room. "Ah, Megs." Mia smiled at the childhood nickname her parents had used when she learned her initials, using her middle name of Elizabeth.

Izzy chuckled, and added, "Remember when you wanted to change your name to Meg instead of Mia?"

Her daughter nodded, and tears fell from her eyes. "I don't think I can do this," she whispered.

Izzy's brow furrowed. "I remember feeling the same way. It's scary, I know, but you'll get through it. I'll be right there the whole time."

Mia shook her head. "No, I mean, I'm nervous about the actual birth, but the being a mom thing. I can't do it." Izzy handed her a tissue. "I can barely handle taking care of myself. How am I going to go to school or work and deal with a baby?"

Izzy put her arm around Mia. "You're stronger than you think. I know it all seems overwhelming and it won't be easy, but the world is filled with moms who felt the same way. I've felt that way more than once, but when you hold your little girl and look into her sweet face and realize she is counting on you, you'll find something inside of you, something deep you didn't realize you had, and you'll do whatever it takes."

Mia sobbed. "That's the problem, Mom. I don't have it. I've decided to give her up for adoption."

Chapter 29

IZZY'S HEART FELL as she tried to think. "Don't you think it would be wise to wait until after the birth? You've never even mentioned the idea before."

"I've been too afraid to say it, but I can't wait much longer. She'll be here in ten days. I kept thinking I'd get a better handle on it, but I know I can't do it."

Colin poked his head into the room. "Everything's unloaded and stacked in the bedroom upstairs." Mia hefted herself from the couch and escaped down the hallway. Colin raised his brows. "What's going on?"

Izzy rose and met him at the kitchen counter. She put her mouth close to his ear and whispered, "Mia is upset and wants to place the baby for adoption. I'm not sure what's going on."

His eyes widened. "I think we better get home. We'll do dinner a different night. She doesn't need a stranger to deal with right now." He kissed her and called Jethro. "Call me later," he whispered, walking to the front door and clicking it closed behind them.

Sunny stood at the entryway, a confused look in her eyes, after her friend left. "We'll see them tomorrow. I promise." Izzy pointed at Sunny's bed, and the dog plopped onto it.

Mia returned from the powder room, her face blotchy and her eyes rimmed in red. "I know you'll think I'll change my mind, but I've done nothing but think about this since I found out I was pregnant." Her chest heaved as she gasped for a breath. Izzy led her to a chair at the island counter.

"Sit down, breathe in through your nose. It's going to be okay. Relax and breathe." She placed a gentle hand on Mia's shoulder. "I've got some chicken soup ready. Let's have a bite to eat and then you can tell me what you're thinking."

Despite the knot in her own stomach, Izzy filled two bowls and sliced the fresh bread she had picked up at the bakery. With the implications of what Mia was saying running through her mind, she cut up some fruit and rinsed a basket of berries. She wanted to support Mia's decision, but was torn, thinking of never seeing her granddaughter after she was born, or perhaps worse, getting attached and having to give her away in a few months.

She stayed calm for Mia's sake, suspecting her daughter needed to eat something. Once everything was on the island, she encouraged Mia to eat, as she loaded her own spoon with the hearty soup. She was sure Mia was overreacting and nervous, not that the whole idea of motherhood wasn't scary, but if Mia had time to adjust, she'd be able to approach everything more rationally.

Images of a few women she'd known in Richland filled her mind. They had all taken in their grandchildren because their children were not fit parents or were too young or irresponsible. She never truly understood why, until now. She was too old to raise a newborn and dismissed the idea. She'd seen the results of older, tired grandparents trying to keep up with youngsters. They provided safety and security, but it wore them down and often they weren't able to keep up with the grandchildren as they became teenagers.

She couldn't do it. As much as her heart hurt thinking about letting her granddaughter go, she couldn't endure what would surely happen as she tried to navigate the stormy waters that always swirled between her and Mia. Adding a baby would only complicate it.

Izzy could offer to do the heavy lifting, but if Mia was truly intent on not being a mother, it would only end in disaster. The soup that normally soothed her and cured any ills, soured in her stomach.

They ate in relative silence, except for Mia asking where Colin went. Something poked at Izzy as she wondered if part of Mia's drama was orchestrated to make Colin leave.

After dinner, Mia sat on the couch while Izzy tidied the kitchen and made sure Sunny was fed. Izzy fixed two cups of herbal tea, and took a seat on the chaise she favored, Sunny snuggling next to her. As Izzy took her first sip, Mia cleared her throat.

"I've already talked to a potential couple about adopting the baby."

"Wow, really?"

"Lauren and Ken." She stared at her mother. "Don't be upset with her. I made her promise not to tell until I had made up my mind. It's my decision, Mom, not yours."

Izzy's heart pounded in her ears and her hand shook as she placed the mug on a coaster. Mia was right. It wasn't Izzy's decision. She practically chewed a hole in her cheek as she resisted saying all the things she was thinking.

"So, what's your plan?"

Mia shrugged. "I thought you could figure out all the legal paperwork, and they could come over and take her home after we get released from the hospital."

Izzy nodded. "Then what?"

"Then, I get my life back, and like you said, I can stay here until I've recuperated and then go back to the city."

"And finish school?"

She shrugged again.

Izzy pursed her lips. That meant Mia wasn't going back to school. She didn't trust herself to say anything. "I'm sure you're tired after the trip. I'll show you where everything is so you can get settled and get some rest."

Izzy collected both their mugs, locked the doors, and turned out the lights, leaving only the soft glow of the tiny decorative lights. She led the way upstairs, and Sunny followed them. Izzy pointed out the extra towels and supplies in the bathroom, and led Mia into the bedroom. "Sleep well. We can talk in the morning."

As Izzy turned and took in the crib, the lovely rocking chair, and all the soft and cuddly pink blankets she had laundered, stacked across it, a tear leaked out of her eye. She didn't think her heart could be more broken.

IT WASN'T VERY late, but Izzy was exhausted. As soon as she got in bed, she called Colin. After chatting with him for almost an hour, she felt better and more in control of her emotions. He didn't say much, but when he did, it was sound advice, especially related to Lauren.

Sabina had been a miracle, and Lauren wouldn't be able to have any more children. She was a lovely mother, and she and Ken would be wonderful parents, if they ended up adopting Mia's child. The whole thing made her head spin. As Colin so logically pointed out, it would be better to have the baby remain in the family, where they could all have influence and a relationship, than to adopt the child out to strangers, where even if they were able to negotiate an open adoption, there may not be a true relationship.

As Izzy calmed, she realized he was right. She felt so betrayed, but also understood Lauren was between the proverbial rock and hard place. Not to mention, she may have made the offer, but may not have realized Mia was serious. She had such a reputation for histrionics, Lauren may have said it to placate Mia, thinking she'd change her mind.

She wanted to wait until morning to talk to her, but couldn't help but text her and ask her if they could chat about Mia and the baby. As soon as the message was delivered, her phone rang and Lauren's name appeared.

"I've been dying to talk to you. I know Mia arrived today, and I promised not to say anything until she had a chance to tell you. I wasn't even sure if she was serious."

Izzy felt her shoulders relax as Lauren apologized, explaining she wasn't sure what to do, but didn't want Mia to give the baby to anyone. She and Ken were serious about adoption and had wanted at least two children, but were so happy with Sabina's arrival, when they had all but given up, they had resolved themselves to having an only child.

Lauren was ten years younger than Izzy, making her a much better fit for the mother of a newborn and the future mother of a teenager. Izzy couldn't imagine being in her mid-sixties and dealing with what she had gone through with Mia. They chatted and wondered how their parents would react, but deep down knew they would be happy to keep the baby in the family, regardless of the circumstances.

"In light of the recent situation with Shannon, I think we should explain to the baby, as soon as she's old enough to understand, who her birth mother is and that we adopted her," said Lauren. "I don't want to be in Mom and Dad's shoes at some point in the future, and I think if she understands it at a young age, it will be easier for her." Izzy smiled. Her sister had expressed exactly what she had been thinking, but of course Mia might have a different idea.

"Do you think Mia's serious about it? She's really set on not keeping the baby?" Lauren's voice was filled with worry. "I don't want to go through all this and get my hopes up, if you think she's not going to go through with it."

"Honestly, I don't know, but she seems set on it now. I think it's more than being scared. I think she doesn't want her life to change or have the responsibility for another person." It saddened Izzy to say that about her own daughter, but it was the truth. "I'll work on drafting some adoption papers and talk to Mia tomorrow. I'm not sure she'll know for certain until after the baby arrives. I'll keep you posted." Izzy's throat went dry. "Lauren, if she's going to place her for adoption, I can't think of anyone I'd rather have raise her than you and Ken."

By the time they disconnected, they were both crying, and Izzy flipped on the television hoping to distract herself and fall asleep.

IZZY WENT WITH Mia to her doctor's appointment, where Max met them to introduce them to Dr. Powell. She was a friendly woman in her early forties, with curly blonde hair and gorgeous gray eyes. Mia took an immediate liking to her, and after Dr. Powell took them on a tour of the birthing rooms and facilities at the hospital, Izzy left Mia in her capable hands for an exam, while she grabbed a coffee with Max.

She told him the latest news, and his eyes went wide. "Well, I'm sure that was a shock, but it's not unheard of and makes sense to keep the child in the family."

Izzy was warming to the idea, though she was still stuck between admiration and disappointment. She respected Mia for speaking up and saying she couldn't handle being a mom, but still thought she was shirking her responsibilities. Although it was best for the baby to be in a loving home, where she'd have every opportunity, Izzy was saddened by Mia's choice.

After the appointment, Izzy went over the adoption papers with Mia, explaining the clauses, and that with the nature of the adoption being within the family, it would be an open adoption with Mia having contact with the baby. Izzy made sure Mia understood she would be giving away her parental rights and would have no say in how the baby was raised. All those decisions would fall to Lauren and Ken. She also advised her it would be best to have another attorney, one who wasn't related, look over things to make sure she was happy.

As she went over each section of the documents, Mia nodded and seemed to relax. Izzy wasn't sure if it would all be so easy once she saw the baby and held her. There was such a strong bond, and although Izzy suspected Mia looked upon the baby only as an inconvenience and problem, she wasn't sure if she would feel the same way after giving birth.

Izzy also explained things to Lauren and Ken via video, giving them the same advice about seeking other counsel, and asked that they talk to her parents and Esther in person, so they weren't caught unaware. She herself stopped by the winery one afternoon and explained it all to Blake and Ellie, who were shocked, but agreed the baby couldn't have better parents.

At least Mia wasn't displaying her usual snarky and petulant attitude. In better spirits than when she arrived, Mia spent some time visiting with Ellie and Blake, where Ellie provided some perspective and her experience as a birth mother to an adoptive child. At Izzy's urging, Mia spent an afternoon with Regi and Nate talking to them about being adoptive parents. She was even cordial to Colin when he came over for dinner. He had an easy-going manner about him, always funny and he even managed to elicit a few smiles from Mia. Izzy wished she could be as relaxed as he was around her daughter. She felt on edge, always waiting for the next shoe to drop, but hoped the last bit of news marked the end of Mia's surprises.

After a long and busy week, including Friday night dinner at Blake and Ellie's, Colin invited Izzy and Mia to join him at The Bistro Saturday night. However, Mia didn't feel like going out, and offered to stay home with Sunny and Jethro, as she binge watched some television.

Izzy was thankful to get an evening alone with Colin. His presence and calming manner soothed her, helping to ease not only the low level of tension that always accompanied a visit from Mia, but also the sweeping emotions she had experienced all week. She still had mixed feelings about the adoption and wondered how it would impact Mia in the years to come. She knew Mia was looking for a solution to end her worries of the moment, but had heard, from clients and friends who had given up a child, that even when it was the best decision they could make, it sometimes tormented them years later. Even more, she worried about the baby, especially after Shannon's experience of never feeling like she fit in.

Izzy ordered another glass of wine, hoping to forget her worries for a few hours. The weather was nice enough for them to sit outside and enjoy the fresh air and the firepit. Colin had paused all the plans he had in motion to organize golf outings and meals for Izzy's parents, now that their upcoming visit would be delayed. Izzy thought it might be best to have them come later in the year, without the issue of the baby and adoption being at the forefront.

As Izzy watched the flames flicker, she realized she wasn't sure she could act like this whole thing was normal, and although she was grateful Lauren was willing to parent Mia's new baby, it was difficult to hide her disappointment and utter sadness over the whole situation. She had convinced herself she could do it and would get through it, but hosting her parents and arranging fun activities, celebrating in a sense, didn't seem appropriate. Truth was, part of her was grieving.

Grieving the loss of her grandchild; the sweet girl she had been imagining, but hadn't even met.

Colin slipped his hand over hers. "You're deep in thought. Something is making you sad."

Izzy nodded, comforted by his gentle manner and concern. "Thinking too much. Worrying about the future, Mia, the baby, even Lauren."

He sighed and squeezed her hand. "I can understand your concern. It's been a whirlwind." He brought her hand to his lips and kissed her knuckles. "In situations like this, I force myself to look for the positives. You'll get to see the baby whenever you like, and you know Lauren is a fabulous mom and she and Ken can provide for all her needs. She'll have the best life possible. You may even have more influence than if Mia had kept her. You said yourself you were afraid she would use the baby as a weapon and keep you from seeing her."

Izzy mouth went dry and her eyes stung. He was right, she needed to snap out of this funk. The baby would be fine and have a wonderful life, and even a big sister who would be a built-in friend and playmate.

Izzy's phone chimed and she dug it out of her purse. Mia texted that she thought she was in labor and needed to get to the hospital.

Colin hurried them to his car and drove the short distance to Izzy's, where he took charge of getting Mia loaded into the backseat and driving them to the hospital. Izzy had called Dr. Powell the moment they had left The Bistro, and she was already at the hospital waiting for them.

Once Mia was settled into a birthing room, a nurse came out to collect Izzy. She urged Colin to go home, promising to call when she had news. He stood and embraced her in a tight hug, whispering in her ear. "I'll wait. Remember, everything's going to be fine. You're going to be an excellent grandma.

Enjoy this time." She squeezed his hand and followed the nurse down the corridor.

SHORTLY AFTER MIDNIGHT, Izzy left the birthing room, having witnessed the miracle she had only been part of one other time in her life. It made her think of that night decades ago when Mia had been born. Where Izzy had opted for a natural birth, which was all the rage at the time, Mia, not one for handling any type of discomfort well, opted for the drugs the doctor offered, and her tiny daughter arrived without much drama.

Izzy hoped the coming weeks and months ahead would be as easy as her entrance. As she held her granddaughter for the first time, Izzy could swear her tiny rosebud lips smiled. She was perfect and beautiful, but when Izzy offered her to Mia, she held up her hand. "I'm too tired. I want to sleep."

Izzy held the sweet girl as long as they let her, before a nurse bundled her off to the nursery. Izzy took several photos and texted them to Lauren, whom she had been talking to throughout the evening. She and Ken would be arriving late in the day, as Dr. Powell suspected both the baby and Mia would be released within twenty-four hours. Lauren texted back and said they wanted to name her Sophia Helen, using the middle name Mia had originally suggested to honor her grandma. They planned to call her Sophie. Izzy shared the photos and the name with Blake, who had asked for updates.

With the baby gone to the nursery for the night and Mia asleep, Izzy, in search of caffeine, found Colin in the waiting room. He stood and reached for her, his eyes questioning.

"They're both fine. Sophie is beautiful and perfect. Mia is tired and resting."

He hugged her close, and said, "How wonderful. I love the name. Let's go home and get some sleep." He slipped his arm around her shoulders and led the way to the parking lot.

It took only a few minutes of travel through the empty streets to reach their neighborhood. Colin walked Izzy to the door, where they opened it to find Sunny and Jethro wagging their tails, excited to see them.

Colin bent down to pet Jethro, scratching him behind the ears. "We need to get home and get some sleep, old boy."

Izzy reached for Colin's hand and pulled him inside. "Stay, please."

Chapter 30

IZZY FELT WARM breath on her face and woke to find Jethro and Sunny staring at her, their heads resting on the mattress. The dogs had slept together on Sunny's soft bench at the bottom of Izzy's bed, but it was later than usual and they were ready for breakfast.

Izzy heard the shower and saw the dent, still fresh in Colin's pillow. She stretched and slid her feet into her slippers before padding into the laundry room to dispense breakfast and refill the water bowl. The smell of fresh coffee greeted her as soon as she made her way into the kitchen.

The sun was shining, and she was anxious for Lauren to arrive. Mia had been exhausted and had shown no interest in Sophie last night, but Izzy wasn't sure what today would bring. She scanned the photos she had taken of Sophie on her phone and smiled. She sent one of them to Shannon with a brief message about her being a new aunt and letting her know Mia wanted Lauren to adopt her. She didn't want any more secrets in the family. As she was admiring her new granddaughter, Blake texted and proposed they meet for breakfast, and then go check on Mia and Sophie.

Izzy suggested they meet at the Front Street Café in an hour. She hurried back to her bedroom where she ran into Colin, coming out. "Hey, do you feel like meeting Blake and Ellie for breakfast in an hour?"

"Sure, I was going to run home and change clothes. I'll take the dogs for a short walk while you get ready." She gave him a quick kiss, and hurried to the bathroom.

She had no idea what to expect, or how long Lauren and Ken would stay, or how Mia would react to all of it. Anticipating that Lauren and Ken would stay at least one night, she moved Mia's things to the other guest room. It may be too hard for her to be surrounded by all the baby items in the nursery. She changed the bedding in the room with the crib, thinking that Lauren and Ken would want to be near Sophie.

This whole situation was uncharted territory and part of her thought it might be best if Lauren and Ken stayed at the bed and breakfast, but she would leave it up to them. She usually had a plan, but this set of circumstances had unfolded so quickly, she had no time to come up with any suitable ideas.

Izzy was ready in under an hour, and when Colin returned, they headed to the harbor. Ellie and Blake were excited about the baby and Lauren's visit, and Ellie offered to cook dinner for everyone at Izzy's place. Izzy gladly agreed and told her to use their key to come and go as she pleased.

The four of them found Mia in her hospital room. She looked rested and was dressed in the exercise wear Izzy had helped her pack into her hospital go-bag, watching television, and sipping on juice. They all inquired how she was feeling and she assured them she was fine.

Izzy placed a hand on her daughter's shoulder. "You were asleep by the time I heard from Lauren last night, but they decided to name her Sophia Helen and call her Sophie."

Mia smiled and nodded. "I like it. Lauren texted me this morning and told me." She set her glass of juice on her tray. "The doctor said I can go home later this afternoon."

"And Sophie?" asked Izzy.

"Both of us." Mia turned her attention to the television.

"Ellie's cooking dinner tonight, so that will be perfect. We'll stay here until they release you, and then get you and Sophie settled in. Lauren and Ken should be here by then."

Mia bobbed her head. "Sounds good."

"Do you want to hold Sophie?" asked Izzy.

Mia kept staring at the television. "I don't think so. I walked down to look at her earlier, but I've been reading that it's not a good idea to form any attachment when placing your baby for adoption. She needs to bond with Lauren."

Blake frowned. "Well, you're still going to be part of her life. You'll see her all the time, and from what Lauren said, they're going to tell Sophie as soon as she is old enough to understand that you are her birth mother. I guess you'll also be her cousin. It's confusing." He shrugged when he got no response from Mia.

A nurse wheeled in Sophie, and placed her in Izzy's arms. As she took in her long eyelashes, perfect features, and examined her tiny fingers, Izzy's heart filled. She was sure the sweet girl in the bundle of blankets would drag her back to Richland more often than she planned. It would be incredibly hard to let her go. She had imagined rocking her to sleep and introducing her to the cute animals and toys she had chosen for her room.

She glanced at Mia, and noticed she was still glued to the television, paying no mind to all the fussing and cooing everyone was doing over Sophie. Izzy's heart broke for her daughter. She passed the baby to Blake and moved to sit on the other side of Mia's bed. She tried to talk to her, but Mia remained silent, keeping her focus on the screen.

After everyone held and fed Sophie, Blake and Ellie hugged Mia goodbye and promised to see her later, as they were off to go shopping and get dinner started. Colin left with them after meeting Izzy in the hallway, where they agreed that with everyone gone, Izzy might be able to talk with Mia.

Even then, however, Mia refused to spend any time with Sophie. She thought it would be easier that way. Izzy had her doubts, but respected Mia's wishes, and while Mia played on her phone or stared at the television, Izzy held Sophie, enjoying the weight of her, the smell of her, the tiny flutter of her fingers against her own.

By the time the hospital was ready to release them, Lauren had still not arrived. Colin had installed the car seat in Izzy's SUV last week, in preparation for the arrival of baby Sophie, and with the help of the lovely nurse who accompanied them outside, she was able to get the baby secured. Mia tossed the basket of baby goodies the hospital provided into the backseat before settling into the passenger seat.

As Izzy drove to her house, she glanced at her daughter. "Are you going to be okay?"

Mia continued staring straight ahead. "I'm fine. Tired of all the fuss."

"I moved your things into the other guest room upstairs so Lauren and Ken could have the room with all the baby supplies." Mia nodded, but said nothing. When they arrived, Ellie's car was in the driveway. Mia hurried inside, leaving Izzy to get Sophie and unload the car.

By the time Izzy got Sophie inside, Mia had already disappeared upstairs. Ellie fetched the bassinette and baby rocker seat that Regi had given Izzy and brought them downstairs. A few minutes later, Blake and Colin arrived and while Izzy watched over Sophie, they helped Ellie set the table and finish up the dinner preparations.

Izzy's phone chimed and she breathed a sigh of relief when she saw Lauren's text letting her know they were getting off the ferry and would be there in a few minutes. She replied that they were at her house, and gave her directions.

Blake went upstairs to fetch Mia for dinner, and Sunny let out a quick bark, which Izzy had learned, meant someone was coming up the walkway. Moments later, the bell rang. Izzy, holding Sophie, asked Colin to get it.

Izzy smiled when she saw Lauren and Ken, holding sweet Beanie, come from around the corner. As they stepped into the great room, Izzy's mouth fell open and she gasped. "John, what are you doing here?"

SHE HADN'T SEEN her ex-husband in a few years and noticed a few extra pounds stressing the buttons of his designer shirt. His receding hairline had eroded a bit more, but there wasn't a spec of gray in his too-dark brown hair, making her think he probably dyed it.

"Hey, Izzy. Mia texted to let me know she had the baby, and I decided to surprise her and show up. Where is my princess?"

Lauren had made her way to Izzy and took Sophie from her arms. Izzy walked across the room to where John stood, reaching for Colin's hand. "Mia's upstairs, but Blake went to get her for dinner. Let me introduce you to everyone."

Izzy caught Ellie's eye, who was checking on something in the oven. "This my friend and Blake's wife, Ellie." John reached his hand out, and Ellie held up her oven mitts and smiled. "John is Mia's father. My ex-husband."

Izzy glanced at Colin, giving his hand a tight squeeze. "This is my Colin." She still hadn't figured out a good word to describe him.

Colin extended his hand, and said, "Pleased to meet you, John." His husky voice and delightful accent comforted Izzy, as did his solid grip on her hand. "We're getting ready to have dinner. Please sit and join us."

A squeal from behind them startled Izzy. She turned to see Mia's face lit up with an enthusiastic smile, as she rushed from the bottom stairs to John. "Daddy, I didn't know you were coming."

"Well, I wanted to surprise you." He hugged her close to him and she wrapped her arms around his chest. "Are you feeling okay, sweetie? I'm sure you're exhausted."

"I'm fine, really."

Despite Blake's cordial greeting, his eyes betrayed his true feelings about John, as he walked by him and into the kitchen.

John released Mia, and clapped his hands together. "I've got great news, princess. You can come back home with me. I've got you a ticket to fly to LA with me, and things are all situated at the house, so you can stay as long as you want. Heck, you can move there and finish your schooling at UCLA."

Izzy frowned. "What about Barbie and the wedding?"

John waved away her concern. "It's over. Barbie wasn't the right woman for me. She's moved out."

Mia's eyes shimmered with joy as she listened to John's news. John checked his gold Rolex and slipped his hand around her shoulders. "We've only got a bit over an hour before the ferry leaves, so let's gather your things."

Mia, with a spring in her step, rushed upstairs.

Izzy stood wide-eyed, staring at her ex-husband. "You realize she just got home from the hospital? Would you even like to see your granddaughter?"

He frowned. "Mia said she feels fine." He glanced across the room at Lauren, holding the baby. Shock and concern were written on her and Ken's faces as they stared at John. "She said it was all arranged and Lauren was adopting her. I don't really see that she'll be my grandchild, and doubt I'll ever see her. If Mia had found other adoptive parents, I wouldn't consider her my grandchild." He turned his eyes toward Izzy. "Because your family is adopting her doesn't change anything for me." With his head he gestured toward

Lauren. "It looks like you've got it well in hand, but if you ever need any money to help with her, I'm happy to send some along. Let me know."

Izzy took a breath, and before she could reply, Blake stepped over to John. "Could I see you for a minute? Outside." He put a hand on his shoulder, and guided John toward the front door.

Izzy closed her eyes, unable to fathom what John must be thinking. She turned toward the stairs. "I'm going to go help Mia."

She found her daughter in the nursery, her suitcases resting beside her. She was in the rocking chair, holding one of the plush toys Izzy had placed in Sophie's crib. "Are you sure you want to leave so soon?" Izzy asked, kneeling beside her.

Mia nodded, tears pooling in her eyes. "I think it's for the best. I didn't know Dad was coming so soon, but told him I didn't want to stay here. Now, with Barbie gone, it'll be perfect, like I had planned before, but without the hassle of a baby." A satisfied smile appeared through the tears. She had achieved what she had wanted and would be back living under John's roof, letting him take care of her and able to do whatever she wanted.

Izzy hung her head as she tried to think of something to say that wouldn't offend Mia. For the first time since this all started, she was thankful Mia had chosen adoption for Sophie. With Mia's words, the scrap of hope Izzy had held onto, that with motherhood Mia might grow or at least realize there was more to life than herself, floated away, like a feather in the breeze.

Mia stood and tugged on the handles of her suitcases. "Barbie was selfish. She thought I was too dramatic and Dad paid me too much attention. He said it would have never worked anyway."

Izzy followed Mia to the landing and hollered downstairs for Colin, asking him to carry her suitcases and the boxes she had brought for her. He bounded up the stairs and took both of them while Izzy slipped an arm around Mia's shoulder. "Could you at least say goodbye to Sophie, and visit with Lauren and Ken before you rush off?"

"Oh, yeah, I'll need to sign those papers before I leave anyway."

Izzy turned away and retrieved the file from her office, following Mia down the stairs and over to the couch where Lauren and Ken were smiling over Sophie, while Ellie held a fidgeting Beanie.

Izzy set the papers on the coffee table. "Mia's ready to sign. Are both of you?"

Lauren looked at Ken, who nodded and smiled. "We're so excited to welcome Sophie as our daughter. We want you to know, you're always welcome to visit and be involved with her life. We'll take care of her and love her and want you to be there when we explain all of this to her. And, before you ask, I had one of the attorneys at work look over the papers and he saw no problems."

Mia nodded. "I'm happy she'll be with you. I know you'll always love her. With me living in LA, I don't think I'll see her often. Probably at holidays, depending what we've got going on." She glanced at her mother, and added, "I'm fine with the papers. I don't need anyone to check them. I trust you, Mom."

Izzy handed Mia a pen. She pointed at the signature tabs flagging the documents. "After you sign them, I'll file them this week."

Mia scribbled her name and initials where indicated, and handed the pen to Lauren. "Do you want to hold Sophie while I sign?" Mia shook her head and bent to kiss Sophie's forehead.

"No, I need to get a move on." She smiled at the baby and said, "Goodbye, sweet girl." She stood and gave Beanie a quick kiss on the head and wandered into the kitchen. "Where's dad?"

"He's outside with Blake."

Sunny, watching out the entry window, began to wag her tail and moments later the door opened. John saw Mia, and said, "We can take your car. I took a rideshare here from the ferry. Are you ready?"

Izzy reached for Mia. "Are you sure you won't eat something?"

John shook his head. "We'll grab something on the ferry or in Anacortes. Our flight leaves in the morning, so we'll have time to find something on the way to the hotel."

Izzy's throat was dry and she felt Colin's hand on the small of her back, reassuring her. She took Mia's hand, and said, "Don't forget to connect with a doctor for a checkup. You were supposed to see Dr. Powell in a couple of weeks."

"I will. Don't worry, Mom. I'll see you next time." Mia hugged her for all of a second, and turned to find Ellie and Blake to give each of them a hug. She met Colin's eyes, and raised her hand in a wave. "See you all later. Thanks for everything."

Blake and Colin carted Mia's boxes to her car, while John took hold of her suitcases and followed her to the door. "Nice to meet all of you," he said, smiling as he met Ellie's eyes. He turned toward Izzy. "I'll make sure Mia texts you when we get home. I've arranged with the dealership to pick up her car, and she can pick out a new one when we get to LA. See ya, Izzy."

Izzy followed them to the driveway and watched, powerless to stop the tears streaming down her face, as John backed out of the driveway and Mia waved goodbye. As the car disappeared, she rested her head on Colin's shoulder and sobbed.

Chapter 31

THE HOURS THAT followed Mia's departure were foggy and muted. Izzy felt like she was underwater, listening to faint conversations Lauren and Ellie attempted to have with her, but the words didn't actually penetrate her mind. Colin stayed with her and brewed tea, to which he added a healthy splash of bourbon. She huddled in her bed, under a blanket, with Sunny snuggled next to her, until she finally slept.

In addition to a heart emoji from Shannon in response to the news of Sophie's birth, Izzy received a text from Mia Sunday night letting her know they had arrived at John's. She didn't even ask about Sophie.

Izzy went through the motions, but was still in shock that Mia had gone. The dream of rebuilding some type of relationship with her daughter, one she hoped a baby might play in a role in mending, had evaporated with Mia's revelation about wanting to place the baby for adoption. With that blow still fresh, and coming to terms with being not only Sophie's grandmother, but her aunt weighing on her, then John's arrival to whisk Mia away left her feeling defeated.

Izzy had learned long ago, life wasn't fair. She had always pulled herself up by her bootstraps, dusted herself off, and moved forward. This time would be no different, but it didn't make her heart hurt any less. She had imagined Mia softening and realizing they didn't have to be adversaries, and had been excited about being involved in Sophie's life and all her milestones. Like a fool, she had believed the baby would bring Mia closer to her.

The vivid family pictures she had allowed her mind to paint, were now discarded canvases. With the way Mia acted toward Sophie, now Izzy feared she would make every possible excuse not to see her and not be involved in her life at all. With time, she hoped that would change, but Mia and John shared the same selfish attitude.

After Mia's abrupt departure, twenty-four hours after giving birth, Lauren and Ken had stayed an extra day, letting Izzy hold and snuggle her granddaughter as much as possible.

As she held sweet Sophie, Izzy kept replaying the last day over in her mind. She wasn't sure if Mia had been the one to orchestrate John's visit and her quick exit, or if it had been John's doing. Regardless, the sad outcome was the same. Despite asking Blake several times what he said to John, he wouldn't say much more than they had a long overdue discussion.

After her early morning walk with Colin and the dogs on Monday, Izzy was in the nursery packing up the clothes and supplies she had gathered for Sophie's stay. As she folded the tiny onesies and collected the diapers to add to the boxes of formula she had downstairs, she felt a hand on her shoulder. "How are you doing?" Colin asked, gathering her in his arms. He had taken the day off to see Lauren and Ken to the ferry, later in the day, but Izzy suspected it was an excuse to check on her.

Hot tears leaked down her cheeks. "I'm not sure. I thought I'd have more time." He led her to the bed and they sat together.

"I'm so sorry, Izzy. I was shocked when Mia left so quickly with John. I can't imagine how you're handling all of this."

She plucked a tissue from the nightstand. "I shouldn't be surprised. It's how the last fifteen years have gone when it comes to Mia and John. There was this sliver of hope I kept clinging to that Mia would change her mind when she met her daughter. That maybe things would change for us. That I'd get a second chance with Sophie." She blew her nose. "Silly, I know, but it all changed in a heartbeat when John arrived."

He slipped his arm around her. "I wish it had turned out differently for you."

She nodded, and sighed. "At least I can be part of Sophie's life. Honestly, I'll probably have more chances to see her at Lauren's than I would have had Mia kept her, like you said. It's all so raw, so fresh."

They sat for a few minutes, without saying anything. She rested against his strong shoulder, comforted by his mere presence. "I need to finish packing up some of this stuff to send home with Lauren."

Colin nodded, and helped her gather the bags she had packed. "If you want to return the furnishings and stuff to Regi, I can get Nate to help me, and we can get it all cleared out of here."

"That's probably best. I won't have to look at it each day." She shook her head and continued downstairs.

They piled the items in the entryway, and wandered into the kitchen in search of coffee. Moments later, Lauren poked her head around the corner, then came to Izzy and put her hands on her sister's shoulders. "I'm so sorry Mia left and I'm heartbroken we have to leave. I feel like we're abandoning you."

Colin stepped closer to Izzy and reached for her hand. "She won't be alone." He kissed her cheek. "Trust me. Jethro and I will keep her company."

Tears spilled down Lauren's cheeks, but she smiled at Colin. She hugged her sister, and whispered in her ear. "You've found yourself a keeper."

Izzy smiled and squeezed her sister a bit closer. "I think so, too."

Lauren sighed and glanced toward the stairs. "I better go rescue Ken and get the kids ready to go. Please let us treat you guys to breakfast downtown before we board."

Through tears she couldn't contain, Izzy nodded. Lauren dashed upstairs and Colin hugged Izzy, as she buried her head in his shoulder. Sunny and Jethro circled around both of them, wanting in on the family hug.

AS THEY DINED at the Front Street Café, Izzy alternated between holding Sophie and Beanie. Sophie would thrive with Ken and Lauren, and Izzy couldn't wait to see the two sisters playing together. Ken had arranged to take some time off at work and was looking forward to being home, helping Lauren with the new baby.

Lauren suggested they set up a video chat call each weekend, so Izzy could keep tabs on Sophie's progress. They also discussed Helen and Gene coming to visit, and Lauren hoped she would be able to join them and bring the girls to spend some time on the island.

"If you drove Mom and Dad, that would make it easier for them. It sounds like a great plan. The Fourth of July is spectacular here, maybe we can plan something around then?" Izzy took another sip of tea from her mug and nibbled at the muffin and fruit she had ordered.

Lauren's brows rose. "That would be such fun. I'll reach out to Mia again when we get home and see if I can interest her in video chatting with us. She may come around once her life settles down. I'll invite Shannon to join us on the trip, too. Maybe by July, things will be better, and she'll feel like reconnecting with all of us."

"Good idea. I'll also encourage her to come. Sam and Linda are always willing to take in guests, so we would have plenty of room for everyone." She sighed and added, "I hope

Mia takes you up on the video chats and visits. With John steering the bus, who knows what will happen?" The sweet sounds of Sophie cooing brought a smile to her face.

The time went by quickly, much too quickly for Izzy, and soon they were gathered outside, helping Lauren and Ken get the girls settled into their car seats before they boarded the ferry. Izzy gave each of them a kiss goodbye, breathing in the sweet scent of Sophie and squeezing her tiny hand, before hugging her sister and brother-in-law, and waving as they drove across the apron and onto the vessel.

Colin put his arm around Izzy as they watched the ferry pull away, the white water churning behind it. He tugged on her arm. "Come on, let's go. I thought we could grab Sunny and Jethro and spend the rest of the day down at the beach, that one you love by the lighthouse."

She smiled and leaned closer as they walked down the street. She didn't know what the future would bring but she knew this place, this beautiful island where she could watch the sun meet the sea each evening, feel the rough sand of the beach under feet, and take solace in the arms of the man she suspected she loved, was where she was meant to be. She knew in her heart, like Sunny, she too had found her forever home.

Epilogue

IZZY HOPES YOU enjoyed her story in Forever Home. If you're a new reader to the Hometown Harbor Series, you won't want to miss the other books. Each tells the story of a different heroine and like this book, they all include dogs.

If you've missed reading any, here are the links to the entire series. All but the free prequel are available in print and eBook formats.

Prequel: <u>Hometown Harbor: The Beginning (free prequel novella eBook only)</u>
Book 1: <u>Finding Home</u>
Book 2: <u>Home Blooms</u>
Book 3: <u>A Promise of Home</u>
Book 4: <u>Pieces of Home</u>
Book 5: <u>Finally Home</u>
Book 6: <u>Forever Home</u>

If you enjoy Christmas stories, a few of my author friends and I got together to create a connected series. The SOUL SISTERS AT CEDAR MOUNTAIN LODGE SERIES releases in October 2020. You can find all the books at the links below:

Book 1: <u>Christmas Sisters</u> – perma-FREE prologue book (available September 1, 2020)
Book 2: <u>Christmas Kisses</u> by Judith Keim

Book 3: <u>Christmas Wishes</u> by Tammy L. Grace
Book 4: <u>Christmas Hope</u> by Violet Howe
Book 5: <u>Christmas Dreams</u> by Ev Bishop
Book 6: <u>Christmas Rings</u> by Tess Thompson

Acknowledgements

Writing this book, during the early summer days of 2020, felt like a vacation. This has been a disappointing year with the pandemic and so many plans and celebrations having to be canceled. I've immersed myself in my writing, which much like reading, offers a wonderful escape. Spending time with my old friends in the San Juan Islands brought me happiness and kept my mind focused on positive things. I hope reading *Forever Home* brings you as much comfort as writing it did for me.

My thanks to my editor, Angela, for finding my mistakes and helping me polish *Forever Home*. She is a true gem and has done a wonderful job. I'm in love with the cover for this book and all the credit goes to Elizabeth Mackey for creating such an inviting and gorgeous cover. I'm fortunate to have such an incredible team helping me.

I so appreciate all of the readers who have taken the time to tell their reader friends about my work and provide reviews of my books. These reviews are especially important in promoting future books, so if you enjoy my novels, please consider leaving a review. I also encourage you to follow me on BookBub, where leaving a review is even easier and you'll be the first to know about new releases and deals.

Remember to visit my website at www.tammylgrace.com and join my mailing list for my exclusive group of readers. I've also got a fun Book Buddies Facebook Group. That's the best place to find me and get a chance to participate in my giveaways. Join my Facebook group at facebook.com/groups/AuthorTammyLGraceBookBuddies and keep in touch—I'd love to hear from you.

All the best,
Tammy

From the Author

Thank you for reading FOREVER HOME. Despite this being the sixth book in my HOMETOWN HARBOR SERIES, I loved writing it as much as all the others. It felt like coming home!

If you're a new reader and enjoy mysteries, I write a series that features a lovable private detective, Coop, and his faithful golden retriever, Gus. If you like whodunits that will keep you guessing until the end, you'll enjoy the COOPER HARRINGTON DETECTIVE NOVELS.

The first book, BEACH HAVEN, in my new GLASS BEACH COTTAGE SERIES is also loved by readers. You met a few of the characters from this new series in FOREVER HOME, so you'll already have a feel for them. It is a heartwarming story of a woman's resilience buoyed by the bonds of friendship, an unexpected gift, and the joy she finds in helping others. As with all my books, the furry four-legged characters play a prominent role.

The two books I've written as Casey Wilson, A DOG'S HOPE and A DOG'S CHANCE have received enthusiastic support from my readers and if you're a dog-lover, are must-reads.

If you enjoy holiday stories, be sure and check out my CHRISTMAS IN SILVER FALLS SERIES and CHRISTMAS IN SNOW VALLEY. They are small-town Christmas stories of hope, friendship, and family. You won't want to miss any of the SOUL SISTERS AT CEDAR MOUNTAIN LODGE BOOKS. It's a connected Christmas series I wrote with four author friends. My contribution, CHRISTMAS WISHES, is the third book in the series and is a heartwarming, small-town holiday story that I'm sure you'll enjoy. The series kicks off with a free prequel novella, CHRISTMAS SISTERS, where you'll get a chance to meet the characters during their first Christmas together.

I'd love to send you my exclusive interview with the canine companions in my Hometown Harbor Series as a thank-you for joining my exclusive group of readers. You can sign up www.tammylgrace.com by clicking this link: https://wp.me/P9umIy-e.

Below you will find links to the electronic version of all of Tammy's books and most of them are also available in paperback

COOPER HARRINGTON DETECTIVE NOVELS
Killer Music
Deadly Connection
Dead Wrong

HOMETOWN HARBOR SERIES
Hometown Harbor: The Beginning (FREE Prequel Novella)
Finding Home
Home Blooms
A Promise of Home
Pieces of Home
Finally Home
Forever Home

CHRISTMAS STORIES
A Season for Hope: Christmas in Silver Falls Book 1
The Magic of the Season: Christmas in Silver Falls Book 2
Christmas in Snow Valley: A Hometown Christmas Novella
Christmas Sisters: Soul Sisters at Cedar Mountain Lodge Book 1
Christmas Wishes: Soul Sisters at Cedar Mountain Lodge Book 3

GLASS BEACH COTTAGE SERIES
Beach Haven

WRITING AS CASEY WILSON
A Dog's Hope
A Dog's Chance

Don't miss the **SOUL SISTERS AT CEDAR MOUNTAIN LODGE,** a connected Christmas series centered around a woman and the four foster girls she welcomes into her home.

Book 1: <u>Christmas Sisters</u> – perma-FREE prologue book
Book 2: <u>Christmas Kisses</u> by Judith Keim
Book 3: <u>Christmas Wishes</u> by Tammy L. Grace
Book 4: <u>Christmas Hope</u> by Violet Howe
Book 5: <u>Christmas Dreams</u> by Ev Bishop
Book 6: <u>Christmas Rings</u> by Tess Thompson

Tammy enjoys connecting with readers on social media. **Remember to subscribe to her exclusive group of readers for your freebie, only available to readers on her mailing list. Sign up at** <u>www.tammylgrace.com</u>. **Follow this link to subscribe at** <u>https://wp.me/P9umIy-e</u> **and she'll send you the exclusive interview she did with all the canine characters in her Hometown Harbor Series.**

Follow Tammy on <u>Facebook at this link</u>, by liking her page. You may also follow Tammy on <u>BookBub</u> by clicking on the follow button.

About the Author

Tammy L. Grace is the *USA Today* bestselling and award-winning author of the Cooper Harrington Detective Novels, the bestselling Hometown Harbor Series, and the Glass Beach Cottage Series, along with several sweet Christmas novellas. Tammy also writes under the pen name of Casey Wilson for Bookouture. You'll find Tammy online at www.tammylgrace.com where you can join her mailing list and be part of her exclusive group of readers. Connect with Tammy on Facebook at facebook.com/tammylgrace.books or Instagram at www.instagram.com/authortammylgrace.